Love isn't in the cards for her...

After her short, failed marriage, Kate tries to rebuild her life and takes a position as a nanny to three small boys. She quickly grows to love them, but their father terrifies her, while igniting a passion she didn't know she possessed. Disturbed by his distant manner with his sons, Kate struggles to make him more involved in the boys' daily lives. Her efforts are mysteriously supported by an entity that cannot really exist. Or can she? And if she does exist, is she really trying to help Kate, or just take over her body?

But when he deals the hand, all bets are off...

Six years after his beloved wife passed away, Matthias Zrin is still trying to become the father she wanted him to be. Not an easy task for a three-centuries-old immortal. His search for the ultimate nanny ends when Kate Rokov stumbles to his home and into his arms. The immediate attraction he feels for her seems like a betrayal of his dead wife, a love he's harboured for over three hundred years. But when Kate is stalked by a deadly stranger, the life he clung to in the past begins to crumble and break down. Can Matthias learn to trust and to love again in time to save his family from disaster, or will his stubborn pride destroy everything worth living for?

He claimed to be immortal, but that was ridiculous...wasn't it?

Kate's heart hammered. The experience seemed so real. A low moan escaped her and she bit her lip. Soon warmth surged through her, causing her body to go limp. Her legs gave way underneath her, but Matthias—or whoever this man claimed to be now—wrapped his arm around her waist. His sweet, musky scent clung to her. Ecstasy filled her and she felt as if she hovered in the air. If he intended to kill her like this, she could imagine no better way to die. A voice echoed through her mind, speaking of undying love in centuries old Croatian.

"Wake up," he whispered close to her ear, his strong arms still locked around her.

"I don't want to." Her head wobbled, exuberant with sheer happiness, a kind she had never experienced before.

"You must." He stroked her hair with tender fingers. "Wake up now."

"No. I want to stay like this. Forever." She focused on his handsome face staring at her through her haze.

His smooth cheek brushed against hers. "Me too, but you must wake."

The fog lifted and his image appeared, clearly now. She blinked once. Twice. What had happened? She pushed away from him and flattened her back against the wall.

"You, you—"

"You," he said, pointing at her, "asked for proof."

KUDOS for *Bonded by Crimson*

With some interesting twists and turns to the plot, *Bonded by Crimson* captured my attention from page one and refused to let go right through the last page. The story was packed with characters I cheered for, laughed with, and even shed a couple of tears over. Our heroine, Kate Rokov, is charming, sweet, determined, and just naïve enough to have you groaning, "No, don't do that," even though you know she will. The hero, Matthias Zrin, is hot, sexy, immortal, and jaded enough to make you shake your head at his stubbornness. Together, these two blunder their way through ghost-busting, parenting three adorable boys, and falling in love across two continents—from Canada to Croatia. Which totally worked for me. I mean, if you are going to blunder into love, you may as well see the world while you do it...It's a well-crafted story with some steamy sex scenes—the very best kind. – *Taylor, Reviewer*

Bonded by Crimson by Zrinka Jelic caught me by surprise. For a first effort by a new author, it is quite enjoyable. I liked the depth of characterization as well as the vivid settings. Having never been to Europe, I truly enjoy books that describe foreign place so well I feel as if I have been there. This book was one of those. The plot is strong and the storyline intriguing—the spirit of a dead wife helping her husband to find a new wife. And while I usually prefer more action and suspense, *Bonded by Crimson* caught my interest and held it all the way through. Jelic took a basic second-time-around romance, gave it a new twist, added a touch of suspense, and came up with something quite good. – *Regan, Reviewer*

ACKNOWLEDGMENTS

Special thanks to everyone who contributed to my book: my wonderful critique partners Anke, JJ Keller, Melania, Tina and everyone in the FFnP critique loop as well as editors and everyone at Black Opal Books. Your brilliant insight has been invaluable.

BONDED
BY
CRIMSON

Zrinka Jelic

A BLACK OPAL BOOKS PUBLICATION

GENRE: PARANORMAL ROMANCE

BONDED BY CRIMSON
Copyright © 2012 by Zrinka Jelic
Cover Design by Black Opal Books
All cover art copyright © 2012 – All Rights Reserved
Print ISBN: 978-1-937329-30-3

First publication: JANUARY 28, 2012

Published by Black Opal Books **http://www.blackopalbooks.com**

CHAPTER 1

The steady droplets of rain glistened in the headlights as the garage door glided up. The wipers squeaked over the windshield, erasing the beads of water. Matthias parked his Audi Quattro next to the recently acquired Grand Cherokee. Not even the new vehicle kept nannies employed for long.

Though Mozart's "Autumn" coming through the speakers suited Matthias's mood, he turned off the ignition, shutting off the music. He opened the door and stepped out of the car. The wall muffled his boys' screams, but the terror in their wails sent him rushing inside in a panic.

The ugly picture presented itself as soon as he entered the house. The nanny dragged Luka across the floor by his arm. Ivan and Teo huddled together in the corner. The woman's fingers had left imprints on their tear-streaked cheeks. The sight broke Matthias's heart. He should have confronted the nanny the first time Rosalia reported the girl took her rage out on the boys.

"You retards can't put your muddy boots away."

The venom in her voice stung Matthias to the core. No child deserved this treatment, let alone his six-year-old triplets. The beast inside him growled and awakened.

The nanny glanced over her shoulder. She shrieked and dropped Luka's arm. His head thudded on the tile floor.

She straightened and turned to face Matthias. "Mr. Zrin, I didn't expect you home so soon." A sweet tone replaced her irate voice. A forced smile stretched her crooked lips, smeared with lipstick.

"Obviously." Matthias balled his hands into fists, struggling to control the waking animal. This nanny had lasted three weeks. She was the fourth one since the beginning of the year, and it was only April. "I want you away from my children and my home immediately." Careful not to strain his neck he leaned to his side and peered behind her. He ordered the boys to their room in their native Croatian tongue. They scurried out of the hallway.

With her fists propped on her wide hips, she narrowed her eyes. "That is rude. Speaking a language I don't understand."

He glared at her. The nerve of the woman. "You have no business working with children. I want you out of here. Now." He pointed to the door. She needed to be told everything at least twice.

"Look who's talking." The strands of her straw-like, bleached-blonde hair fell from its clip when she shook her head. "It's not like you're the world's greatest dad. Your boys don't even know you exist."

"That is none of your concern."

Though she was right. He had been a distant parent, but her attempt to make him the bad guy was pathetic. "I don't care what they've done to make you so angry. This is not how you treat children. You have fifteen minutes to get out of my house."

She folded her arms over her heaving chest. "You have to pay me two weeks in lieu."

The familiar pain stabbed his eyes. He blinked fast in an attempt to stop the color fading from his irises, but the sensation intensified. Avoiding the eye contact with her, he pressed his hand to his brows and closed his eyes. Money. All any of them ever wanted.

"You'd have to take that up with the agency. I could call the police and have you arrested for the assault. You should consider yourself lucky."

He blinked once again, as the pain in his eyes eased off, and returned his glare to her. The frown on her face made her double chin look grotesque.

"It's no wonder your wife died." Her breath carried the smell of stale coffee and tobacco.

He tightened his fists and narrowed his eyes as he pushed away the raging demon brewing in the pit of his stomach.

She tapped her foot. "I'll have to call my boyfriend. He may not be able to come and get me out here, away from civilization."

Matthias snapped his wallet open and pulled out twenty dollars. "Call a cab." With the bill in between his fingers, he extended his arm to her.

Her beefy fingers slipped the money out of his. "You're all so weird."

Fortunately for her, she spun on her heels and headed toward the stairs. The black leotards stretched over her large buttocks left nothing to the imagination.

Matthias retreated to his study to calm down before he tended to the boys. The girl had been but a few seconds away from an untimely death. The fiend inside him had stayed dormant for decades, and he had never expected that the mistreatment of his little ones would awaken it.

Twenty minutes had passed and her boyfriend had still not arrived. Finally, the screech of the tires on the driveway, coupled with the thumping music and an impatient honking ensured Matthias that Mr. Baggy Pants had come for his girlfriend, late as always. Profanity poured out of the nanny's mouth as soon as she stepped out the door. Her sweetheart replied the same way. The engine revved and the car disappeared in the distance. Well, those two wouldn't raid his fridge anymore.

He went upstairs and checked on Luka while the other two sat on the big bed in his chamber, flipping through the television channels in search of cartoons.

"Will Rosalia stay with us while you're at clinic, Papa?" Luka squirmed while Matthias examined his arms and head. Multiple bruises in various stages of healing above the boy's elbows confirmed Matthias's suspicion—he had been manhandled.

"Uncle Fortuno and Aunt Adriana will."

Rosalia, the maid, loved the boys dearly, but she was old, and Matthias couldn't burden her with their care. She had plenty of work as it was.

"Awesome." Luka threw his arms in the air. "We get to play vampires with him."

Matthias gave his son a weary glance. Fortuno would have to stop filling the boys' heads with this 'vampires' nonsense. Unlike their unusual family, the children were mortal. "Only till the new nanny arrives." He was glad his friends were still in Canada. They had agreed to help him until he found a new nanny. Nonetheless, they'd had to postpone their trip to the old country. Hopefully, their staff would be able to open their restaurant in time for the season.

"Not a nanny again," Ivan said with a winy voice.

Matthias cast him a scornful look. "We'll find her. I know we will."

He propped his hands on his hips, reminding himself not to give up hope. "Now, who's up for dinner? Rosalia's roast smells delicious."

The three boys scurried out of the bedroom and down the stairs. Matthias exhaled then pulled his laptop from its case. He'd try the nanny agency's database one more time. After entering the usual search criteria, he also added Croatian as a language preference.

"Help me, Emina. I beg you," he whispered before submitting his query.

An hour later, he returned to the computer, expecting to find "no results" flashing on the screen. To his delight, one hit matched his requirements.

Downtown Toronto's dreary and gray skyscrapers sank into the distance in Kate's rear-view mirror as she drove on the Gardiner Express Way. The ridges of the steering wheel pushed against her palms. The thought of working as a live-in nanny in a strange household knotted her stomach as she took a note of the first upcoming highway exit. There was still time to call it quits.

No. No more waiting on tables. It was time to go back to working with children and put her teaching degree to use. Besides, what was she afraid of? Mr. Matthias Zrin, the boys' father? He couldn't be an ogre like Mr. Wilkins described. The recruiting agent from the Nannies' Care had tried to discourage her from accepting this job and he'd warned her of the client's odd behaviour. Mr. Zrin chose her from all the other applicants and not just for her fluent knowledge of the Croatian language.

If Mr. Zrin were a typical Croatian man, he'd speak his mind, curse, swear, and pound his fists if the job at hand wasn't going smoothly. Her father was no different. Well, just because other nannies the headhunter had placed in the

Zrin's household had not lasted a month didn't mean that she would not.

Mr. Zrin had triplets, but then so did Shrek. A giggle escaped her and she loosened the hold on the wheel.

"You must do this. There aren't any other job offers. Your last dime is lonely on the bottom of your purse, and the landlady increased the rent." Her short pep talk filled her with a newfound courage, and she pressed her foot on the accelerator.

Hectic morning rush-hour traffic thinned as the eight-lane freeway reduced to two lanes, though semi-trucks dominated the road. Lush green hills replaced the urban asphalt. Yep, she was out of the city.

You are now entering the Niagara escarpment, a sign read. The clock on the dashboard displayed twenty minutes passed seven. She had forty minutes to arrive on time.

The hiccupping under the hood caused her to hold her breath in hopes the car wouldn't stall. She gunned the engine. The gauges leapt as the old Corolla picked up speed.

A few scattered farmhouses came into view along the dinky, country road as she took the highway exit. No safe place to pull over—even worse, no one to ask for directions. Would the sign for Concession Road Six even be posted?

She glanced over the map again. It had to be here. With all this untamed greenery, she must've missed the turn. So, this house was in the middle of nowhere, not in the suburbs as she had expected. It was no wonder city nannies couldn't last out here. The closest shopping mall must be miles away.

Just when she thought she was on a never-ending road to who knew where, a green sign displaying *Cons. Rd 6* appeared. A breath of relief escaped her. She made a right turn, and the car sped down the gravel path.

There should be a manmade pond around this bend. There was. She shivered as she passed the small body of water mere seconds later. On the field to her left, there would be longhaired cattle grazing. The sight of shaggy livestock caused her to flinch. None of this was in the driving directions. How did she know? She couldn't have been this way before. She'd remember.

The private driveway appeared on her left. She turned onto the circular pavement as if she'd done this for years, causing her tires to screech.

A two-story house with a gray-stone façade and a round tower in the middle, stark against the blue sky, loomed over her. Tall pine trees surrounding the building reflected in the enormous bay windows. Intricate cast iron filigree displayed number twenty-six above the door. Of course, the agency wouldn't want to lose this client. Everything about his place spelled cash.

Silence surrounded the modern castle. Where were the children? Not a single cloud spoiled the sky. Kids should play outside, in these landscaped gardens. Once the buds blossomed, their scents would attract many insects and birds. But it was early May in Toronto. The weather could change from one moment to the next. They could still get snow.

She flipped the visor down and inspected her face. Mascara was smeared under one eye and liner dye had seeped into her eyes, turning them red so that the green of her irises stood out. She reached for a tissue and eye drops. Bother, why did she put this stuff on? She had stopped wearing makeup long ago. Cosmetics only made her eyes itchy and teary.

"Okay," she muttered as she gathered her long hair into a ponytail. Then she opened the envelope on the passenger seat and read the employment package one more time.

Papers crinkled as she flipped straight to the page containing the family history. Three boys, six years of age, left motherless at birth. Poor little darlings to have experienced that loss at such a young age.

There was no mention of the lady of the house in the papers. Hadn't their father remarried? Kate shoved the sheets back into the envelope.

Three sweet boys, growing up in this world without their mother, left to the mercy of nannies. So vulnerable and defenceless. How much love had they known? Would the children like her? They were still little, and she hoped they'd love to cuddle. This would be the closest she would come to being a mom.

No. She mustn't get carried away. They weren't her boys.

The car door opened with a clatter. She stepped out, scanning the estate. Could she take this on? She must. She couldn't push another mile through the exhaustion.

Her shoes clicked on the stone steps as she walked to the double front door. The doorbell didn't chime when she pressed the button. So she used the knocker. The silhouette of a stout woman appeared through the stained glass.

The white apron on the waist of the woman's black dress stood rigid when she opened the door. What would laundry starch manufacturers do without Croatian women?

"Miss Rokov?" When Kate nodded, the woman knitted her thick eyebrows. Deep creases formed on her forehead. "We've been expecting you. Come in." She gestured with a meaty hand.

Kate detected a dialect from the province of Dalmatia when the woman spoke. They seemed to be from the same part of Croatia.

"I'm sorry I'm late. This place wasn't easy to find." Kate stepped into a large hallway with tall ceilings. "Once I turned on this road everything became familiar."

"Have you been here before?" the housekeeper demanded, closing the door.

"No, I can't say I have."

"The children are not up yet. I can show you the house." She straightened the small woven rag in front of the door. "I'm Rosalia," she continued, her voice echoing in the spacious area, bouncing off the marble floors and sage tinted walls. "I've been working for the Zrin family for fifteen years."

"So, you're not the lady of the house?"

Rosalia's stern expression caused Kate to wince.

"I'm the only maid here, but this is the real lady of the house." She stopped by the portrait of a young woman. Larger than life, it hung on the wall separating dining room from kitchen.

"This is the boys' mother?" Kate couldn't take her eyes off the oil painting. The woman was seated, her golden hair cascading down her shoulders. The artist had captured her with life-like accuracy. Her piercing, pale-green eyes stared from the canvass as if she were trying to say something. Her peach complexion and soft features had an odd familiarity. The rose dress she was wearing seemed old fashioned, as if the late Mrs. Zrin was nostalgic about the times long gone.

Kate rubbed her bare arms as a sudden burst of cold air brushed against her. Did someone turn on the air-conditioning in the room? A strange intuition dragged her attention back to the painting. An ink like dot appeared above the woman's head and spread over the entire canvas.

Kate leaned closer, her body tingling, her pulse quickening. The drive must have torn on her nerves, because somehow the lady's face blurred, and in the next moment Kate was looking at herself.

Her double's eyes filled with blood. Kate gaped at the painting, struggling to breathe.

"Yes," Rosalia said, snapping Kate out of the vision. The maid sighed. "The Master loved her so. He hasn't been himself since."

Kate nodded and swallowed hard. Had she really seen that? She looked back at the painting. Mrs. Zrin's face had returned. The illusion of ink was gone. She glanced at Rosalia. The maid didn't seem to notice anything strange about the portrait.

Kate licked her lips. Should she say something? Rosalia might think she was on drugs and report her to Mr. Zrin and she'd lose the job before she even started.

"What was her name?" she asked.

"Mistress Emina Zrin." Rosalia smoothed a strand of her dark hair touched with gray, in a neat bun she wore.

Mistress. Kate frowned. Those titles were long gone from Croatia. There were no more Masters or Mistresses, although she had heard some older women refer to their husbands as *Gospodar.*

"Zrin," Kate mused aloud. "I haven't heard of that last name even in Croatia."

"It is short from Zrinski."

"Zrinski?" Kate turned to Rosalia again. "That line of nobles died out. With the beheading of Viceroy Petar in Vienna in sixteen seventy-one."

"I see you know the history of our country." Rosalia gave her an approving nod and gestured to her left. "The kitchen is that way." She turned towards the curving stairs. "Let me show you to your quarters."

Her quarters? Kate arched an eyebrow. Where was she? On board the Federation Star Ship Enterprise?

She glanced over her shoulder at Emina's painting. Just where had she met her before? Emina's face wasn't one she would forget.

The hem of Rosalia's dress rose with each stair she climbed, exposing her thick calves hosed in black nylons.

She held onto a dark wood banister as she led Kate down the long hallway then stopped in front of the door at the end.

"You'll stay in here." The saffron walls welcomed them as Rosalia opened the door. "When you have settled in, come down to the kitchen. Master left some papers for you."

Kate scanned the spacious bedroom. Two square windows allowed sunlight to wash over the walls, making the interior bright. The double bed with its fluffy pillows called to her. Hopefully, she'd be able to make it an early night. It must have been well after midnight last night by the time she had fallen asleep, only to be awakened, two hours before the alarm went off, by a nightmare she hadn't had since her childhood.

"Please be quiet when you bring your belongings in. The Master's chamber is at the other end." Rosalia pointed to the double doors at the top of the stairs they had passed on their way here. "You're to get the boys up and ready for the day. Do keep them as quiet as possible. The Master works nights."

"The Master is here?" Kate asked, her voice raised a pitch. It sounded odd to call him Master. With any luck, she wouldn't have to.

"He returned from Croatia late last night. It has been six years since the Mistress passed away. He buried her on an islet they own there." Rosalia sighed, lacing her fingers over her round midriff.

"How sad." Kate's throat closed. She blinked to push away the tears that threatened, not understanding her sudden outpouring of emotions.

"She was a good mistress. May she rest in peace." Rosalia made the Sign of the Cross and turned. "The children's room is in the middle." She pointed to the white doors facing Kate's suite. "They'll be up soon, so go get your things in. I have to return to my kitchen duties."

"When do I get to meet Mr. Zrin?" Kate followed Rosalia down the stairs.

"Later perhaps. He never took time to meet the other nannies. He's a very private man. Even the boys are shy of him." Rosalia reached the bottom of the stairs and turned to Kate. "You are to call him Mr. or Doctor. He'd prefer the latter. I'm old so he doesn't mind me."

Kate nodded. "He's a doctor?"

"Yes, a surgeon."

A shudder rushed through Kate, causing her weakness in her knees. "How old is he?"

"He turned forty-four last week." Rosalia scurried to the kitchen, leaving Kate by the front door.

What kind of father was this Master or Doctor or whatever he liked to be called? His own children were shy of him.

Kate carried two stacked boxes and made it to the top of the stairs. The smaller box tipped and the contents spilled out, scattering over the hardwood floors and under the door of her new "Master's" chamber. She cringed, so much for her being quiet.

The door swung open, causing her to snap her gaze to the man standing in the entrance. Mr. Zrin wore pyjama bottoms, an unbuttoned shirt crumpled around his biceps. She swallowed hard at the sight of him. Her heart drummed as she scanned his face. His eyes—narrowed, blue crescents—and dishevelled ebony hair caused her to force a smile in spite of her clenched teeth. No way could this man be forty-four. He appeared much younger.

She peered behind him. The tangled sheets on the large bed meant she woke him with her clumsiness.

"I am so very sorry—I apologize—I didn't mean to." Words rushed out of her mouth. She knelt, scooped up her belongings in haste, and shoved them into the box. Darn, she'd had one chance to make a good impression on her new boss and she blew it.

Gathering the scattered pens and papers, she trembled on her knees in front of him. Would he help her or just stare down at her? He closed the door. She exhaled, balling her hands into fists, fingernails digging into her palms. Could the doctor have been any more lacking in good bedside-manners?

She picked up the box and got to her feet. The door of the children's room popped open before she entered her suite. Two dark haired boys tumbled out while a third golden blond one meandered out, rubbing his eyes.

CHAPTER 2

Shivers ran up Kate's spine. *Well done.* She managed to get the whole household out of bed. The maid ran a tight domestic establishment. How could Kate explain this mishap? Her duty was to get the boys ready for the day and keep them as quiet as possible, so "Master" could rest. No chance he would get any sleep now. With a box in her hands, she scurried through the door of her suite and dumped the cardboard container on the floor.

She returned to the boys, fighting an overwhelming, unexplainable urge to wrap her arms around them. *God, they are cute with those rosy cheeks.*

One of the dark haired boys stepped up to her. "Are you our new nanny?" he asked in English.

"Yes, I am," she answered in Croatian, crouching in front of him. After all, Mr. Zrin hired her to increase the boys' knowledge of the language. "And you are?"

He furrowed his brows as if struggling to understand her. "Ivan."

Kate stroked his dark hair. "I knew you'd understand. I'm Kate."

The other dark haired boy joined his brother. "Are we not going to call you Miss Kate?" He too spoke English.

"Just Kate is fine. What's your name?" she said, persisting with Croatian.

His lips scrunched and his eyes widened. "I'm Luka," he answered, also in Croatian.

"So nice to meet you both. Who is this?" She turned to the blond-haired boy who hadn't moved from his spot.

He stared at the floor for a brief moment then disappeared back into his room, shutting the door. Kate stood and approached his bedroom.

"That's Mateo, but we call him Teo. He doesn't like strangers." Ivan tugged on her elbow. "Can you get us dressed?"

With her hand on the doorknob, she looked down at the child. "What about Teo?"

Luka stretched. "He dresses himself."

"If he can do it, why can't you two?"

Ivan burst into a silly laugh. "But, he does it all wrong. See." He pointed at Teo when his brother stepped into the hallway.

She crouched in front of Teo, fixing his misbuttoned shirt. "If you never try, you will never learn."

Rising, she turned to Ivan and Luka. "Let's get you two into your clothes. Teo and I will show you how it's done."

Half an hour must have passed before the two boys got themselves dressed and ready. She helped with zippers, buttons and brushing teeth.

"See, that wasn't hard. You did it." Their little fingers wrapped around her hands, and she smiled at them. "Breakfast now."

They headed towards the stairs. Her eyes narrowed as the door to "Master's chamber" shut with a thud. Why wouldn't he step out and introduce himself? Well, she had been warned of his odd conduct, but he was rich and the world saw him as eccentric. If he were poor, he'd would have been plain weird.

Mr. Zrin could act as strange as he wanted. If he didn't feel like meeting with her then let him be. Suited her fine. With all the other nannies who quit, no wonder. He must be terribly disappointed. She planned to do her job beyond the call of duty. His little boys had already stolen her heart.

Two little hands snapped out of hers as they reached the bottom of the stairs. The three boys ran into the kitchen, embracing Rosalia.

"My angels are up." Rosalia placed a kiss on each boy's forehead. "There now, sit at your usual spots. I'll get your breakfasts." She cast Kate a stern look pointing to Ivan and Luka. "These two need to be fed."

Fed? According to their records, they are in Senior Kindergarten. Kate squeezed in between the two boys at the kitchen island. Ivan took a remote control in his hand and pressed the button. Sound of cartoons came from the small, flat TV screen nestled in the corner of the counter.

Rosalia ceased pouring milk over their cereals and turned to the television. "I don't like them eating and watching this but they know how to turn it on."

"Can hardly blame them, there's one in every room." Kate reached for the two bowls Rosalia pushed her way, scooped the spoonful in Ivan's mouth and turned to Luka till his brother chewed. So far so good, Rosalia didn't give her any of those scolding looks, so she must have not heard when Kate dropped the box.

Kate lowered the spoons in the boys' bowls. "I'm surprised you two need to be fed. You're starting grade one in the fall. No one will spoon-feed you at school. How about you try to do it?"

"They'll just make messes for Aunty Rosalia to clean up. Won't you boys?" Rosalia turned to Kate handing her a small stack of papers. "The size of this kitchen keeps me plenty busy. Master wants you to read this."

"Don't worry, Rosalia. I'll clean up after them, but at least let them try." She took the reading material in her hand, trying to think of a way to gain Rosalia's trust. "Ivan and Luka are not disabled they should learn how to do things for themselves."

The two boys stared at their bowls, appearing uncertain.

"Come on." Kate tapped her hands on the counter. "Unless you want to stay hungry."

Cheerios and milk dribbled on the ivory tiles around Ivan and Luka's stools as they fed themselves. Kate praised their efforts despite Rosalia's disapproving shake of the head.

The coffee machine beeped. Rosalia stood. "The Master cancelled all of their activities for today so they can get familiar with you, but they can't miss school tomorrow."

The smell of freshly brewed beverage drifted to Kate as Rosalia poured the liquid in two mugs.

"We'd be at our riding lessons right now." The sight of Ivan's shaky hand as he aimed the spoon with one ring of Cheerios at his wide-opened mouth caused Kate to giggle.

"Yes, I can see that here." Kate glided her finger over the boys' daily schedule on the table in front of her. "You're in riding, fencing, archery, swimming, karate, and the church choir. It's cool you can do all this stuff. You should also be able to use the spoon. What do you think is more important?"

"I always pack finger snacks in their lunch bags." Rosalia cast Kate a wary glance, passing her the black mug. "You should eat too. Put some meat on your bones. You look like a starved rabbit in the winter."

Kate stifled a laugh. Rosalia seemed to be one of those ladies who didn't have trouble speaking her mind.

"Thank you, Rosalia. At least someone thinks I'm skinny." She took the beverage from Rosalia's hand and placed the coffee mug on the island in front of her.

Rosalia climbed on the stool at the kitchen island. Kate cringed as the stool creaked under her weight. She should sit at the table, instead of this high island.

"Miss Rokov is right, Rosalia." A man's deep voice startled Kate, causing her to turn her head sideways. Mr. Zrin stood in the doorway. How long had he been listening in on their conversation? A black T-shirt and dark pair of jeans replaced his previous attire. However, it didn't remove the image of his tight body from her mind.

"Master, you're up already? Can I get you some breakfast?" Rosalia's eyebrows arched. Kate darted a glance at Rosalia then back at him. Rosalia had no idea what woke him.

"Just coffee, thank you." He turned to the boys. "Good morning, children."

"Morning, Papa," all three replied, keeping their voices low and staring at their bowls. A memory of her own father demanding a greeting from her stabbed at Kate's mind. Just like her father, Mr. Zrin too was a stranger in his own house, feared by his own children.

"I'm sure you can speak up." Kate nudged the boys. "Let me hear you greet your papa like you mean it."

They sat in silence and stared at the food in front of them.

"It's fine, boys." Mr. Zrin turned to Kate. "Miss Rokov, I'd like a word with you."

She straightened her back at his stern voice, and her knuckles whitened on the handle of her mug.

"Bring your coffee to my office. Rosalia will watch the boys for a few minutes." His voice changed to softer tone, more reassuring.

Leading the way out of the kitchen, he opened the door of a small office nestled between the family room and the stairs.

"Have a seat." He gestured to a chair in front of the black desk of his study. "And before we begin." The leather of his armchair puffed when he sat. "I apologize for my behaviour earlier."

She relaxed her shoulders as his smile sent tingles all over her.

Silence followed. She cleared her throat and flashed him half a smile then placed the mug on his desk, searching her mind for an appropriate conversation starter. "Good coffee."

"Indeed." A paper rustled in his fingers as he picked it up off his desk and scanned over the page. She recognized the copy of her resume. "You graduated with honors from two teacher's colleges, first from the University of Split then from Ryerson's in Toronto."

He winced when he raised his head towards her. His expression made her draw her eyebrows closer. Could the doctor have seen someone else in her?

"You like teaching?" He spoke with an effort as if a sharp pain constricted his chest.

"My mom was a teacher. I used to help her by marking papers and managing kids on the field trips. You can say I've been destined to teach, but those jobs are scarce in this recession."

He nodded. "You're one of a lucky few who knew what they wanted to be when they grew up."

"I suppose." She shrugged. "But, I don't believe in luck."

"Don't believe in luck?" He leaned back, his voice resonating with surprise. "What do you believe in?"

She sighed and looked away, biting her lip. Once she believed in angels but dared not to tell him that. It seemed she had said too much already. Now he was getting curious. "I don't know anymore," she said. Her gaze returned to him. "I used to believe hard work would be rewarded, but I've learned people can go a lifetime without receiving any recognition for their efforts."

"Most never do." He gripped the armrests of his chair. "This family requires hard work—if you're up to the challenge."

She nodded with determination. "I am."

"I've been an absent father. It's an unfortunate situation I must remedy before it's too late. Teo worries me. He was inconsolable and cried for the first four years of his life. When he stopped, he closed himself into a shell and refuses to come out. As you gathered, he is independent, but he doesn't say much." He sighed, letting go of the armrests, and planted his elbows on the desk.

She rubbed her fingers. "Love can bring him out. Well, from the brief moments I've been with him and seen the interactions with his brothers, he seems to retreat when they step in his space."

He levelled his eyes with hers. "You're right. I haven't spent much time with the boys, but it took you one morning with them to figure out Teo. How much of a little boy is still inside him?"

"Teo is still a little boy, no matter how grown up he acts. Children need love more than anything." Kate blinked fast, lowering her gaze to her hands. Tears stung her eyes, but she couldn't show her new employer how wimpy she was.

"Now, how's your first day going?" he asked, casting her cheerful smile.

"Pretty good." She gave him a shy smile of her own. *Please, don't look at me like that.*

She darted her glance left, then right, then focused on his face again, frowning. Ice spread down her spine. "What was that?"

"What was what?"

"I heard a whisper." She tilted her head, straining to listen.

"A whisper?" He cleared his throat, but dropped his glance as if trying to avoid looking into her eyes. "I heard none."

A cold sweat washed down her back. It had been years since the whispers had occupied her mind day and night. At times she had feared she'd gone insane. It couldn't be happening all over again. Not today.

"What did you hear?" He leaned on his elbows, appearing eager for more information.

"Not sure. Someone asked me to not to look at him." Heat seared her cheeks. She waved her hand, chuckling. "Silly, I must be worn out. I've started hearing ghosts."

Ghosts. You've no idea how right you are.

The leather of the seat crinkled as she shifted uneasily, wrinkling her nose. Her laugh wasn't confident any more. "I guess you didn't hear that either?"

He raised an eyebrow and shook his head.

Her fingernails scraped her thighs. She mustn't panic. She was overtired. That's all. Nothing a good night's sleep wouldn't cure.

"Tell me more about your first day. Other than it's going pretty good, how do you find your room?"

A load lifted off her shoulders when he changed the subject. "I love it. Can't wait to try out the big bed. I didn't get much sleep last night."

He shifted in his chair, coughing. "The boys go to bed early. I suggest you do, too. Their schedule may wear you out."

"They should have some free time." She creased her forehead, pleading with him. How could he pack the boys' days with all those activities? One couldn't help but think he didn't want to deal with them.

"They will." He nodded. "We'll travel once the school is out for summer. I expect you to accompany us. Do you have your passport in order?"

She shook her head. "No. I'll have to renew it. The process is faster if I fill out the forms online. I need access to the Internet though." Would he allow her to use the computer? She was here to take care of his children not to surf the net.

"I'll get you set up with wireless connection," he said, leaning back. He appeared relaxed now.

"May I ask where are we going?"

"Croatia."

She gasped and clapped her hands over her mouth. This time she couldn't contain her tears. "Home."

"The children will spend two weeks with our friends. That will be your paid vacation. Then we'll go to the islet of *Aba Vela* and stay there until we return in late August."

She couldn't believe her ears. "*Aba Vela*, close to *Sali?*"

He nodded once, his lips pressed into a thin line.

"Straight to my neck of woods."

"I can see how happy this makes you, but don't forget it's still work," he said, wagging his finger.

"Yes, of course, Mr. Zrin." She shouldn't let her happiness get the best of her, but she struggled to restrain from bouncing. "I haven't been home in ten years. My first day just went from pretty good to fabulous."

"Kate," he croaked. "I like the excitement you have brought to this home and from the look of it, the boys take to you. Rosalia won't show her joy, but I know the old lady is grateful she has someone to talk to."

No Miss Rokov. She loved the way he said her name and couldn't stop the smile. If she didn't know better, she'd think he longed for her. That was probably just her overtired imagination playing tricks on her again. "Thank you, Mr. Zrin. I like it here."

"Before I forget." He stood, taking the garage door opener from the top drawer. "Let me show you the car."

She cocked her head. This wasn't mentioned in the employment package. "The car?"

"The roads around here get very treacherous in the winter. I saw your rusty Corolla on the driveway."

Not very gentlemanly of him to badmouth her car, but he was right.

He jerked his head toward the door. She followed him down a long hallway with large windows on both sides.

"The garage is attached to the house by this corridor." He pointed to the rack on the wall next to the white door. "The keys hang here. These doors lead into the garage, but let's step outside." The sun reflected on the glass as he pulled the side door open.

The warm asphalt of the driveway burned her soles when she stepped outside. The heat didn't seem to bother his bare feet. The doors on the three-car garage glided up when he pressed the button.

"Think of it as a company vehicle." He pointed to the silver Grand Cherokee parked in the middle. "I had the interior steam cleaned. The previous nanny spilled her mocha Grande Frappuccino after I specifically requested no food in the car. Feel free to take the Jeep for a spin."

Her legs froze. "I will," she whispered. "Is it okay with you if I take the boys for some ice cream?"

"Yes, by all means, but no eating in the car. Leather interior." He shrugged and pulled the wallet out of his jeans' pocket. "And if you wouldn't mind, take Rosalia once a month to the farmers' markets. It's her treat, reminds her of the *piazza* back home."

"It's my treat, Mr. Zrin." Kate said with a quick smile, refusing the money for the ice cream. She glanced back at the garage. "I take it you drive the Audi."

He cocked his head and shrugged as if he wanted to apologize for being rich. "I do."

"Is that a red convertible?" She jerked her chin in the direction of the third car, hidden under a tarp.

His mouth dropped open, but he snapped it shut fast. "Emina's Porsche. It hasn't been moved from this garage since her death."

How could she know this? His puzzled look met hers. She should say something to him, but she was a new employee, and he would perceive her as crazy. No reasonable parent would allow a demented person anywhere near his children. No. Better to stay silent.

He reached his hand out toward her.

She pulled back, suspecting he wanted to touch her hair.

"I have to return to my work." His hand balled into a fist and dropped to his side. "I'll let you go for now. We mustn't leave Rosalia with the boys for too long," he said then hurried away.

Kate followed him. "Mr. Zrin."

He stopped and faced her.

"I noticed the boys' self-help skills are poor. We need to work on them, but I don't want to step on Rosalia's toes."

"Do what you need to do and don't worry about Rosalia. She loves the boys too much and is doing them a disservice. What can I say? She can't help herself." He shoved his hands into his jeans pockets. "I'll talk to her. Enjoy your first day. Tomorrow, the busy routine returns."

He pulled one hand out of his pocket and tapped Kate's arm, then continued walking, leaving her behind.

Once alone, she jumped up and down, pressing her hands together. Three wonderful boys, a new car, trip home, huge bedroom with en suite bathroom and nice furniture. Mr. Wilkins had her so worked up, she had almost changed her mind and turned around. Mr. Zrin must be the world's greatest boss. What did she do to deserve all this luck? Oh yes, luck didn't exist.

Sweet mamma, Mr. Zrin made her heart race. The emotions took her by surprise. She had considered the yearning dead since the break-up of her short marriage.

The whispers she had heard in his office had been a close call. For a moment there, fear had gripped her mind and body with a thought that Miles could have returned.

Why would he? All he had wanted from her was for her to write about his life. Then he vanished. Nonetheless, her ex, or rather his lawyer, used her obsession with the legendary character in the divorce settlement. As if a man, who had lived three centuries ago and loved his sweet Dobrila could pose any kind of a threat now. Maybe someday she'd be able to forgive Craig's ugly words, but today was not the day.

She froze. The box she had dropped earlier at Master's door contained the memory stick with the copy of the novel. She was certain she had not picked the device up off the floor.

Matthias retreated to the solitude of his bedroom, flattening his back against the cool wood of the door. He held his breath and studied the stucco ceiling. A thorough kick in his backside is what he deserved for leaving the girl in the dark, but he couldn't help himself. The shapes overhead floated before his eyes as he let the air out of his lungs.

Kate practically staked him with her tenderness. Although it had been years since he severed the telepathic connection with her, he cared too much to leave her completely and had remained at the fringes of her mind. Could she possibly still hear him?

Whispers in this house were not so unusual once. He remembered the time when he and Emina had shared a mental connection. It allowed them to hear each other's thoughts in their minds.

He stepped to the bed and plopped down, bracing his head with one arm. At least Kate had dismissed the voice inside her head as overtiredness.

A glimpse of red under the mahogany dresser next to the door caught his eye. Damn, he was ready for a nap, but he stood and walked to it then squatted and retrieved a memory stick that didn't belong to him. The storage device must have slid under the door when the box containing Kate's stationary spilled.

Maybe a brief look of what was on the stick? What could it hurt? He glanced at the leather case propped against the nightstand and closed his fingers around the item as he rose from the floor. Who was he to snoop in her private things? He must return this to her.

The ring of his cell phone stopped him on his way out of the room. Nannies' Care displayed on the cell's screen. Sighing, he pressed the talk button.

"Yes, Mr. Wilkins. What can I do for you, today?" he said, struggling to keep his voice steady.

"Doctor Zrin, we sent a nanny your way." Mr. Wilkins's voice blared in his ear. "Has she arrived?"

"Yes, I just met her."

"Just now? She was supposed to be there by eight. I can assure you, Doctor Zrin, we have zero tolerance for tardiness. I have another nanny standing by. I can send her there right away."

"That will not be necessary. Miss Rokov arrived on time. I was the one running late." Matthias paced in front of the bed. "Besides, I was clear in my request for a nanny to be fluent in Croatian. It's something very important to my late wife and me. None of your other applicants qualified. Now, if you'll excuse me, I've got things to attend to." He ended the call and threw the phone on the bed. Mr. Wilkins suddenly seemed a little too eager to do the job He had never checked on any of the other nannies he sent to this house.

Matthias returned his attention to the memory stick in his hand. One little peek, no more, he promised, as he pulled the laptop out of the case and inserted the device into the USB port. The computer booted up and displayed the file folders on the screen.

"It's here," he whispered in awe, not expecting to find his life's story stored away on this small stick. "Last modified six years ago." No wonder Kate's memory was fuzzy. It must've been quite some time since she'd thought of him and Emina.

He double-clicked on the icon named *Rose*. Everything was here, the query letter, the synopsis all ready for submission. Had Kate ever found the courage to send them? How would he explain all this to her? One small detail at the time. No mortal could take this in all at once.

The image of her doe-like eyes, soft face, and hazel hair danced in front of him. So different from Emina, and yet Kate's mannerisms reminded him of his beloved. No, to love another would go against his vow of eternal love and faithfulness to Emina.

Why then, couldn't he stop thinking of Kate?

CHAPTER 3

Barry Wilkins pulled a form with Nannies' Care logo from his brief case and clipped the sheet to the clipboard. The large Zrin's estate sprawled in front of his car. Canada was once a proud country. Damn government had to help every crying baby, allowing migrants to come here, take over good jobs, and own nice homes. He'd never *been* in a place like this, much less owned one.

No wonder the economy was in the crapper. Fine, if they must come here, let them work at the jobs no one else wanted. There was plenty of Canadian geese poop they could scrap from the parks. That was what foreigners were for.

With his clipboard in one hand, he stepped out of the car. The overcast sky threatened a downpour. The first drops dampened his plaid shirt as he scurried to the front door and rang the bell.

"Good morning," he said, greeting the ever-ungraceful maid. The woman frowned in disgust. If it were up to Barry, he'd ship her back wherever she came from. "I'm from Nannies' Care, here to check on Miss Rokov, your nanny."

He jerked his head back when she slammed the door in his face. What kind of rude and illiterate peasants lived here?

The door opened again, and he forced a grin at the sight of Doctor Zrin.

"Mr. Wilkins?" Zrin blocked the entrance and appeared as if he had no intention of letting him in.

"Good morning, Doctor Zrin. I'm here to observe Miss Rokov." Barry straightened his lips at Zrin's stern face. "We must ensure both parties are happy."

"Come in, then." Zrin stepped aside.

The beauty of the house increased once inside. Bizarre abstract paintings decorated each wall of the sitting room where Zrin led him—all of them an unrecognizable disarray of lines and circles. Originals no doubt. The rich didn't hang copies. Judging by the size, the frames alone must be worth a fortune.

"Mr. Wilkins." Zrin gestured for him to sit on the white sofa facing his chair.

Barry lowered himself onto the nice, firm seat. Must've not been used very often. "Did you know our agency also places professional housekeepers?" Such a beautiful home deserved a maid who can perform her duties without a dictionary.

"No, I did not. I'll keep that in mind, but our maid is as professional as they come."

Was Zrin bluffing? Barry was good at reading people's expressions but could never read the Doctor's pale face.

Zrin took his seat and crossed his ankle over his knee. "How much do I still owe the agency for finder's fees?"

"Excuse me?" Barry straightened, taken aback with Zrin's bold assumption.

Crap, he hated it when Zrin stared at him as if reading his mind. Barry averted his eyes to the questionnaire on the clipboard in his hand.

"The finder's fees, Mr. Wilkins? The same ones I paid time and again for every nanny you sent here." Zrin's eyebrows rose as annoyance filled his voice.

"I'm here to observe Miss Rokov interacting with your children. I wouldn't know the financial side of your account." Barry laughed to ease of the tension. What was Zrin up to?

"Miss Rokov is not here. She took the boys to the school, and I sent her on an errand. It may take her the whole day."

"In that case, I'll have to return another day." Barry flipped the clipboard down. This may work to his advantage. If Kate's observations weren't completed in time Zrin couldn't take her into permanent employment.

Zrin shook his head. "You can't come here unannounced."

"The surprise visits give us the true insight in the nanny's work."

"I'm very satisfied with Miss Rokov and will hire her full time."

"You're satisfied?" Barry's mind raced. "Why be merely satisfied when you could have a nanny who would do the job so you could be ecstatic?"

"My children are used to her by now. They adore her. I'm afraid replacing Miss Rokov with someone else at this point would cause us all unnecessary grief." Zrin's eyes narrowed as he stared at him.

Shit, Zrin wasn't biting. Think Barry, think for crap sake. If he failed to place someone he could manipulate, he wouldn't be able to gain access to Zrin's bank account. If he couldn't pay the loan shark back, he'd be in for some serious trouble. The last time the man threatened to send his collectors after him. They were known to break kneecaps.

Zrin lowered his foot and sat up straight. "She even cooks dinner once a week. I don't know how she managed to get our maid to agree. Rosalia wouldn't have given up her kitchen that easily."

"That's all fine and dandy, but her ninety-day probation period isn't over yet. You'd be in breach of your contract. Plus, her work must meet our high standards. We're a prestigious placement agency. Once we match a nanny with the family, we must make sure both parties are satisfied."

Zrin already knew he could pay the fees before nanny's trial period was up. So playing on the conditions of the agreement was the only thing Barry could use to discourage him.

"Yes, you already said so and we are pleased. That is why I'm willing to pay the finder's fee upfront. I can write you a check right now."

Barry's temper flared. The rich were all the same. They thought they could buy anything with their money, but not everything was for sale.

"I'd have to run this by my supervisor, but I don't think she'll agree. It's never been done before. You signed a contract with us."

"I'd like a word with your supervisor. I'm sure we can come to some sort of agreement."

Zrin smiled, exposing straight, white teeth. Barry pressed his lips together to hide his yellow, crooked ones. The latest laser whitening treatments were for those with deep pockets. Hell, he couldn't even remember last time he went to the dentist.

"All I can do is pass along your message, Doctor Zrin," Barry lied.

"Will that be all?" Zrin stood and stepped to the door. "You caught me at the bad time. I must return to my work."

"Yes, that's all, Doctor Zrin." What work? The check mark logo on Zrin's gym clothes caught Barry's attention. He rose, drawing in a long breath, and tried to think of anything else to say.

"Have a nice day." Zrin held the front door open for him. "I'm sorry you drove all the way here and missed Miss Rokov. Please have the release forms mailed. I'll make sure I sign and send them back along with a check for any outstanding fees."

"I can't promise anything." Barry stepped out, the anger inside him about to burst. "Goodbye, Doctor Zrin."

"Good bye," the Doctor said and added. "And, Mr. Wilkins—"

Barry stopped at the bottom of the steps and turned to face him.

"Thank you for finding Miss Rokov. Life has returned to our house at last." Zrin even dared to cast him a smile.

"You're welcome," Barry said through gritted teeth. Sour bile rose up his throat. He scurried to his car.

"Hell's bells." He pounded his fists on the steering wheel, ignoring the pain. How could he have underestimate Kate? He should've placed her somewhere else while he had the chance. Other families had requested her again, but he had shoved her file in the lowest drawer. He would have sent her to one of them if Zrin had not insisted on Kate once Barry faxed him her resume. She was the only one in the agency fluent in Croatian. It wasn't like Croatian-speaking nannies were wildly available in the middle of Canada unless they were straight off the boat. From what he gathered, youngsters were rarely taught the language at home.

The tear on the polyester cover of the headrest scratched through his thin hair as he pondered his dilemma. There wouldn't be enough time now to put his plan into action. He'd have to change the dates on Kate's files. It wouldn't be the first time he'd had to forge the documents. By the time anyone noticed, he'd be rolling in Zrin's money.

Though he stole a bit from every client, he was in an urgent need of big cash, and Zrin owed him big time. After Barry cleaned out Zrin's account, he'd go incognito.

However, he had to be smarter than the last time, when he had been employed in the nursing agency. The fake nurse he had sent to tend to pregnant Mrs. Zrin had screwed up, costing him the job. The wench had not even gotten him the information he needed to get to Zrin's business account. That was where the most of the money was, not the doctor's personal account. With multiple signing officers, business accounts were easier to manipulate.

Good thing Barry's signature hadn't appeared on any of the documents, so the management couldn't pin the mishap of an unqualified nurse on him. She was the one who had overdosed Mrs. Zrin. The agency hushed it all up nicely. And the management at MedEx thought if they kicked Barry to the curb, their problems were over?

No. They had just begun.

What did Zrin say? He had sent Kate on an errand. Zrin should know nannies were there to benefit the children. It was in his contract. He'd write this up as wrongful action. Two more incidents like this, and Kate would be out of there.

The wiper blades swished over the windshield at full speed. Water sloshed under the tires. Her seatbelt pressed against Kate's chest as she jammed the brake to stop at the red light. Dark clouds hovered low, and she flipped on the headlights in the middle of the day.

What good had it done her to fill the application out online? Once at the passport office she spent most of the morning waiting for her number to come up on the screen only to be done at the clerk's window in one minute.

Despite her frustration, warmth flooded her. She could hardly wait. Ever since Mr. Zrin informed her of the upcoming trip, the days, although busy, passed by so slowly. Just as her boss becoming involved in his boys' lives progressed at a snail's pace. At least he made a point to sit with them at the dinner table. Even if he didn't eat every time, he was there and the boys were getting used to him.

She'd been working in the Zrin household for a month now, and she still waited for things to go bump in the night. Nothing unusual happened anymore when she stared at Emina's portrait. No ink-like dots spread over the canvas, Emina's eyes and face didn't change.

However, Rosalia complained Kate spent too much time examining the painting and not concentrating on her duties. So Kate knew she'd have to be careful about that.

Emina's pictures, portrayed in authentic period costumes, dominated throughout the house. Even her hair was styled as the fashion of the times dictated. Maybe she was an actress and played in movies depicting lives of past centuries.

Strange that there weren't any pictures on display of Mr. Zrin.

"*Up-side-down, boy you turn me...*" sounded from the radio and she turned up the volume.

Mr. Zrin. Kate smiled as her mind drifted to him. Even though she was thirty years old, she giggled like some teenage girl at the mere thought of his name. She moaned as his image replaced the streetlight in front of her. The tug on the corners of his lips could hardly pass for a smile, but it jump-started her heart every time. Not to mention the dimples in his cheeks.

She sighed. Better not think of him that way. They shared a professional relationship. Besides, a single dad falling for his children's nanny only happened in romance novels, and her life couldn't be further from such tales. He most likely dated, anyway. A man such as he would enjoy a company of a rich, overeducated, sophisticated lady, not her—plain Kate.

A honk from behind her snapped her back into the moment. She cut a glance at the traffic lights—it must have been green for a while.

"Alright, hold your horses." She eased of the brake and rolled down the narrow street lined with small shops.

With the traffic jam, she'd be late to get the boys from school. Her knees shook with the sight of a white Elantra with Nannies' Care logo signalling to get in her lane. The agent warned her he'd be watching her like a hawk. If he paid the Zrins a visit, and she wasn't there, who knew what he'd write on the report? The thought ignited a shudder. Barry Wilkins gave her the creeps. Might not have been him in the car, though. The agency may have a branch out here.

Her attention returned to the road. She pulled up in front of the school and got out of the car. The dismissal bell rang. Luckily, it had stopped raining just as kids poured out of every door.

Her eyes widened and her stomach dropped at the sight of Ivan's bruised face. She crouched in front of him and struggled to hide the tremble in her voice. "Honey, what happened?"

"We had an incident."

Kate raised her head at casual tone of the boys' teacher. According to her young looks, this might be the girl's first year on the job.

"It happened during the afternoon recess. I wasn't present, but some boys bullied Teo and Ivan came to his brother's defence." She extended a paper to Kate. "We called home but there was no answer so we wrote up an accident report."

Kate levelled her eyes with the teacher's. "You're putting me in a very difficult position. I'm the boys' nanny and I cannot explain this to their father with a piece of paper. Doesn't the school have my cell number on the record?"

The teacher frowned, shrugged, and shook her head. "I guess not."

Kate blew air out. "Can I give it to you now?"

"I suppose." The woman produced a sticky notepad and pen from her pocket and handed it to Kate so she could write the info. "The instigators have been reprimanded," the teacher said. "In fact, they're still in the Principal's office. Their parents have been called in. I'm quite sure the students are facing expulsion. Mr. Zrin can press charges if he wants to." She cocked her head, a frown creasing her brow. "But he should keep in mind these are minors."

"Has this happened before?" A hint of anger mixed with fear inside Kate, tensing her shoulders. If Mr. Zrin reacted badly to this, it was his fault. He had failed to inform her something like this could happen.

"Once or twice," the boys' teacher said. "Their dad spoke with the Principal each time. The school is not in the position to release the names of the children involved, but we will not tolerate bullying." She took the sticky notepad and pen from Kate's hand. "They are under the Minors Protection Act." The teacher looked away and waved. "Excuse me," she said, and took her leave.

Kate crouched in front of the boys again.

"Don't worry, Aunt Katie." Ivan's grin melted her heart. "The other boy looks worse."

She pulled all three into a bear hug. The tingling started in her fingers, and the sensation travelled through her arms then spread all over her. With her pulse quickening, she trembled. The feeling was familiar. The same experience had happened the very first time she had looked at Emina's portrait. For a fraction of an instant, Kate had the sensation that someone else had taken control of her body. Like someone had invaded her when she reached out for the boys. But this was insane. She flexed her neck to shake off the feeling.

"My sweet darlings," she heard herself say in a hoarse voice through her tight throat.

What had provoked the strange reaction? She had hugged them before, but this was the first time she had held all three in her arms at once. This wasn't a déjà vu or some kind of coincidence. Something odd was going on, and she intended to find out what.

"Aunt Katie, are you alright?"

Ivan's voice startled her and she loosened her grip on them. "I'm fine, honey. Did I squeeze you guys too hard?" She pulled back and the sensation dissipated the same way it started.

"I like your hugs." Luka threw his arms around her neck. "Can we do it again?"

"Not now, Luka." She tickled his ribs and he squirmed away. "We have to go. It's starting to rain again."

Droplets bounced off her raincoat while she hurriedly strapped them into their seats. She got into the driver's seat and buckled in. First, she had to teach the boys to stand up against the bullies with their wits, not their fists. A challenging task with ten school days left, but they'd be prepared when they started first grade.

Kate nibbled on her lips as Mr. Zrin examined Ivan and determined no damage was done to the boy's eye. She relaxed and rubbed her temple. The migraine pounded against her forehead. Thinking about his possible reaction had her worried during the entire drive home. Yet it turned out, he took the news a tad too calmly. His words echoed in her mind. *'The world will keep on spinning.'*

Despite their protests, the boys went to bed early. She retired early, too. The bedding rustled as she turned to her side, but the headache wouldn't allow sleep to take her. Frustrated at the relentless pain, she crept out of her room and into the quiet house, looking for a diversion from her discomfort. Light under the door of the "Master's chamber" drew her attention. Mr. Zrin was awake. No, as much as she would like it, he would not be a good diversion. Her feet threading on the lush carpet, she scurried down the stairs to the sitting parlour. The edges of the hard covers of the books on the shelf scraped her finger as she traced it over them. Where did she see the one she planned to read if she could focus her eyes on the lines?

She pulled out a book with a red cover and golden letters. The yellowed pages and stale paper smell assaulted her when she flipped the volume open. She glanced to the bottom of the first page and stared at the "eighteen-seventy"—the year of publication. The fabric of her pyjamas bottoms bunching behind her knees, she sat on the sofa and switched on a lamp on the corner stand.

Yawns started to plague her after the tenth page. She lowered the book onto her lap. The knight's tale was a captivating narrative, but she sensed what would happen next—although story was in no way predictable—quite the opposite, in fact. So how could she know the outcome if she'd never read the book before?

"How do you find *Templar's Journey*?"

She gasped at Matthias's voice and sprang to her feet. The book dropped to the floor with a heavy thud.

"You startled me, Mr. Zrin." She reached for the novel, not taking her eyes away from her barely dressed boss. A strap held his robe in place around his hips. The collar hung casually open to reveal the pale skin of his chest.

He leaned on the doorframe. "How come you are up this late?"

"I have a headache."

He disappeared behind the coat closet door and brought out his doctor's bag. "I can give you something mild to help you sleep."

"Thanks, but aspirin won't help."

He rummaged through his bag. "You have a migraine. I know."

"How did you know?"

"You were quiet during the dinner and kept pulling on the same eyebrow. Rosalia's stew was delicious but you didn't taste it. Having a sick stomach is normal for a migraine." He wrinkled his nose and gave her a sympathetic smile. "But what really gave you away was the fact you evaded sitting at your favourite place in front of the huge window. The light hurt your eyes, I believe?"

She shrugged one shoulder, frowning, trying not to let him know how pleased she was that he was paying so much attention to her.

"Here, take this." He held a pill on his palm.

She picked the capsule and examined its triangle shape. "What is it?"

"The new drug for migraines. I had a pharmaceutical sales rep in my office yesterday. He left me the physician samples. If it alleviates the pain, I'll write you up a prescription." Mr. Zrin left the room, apparently headed for the kitchen. "You'll need water," he called over his shoulder.

Wouldn't it be interesting to see if he could find his way around the kitchen?

To her surprise, he returned with a tall glass and handed it to her. "You're upset over the school incident, aren't you?"

She popped the pill in her mouth and chased the pink capsule down with a long gulp of water. "Yes, your boys are the sweetest little things. How can someone bully them?" Her throat tightened and she closed her eyes for one brief moment. When she opened them again, his face was a few inches away from hers.

"Ivan is fine, and the school will do whatever is in their power to stop this from happening again. And so will we." His tender voice had a calming effect on her frail nerves. He took the glass from her hand and placed it on the coffee table.

A tear rolled down her cheek. He cupped her face and wiped the droplet away with his thumb. "Don't cry. Please."

She shivered at this touch. He slid his hand behind her neck, pulling her into his embrace.

In spite of her better judgement, her arms rose and slipped around his neck. She was in Heaven, enveloped in his masculine scent.

"Matthias, at last, at last. I waited for so long." What the heck was she saying? The yearning inside her tightened her chest.

"No, my dove. You mustn't do this." He brushed her hair back. A pained smile stretched his lips before he let her go.

Kate took a step back, holding her hand pressed against her heaving chest. "I—my head feels better. I'll return to my room."

He bowed. "You do that." The cushions of the white chair bent under him when he sat.

She charged up the stairs. Had she gone insane? Acting on impulse was so not her. *His dove*, he called her. She snorted. Only Miles would use this special pet name for her.

Miles. The last time she'd thought about him had been during her talk with Mr. Zrin that first day. Could her creation of a fantasy lover possibly have returned in the body of a human? Of Mr. Zrin? Maybe the ghost of her past had entered the doctor's mind so he could be together with her again. Miles hadn't occupied her mind once since she wrote his life story—when his constant presence in her thoughts almost drove her crazy. But a terrible emptiness had swamped her after he disappeared, leaving scars in her soul.

Mom had taught her not to believe in fairy tales, not to be a dreamer, because life was too hard for nonsense. Mom's word was law in her life and yet, Kate had written a fantasy novel.

The bedding crinkled as she pulled the coverlet over her head. The pill Mr. Zrin had given her had kicked in fully. Her eyelids drooped. Right now wasn't the best time to sort out her confused feelings between the real Mr. Zrin and the imaginary Miles.

CHAPTER 4

The ropes of the hammock creaked as the hanging bed swayed on the terrace overlooking the Adriatic. Kate relaxed, listening to the chirping of night crickets. For the past decade, she'd missed the warm, salty air. She drew in another deep breath, delighting her senses.

Twenty-six hours, three planes, and a car ride after they left Canada, they've arrived in Croatia.

Upon landing, Mr. Zrin appeared invigorated. No wonder. He'd covered his eyes with a black patch and slept, waking up only when the meal cart came around. Kate wished she could drop off and be dead to the world on long hauls. At least the boys had provided plenty of entertainment.

Rosalia's relatives had waited for her at the airport. She'd bid her goodbyes and started her two-month vacation. The image of her attempting a happy dance made Kate chuckle. The old lady deserved the time off work.

Secretly, she was glad Mr. Zrin slept most of the journey. After their shared embrace in the library, Kate had been certain he'd fire her. With fear infesting her mind, she'd wondered if she would ever get to take him in her arms again. No, it wasn't likely to happen. He'd avoided her for the whole week. When he spoke to her, he never once looked her in the eye.

The warm night breeze rustled the leaves of an aged fern tree. Aware of every little thing, Kate revelled in her surroundings.

Mr. Zrin stepped out through the wide doors. "How does it feel to be back home?"

"It's breathing new life into me." She attempted to sit up. Dizziness pulled her back.

"Do you want to stay with your family until the boys visit our friends? I know the boys would love to have you around, but if you wish to go—" He shrugged, not meeting her gaze.

"Yes I do. My parent's place is not far from here."

"We can take you there in the morning. The boys won't see you for two weeks. They'll be disappointed if you leave without saying goodbye."

"Of course, Mr. Zrin. Besides, wild horses couldn't drag me away from this hammock right now." She pressed her hand over her yawning mouth.

"Sorry, but you're a little too late to crave this special place. I claimed this hammock years ago." He winked at her and cocked his head. "And just so you know, here I'm Matthias, or Matt, if you will. No Mr. nor doctor or, God forbid, master."

She examined his face. He appeared different. Relaxed and smiling. As if he left Mr. Prim and Proper Zrin on the plane. He even had a glass of beer in his hand. The Dalmatian coast apparently loosened the stiffest of men.

"Okay, Matthias." She gave him a reluctant smile. "I'm just Kate. And I'm sorry, but I'm so tired I can't move."

"I'll let you off this time. Scoot over."

The hammock swung when he dropped down beside her, taking more than half of the space and leaving her no choice but to move to the edge.

"Look at those stars." He sighed and pointed at the sky. "Beautiful, aren't they?"

She covered another yawn with her hand without taking a look at the nightly firmament. Tired, she didn't have strength left in her to star gaze.

His laugher sounded from far away when she mumbled some undefined words before the sleep claimed her.

Soft breezes rustled the leaves of the tree and woke her twice. Her head rested on Matthias's shoulder, but the sweet smell of his skin drifting to her and the gentle sway of the hammock lulled her back to sleep within a minute.

She must have slept for hours nestled against him, and he appeared as if he never so much as stirred a muscle underneath her cheek. But when she woke for the third time, he insisted she needed the comfort of a cozy bed. Half asleep, she staggered out of the hammock. He steadied her on her feet. With his arm wrapped around her waist, she wobbled to her room and collapsed on the queen-sized bed. Her heavy eyelids refused to stay open. The last thing she remembered was his knuckles brushing down her cheek before settling on her cleavage.

The boys' Aunt Ana, as they called her, dressed and fed them. Guilt stirred in Kate, her vacation hadn't started yet, but she was letting someone else do her work.

Mixed with her guilt was confusion and she frowned each time Matthias and the host of the house, Petar exchanged looks and nods. They must have communicated some plan or a mission in some way or played a silent guessing game. Would they have to kill her if she ever found out about it? She scolded herself for her overactive imagination, but at least it took her mind off her depression about leaving the boys.

She dreaded being away from them, even if for a short while.

All three boys clung to her. "Don't go, Katie. We'll miss you." The tears in their eyes broke her heart.

"I'll miss you, too, but I'll be back, I promise. No crying now." She hurriedly planted a kiss on each boy's forehead and rushed out to the car, feeling the sting of her own tears.

Two weeks of paid vacation. She had hoped to connect with old friends, spend days laying on the beaches, and nights sipping drinks on the patios of her favorite cafes. But time had changed everything. All her friends were married or had moved away. She didn't recognize anyone in her own town. The beaches were privately owned and opened for hotel guests only. One of her favorite bars still stood, but it was degraded to a local watering hole.

What would she do with the rest of her free time? She reminded herself that Zadar had a rich history, and she should re-connect with its heritage and perhaps even try to write again. Something she hadn't done in over six years. Her ex had crushed her dreams of becoming a writer with one demeaning remark: *'Get real. You have no talent.'*

She left her mother's small apartment and passed through the Bridge Gate under the steep medieval-defense walls then continued on to the Forum. A central market and public area during Roman times, it lay in ruins for almost two thousand years. Now it was a tourist attraction. Unable to resist the temptation, she ran through the remains and pretended she was a child again, playing hide and seek.

She crossed the square to the Church of Saint Donatus. Religious services had not been held here for centuries, but the place made her feel as if she had stepped out of the busy modern world into an unchanging, ancient realm, wrapped in a shroud of mystery, waiting to be awakened again someday.

A few tourists, fascinated with the unusual round structure of the building, *oohed* and *aahed* at the entrance. She paid the admission and strolled across the three apses cloister. An amateur sang an unrecognizable tune on the small stage. Anywhere else in the world, his singing would sound like strangling a cat, but the stark interior provided acoustics that made his voice bearable.

The steep stairs took her to the first floor arcade where she walked around, looking down on the ground level until she completed the circle. This was her little ritual each time she visited here.

The thick, stonewalls kept the heat out. She took a deep breath, sat, and pulled the laptop out of her bag. So, what else was new here, besides the marble floor? She scanned the interior while her computer booted, taking note of the plexi-glass coverings on the windows. Good, it kept the pigeons out. Street noises mixed with the clunking sounds of guys setting up chairs on the lower level for the concert venue of the Annual International Festival of Renaissance Music.

Staring at the flashing cursor, she searched her mind. Maybe something would come to her if she touched the ancient walls.

"Come on, talk to me," she whispered, pressing her palm on the Roman pillar that early Byzantine settlers had incorporated into the edifice. Nothing. It would probably take some time before her muse returned.

A quiet chuckle echoed. She looked around. The upper level stood empty apart from the honeymooning couple she pretended to ignore. Their display of affection in this public place rushed the heat to her cheeks. A camera flashed again and they left, holding hands. Ah, yes love. Her heart ached with envy.

"Tried that many times, but these walls are stubborn." A shape rounded the pillar. "The pillars won't talk."

Shoving the screen of the laptop down, she scrambled to her feet. She never thought she'd crave his company, but seeing him after three long days, the realization that she'd missed him hit her hard.

Matthias approached with slow steps. His devilish little smile stirred butterflies in her stomach. Her hands trembling, she played with her fingers.

"How are the boys?" she asked to break the awkwardness.

"Their usual, can't stay still for one minute. They ask about you all the time." Matthias's voice echoed in the stark church interior. "How's your vacation going?"

"Slow. I'm not used to sitting around and doing nothing." She laughed, his smile widened.

He nodded. "Enjoy while it lasts. In a week's time it'll be over."

She lowered her gaze from his face to her feet. "I can hardly wait." Her so-called vacation had left her with an empty feeling only his boys could fill.

"Your family must have been happy to see you?"

Pain stabbed at her chest. "They were, but it was hard. My dad passed away four years ago and—" She took a deep breath and stared over his shoulder. How would she explain she had not come home for Dad's funeral? "I requested time off work, but couldn't get it. Besides, I didn't have the money."

"I understand." His soft voice eased the tightness in her ribcage. "So, you like coming here, too?"

Glad he had changed the subject, she relaxed her shoulders. Her family had become smaller and, as their numbers declined over the generations, the more estranged the current members had become. Not something she liked to discuss with anyone, let alone him.

"Yes I do. This place takes me back into history." She sighed. "Wouldn't it be great to see this church in its former glory?"

"It would." He pressed his back against the balustrade and shoved his hands in the large side pockets of his cargo shorts, staring at her in silence for an eternal moment. "Will you do me a favor and sign this?" He extended a book to her.

She took the pages bound in a cover of red and white squares with a rose across the middle. Funny, she'd chosen this picture for her novel to have on the sleeve, if it ever got published. *Rose of Crimson, by Kate Rokov* was printed on the front. The words started to sink in as she leveled her eyes with his. "You want me to sign this for you?"

He drew a long breath and nodded again.

"How?" she asked. "This never left my computer." Puzzled, she searched his face.

His smile vanished. "I found the files on the memory stick on your first day."

She shook her head in disbelief. "You returned it."

"Forgive me." His gaze travelled back and forth from her face to the floor. "I copied the files."

Silence followed. She stood transfixed. He had copied her files? Why would he?

He reached out to her. "Wasn't this what you wanted? To see it published one day?"

She lowered her gaze to book in her hands. Her book. Not just an electronic file anymore, but pages with a hard cover and a sleeve. How did he know she was dying to see it as a book one day?

He took a step closer. "This is the only copy. Just for you." His breath caused wisps of her hair to flutter. "Please say something."

A tsunami of joy, disbelief, and anger rose inside her. "Why did you do this?"

He turned his head to his right. A pained expression filled his rugged features. "Miles and Dobrila's story is mine and Emina's."

Kate frowned, still examining his face. "You mean their story reminds you of your and Emina?"

"No." His brows arched and he tensed. "It is our story."

"You lost me." She faked a laugh to mask her confusion. "Miles and Dobrila lived in the seventeenth century. How can it be your story?"

His broad shoulders rose and fell when he blew air out. "What happened to them at the end?"

"They died. Didn't you read it?" Wide-eyed, she pressed index finger of her free hand to her lips. She got it. He'd point at her any moment now, say something like *gotcha* and burst into laugh.

"I did, even if I didn't need to. It's my life story. I held Dobrila in my arms through the night as she was dying. It was me who made her immortal and me who helped her out of the grave."

"Yes, and they walked away holding hands. The ending is fiction. Are you trying to tell me its real life?"

She waited for him to tilt his head and wink. Her heart sank when she realized he wasn't joking. Typical, just when she started to like a man, he turned into a weirdo. How could he come up with lies like this and stay so collected?

"I've been living like this since sixteen-ninety." The sadness in his voice caused weakness in her knees, but she steadied herself.

"Miles was barley nineteen when Dobrila's father shot him. You're older." Yes, Rosalia had said he turned forty-four, but to Kate he appeared to be in his mid-thirties.

She thought about trying to escape, but her ankles felt as if they were attached to a ball and chain. No way could this man be Miles. Could he? Miles and Dobrila existed once. Kate didn't pull their story from her head. Only the ending was fiction, but she wasn't sure whose imagination was at play there, hers or Miles'. What kind of force made them immortal? Could immortals have babies? Why then didn't he save Emina? No, this was too far-fetched.

"I do age." His solemn voice startled her. "And to answer your other questions would require more than a pot of coffee."

She cast him a sharp glance. He heard her thoughts? "I get it. Now you going to tell me you're an immortal."

"I am."

"Prove it." Surprised at her actions and words, she forced out a laugh to mask her fear and wagged her finger.

"Prove it?" His forehead creased. "What do you want me to do?"

"You started this charade. It will be interesting to see how you're going to get yourself out of this. There's something crucial about Miles I didn't put in the book." She'd be lucky if he didn't fire her after the way she talked to him.

"I'm not in the position to show you my heart shaped mole." He shifted his feet and lowered his voice to a whisper when another couple of tourists came in. "It's higher up my inner thigh than you thought."

"That's not what I meant." How could he know this? "Try again."

He stepped closer to her and lowered his head to her ear. "You assumed I'm a vampire."

Not believing her ears, she jerked her head back. "Not you, Miles. I mean, he is. I mean—argh—you know what I mean." In the book, she might not have spelled out that Miles became a vampire, but she had hinted at it.

Matthias's lips stretched in a tight smile. "I'm immortal but not a vampire."

"Miles fed on humans." She hissed when a tourist strolled by them.

"You're wrong." Matthias kept his voice low. "I was merely ending the agony of those near death."

"What do you mean 'ending the agony'? How do you think Miles did it? What am I saying? You're not him. You can't be." She gave an exhausted sigh, annoyed because Matthias had her babbling as if fiction were fact.

"I've been a doctor for a long time. I can ease the dying, so they don't die alone and scared."

"What are you then or rather him, Miles? What is he then?" When had she started to believe this nonsense?

"Still searching for an answer myself. I'm alive, but not a beast. Let's leave it at that."

"What does that even mean?"

"Means, I don't have fangs. You're safe. Do you need more proof?" He mocked her with a wide grin exposing his human teeth. Perfectly white and straight, she had to admit.

"Are there others like you?" She frowned, not yet convinced.

"Not many." A muscle on his jaw twitched. "I see you still don't believe me. Let's step behind this." He pointed at the enormous poster of upcoming exhibition at the archaeological museum on Iliryc's artifacts.

"Why?" She turned at the placard.

"I want to show you something."

"Not your mole, I hope." Although under the different circumstances, she wouldn't have minded checking his goods.

"You'll see." He reached out to grab her hand. "Trust me, Kate."

"Crazy kook." She sighed, shaking her head, and stepped behind the advertisement without taking his hand, asking herself why she wasn't running the opposite direction.

He blinked, looking toward the ceiling and let out a loud laugh. "I only wish."

She raised an eyebrow. "You *are* making fun of me."

"No, but you've made me laugh for the second time today. That's nearly impossible." He took her hand in his and brushed his thumb over her fingers. His soft touch flooded her with ease.

She gave a half smile. "Can't help but think about what the good, old Illyrians would think of this?"

"Illyrians were regarded as bloodthirsty, unpredictable, turbulent, and warlike peoples by Greeks and Romans. They were seen as savages on the edge of their world. I don't see how that made them good." He frowned, his expression puzzled.

"Never mind, it was a joke." Her voice trembled. She refused to believe he didn't have a sense of humour. He had laughed at her joke a minute ago, but her attempts at humor could be odd at times so maybe he hadn't understood it.

His breath tickled her knuckles when he brought her hand to his lips. The kiss he gave her was no more than a brush of his lips on her hand, hardly a real kiss, but it seared her skin all the same. He cradled her chin in his fingers and tilted her head, locking his gaze with hers.

"How do you change the color of your eyes like that?" Her own voice sounded from afar.

"It's a skill. No more questions now," he whispered.

Tunnel vision replaced her clear sight.

Images of a time long ago appeared before her. A young girl held hands with a boy. Her golden blonde hair swayed with the breeze, like sun-ripened wheat. They spun till they were dizzy then dropped on the lush grass and laughed, staring at the sky and gasping.

Kate's heart hammered. The experience seemed so real. A low moan escaped her and she bit her lip. Soon warmth surged through her, causing her body to go limp. Her legs gave way underneath her, but Matthias—or whoever this man claimed to be now—wrapped his arm around her waist. His sweet, musky scent clung to her. Ecstasy filled her and she felt as if she hovered in the air. If he intended to kill her like this, she could imagine no better way to die. A voice echoed through her mind, speaking of undying love in centuries old Croatian.

"Wake up," he whispered close to her ear, his strong arms still locked around her.

"I don't want to." Her head wobbled, exuberant with sheer happiness, a kind she had never experienced before.

"You must." He stroked her hair with tender fingers. "Wake up now."

"No. I want to stay like this. Forever." She focused on his handsome face staring at her through her haze.

His smooth cheek brushed against hers. "Me too, but you must wake."

The fog lifted and his image appeared, clearly now. She blinked once. Twice. What had happened? She pushed away from him and flattened her back against the wall.

"You, you—"

"You," he said, pointing at her, "asked for proof."

She stared at him in horror as panic claimed her body and mind, rendering her helpless. Every fibre of her being wanted him to be Miles, but reason prevailed.

"Please, I beg you. Do not fear me. You're safe," he whispered as voices of more visitors neared. "I could have carried on the charade and pretend to be someone I'm not. You're smart. You'd have figured it out sooner rather than later. I hoped you, of all people, would understand."

She should understand, and maybe one day she would, but right now, she had to get away. Away from this crazed man.

"I can't." She grabbed her bag and stormed away from the only man she had allowed herself to befriend in years.

At the top of the stairs, she paused and glanced over her shoulder. He stood on the same spot, his arms dangling at his sides. The longing in the look he cast her split her heart. Did he speak the truth in his words? Could he be some kind of a hypnotist? Or maybe it was she who was crazy.

No, it must be him. There wasn't any other reasonable explanation. She had heard of cheesy pick-up lines and the strange things men would do to get the girl, but this was beyond normal.

CHAPTER 5

Perfumes and colognes mixed around Kate as she pushed through the happy crowd. The city's famous nightlife was in the full swing. Some of these youngsters would find love tonight, while she seemed destined to roam this world alone. Her lips quivered as she struggled to keep her sorrow intact.

A storefront on Kalelarga Street drew her attention and she slowed her frantic pace. *Psychic advisor and spiritual counsel*—just the kind of nonsense she needed. People changed when they became accepting of perceptions without a scientific explanation. Her breath shuddered as she exhaled, trying to ease the tightness in her chest.

A girl stepped out, keys rattling as she locked the door. "Sorry, we're closed."

Kate cast a glance at her. "No worries." Her eyes widened when she recognized the girl's curly, brown hair. "Dyane?"

Dyane turned to Kate. Her mouth dropped open and her eyes widened. "Kate." She threw her arms around her. "When did you get back?"

Kate hugged her, finding some comfort in her old high school friend. "Three days ago. I thought I'll never see a familiar face in this town again."

"A few of us are still kicking around." Dyane gestured to the street patio next door to her shop. "Come, let's have a drink. There's so much to tell and I want to hear everything about you."

Kate nodded. She could use a real drink.

The patio lights flickered to life as they stepped up to the only empty table—one with two wicker chairs in the corner.

"No shortage of cafés here, and they're all packed." Kate adjusted the cushion to cradle her back. "You're still reading fortunes?"

Dyane chuckled, flipping the end of a bright colored scarf behind her. "I am, but right now I want to know about you. Let me see your hands."

Dread filled Kate when Dyane's fingers wrapped around her wrists and pulled them closer. Her friend would try to interpret the lines on her palms into how her life had changed and what would transpire in the future. Her family bombarded her with the same questions when they knew all too well how and why her short marriage ended. After ten years away from her homeland, she had neither a family of her own, nor a satisfying career.

Dyane's face crumpled. She looked Kate in the eye and squeezed her hands. "Love is tricky. Don't fret. We'll fix you up with someone, and you'll have a time of your life."

"No, thanks. I don't want you to fix me with anyone." The last thing Kate needed was to get stuck on a blind date, looking for a polite way to escape. "Tell me about yourself?"

Dyane crossed her long, tanned legs, flashing her pedicured toes in her gladiator sandals. "Remember in our senior year how you read in my coffee sediment that I'd marry someone close to me?"

Amusement had Kate chuckling. "Don't tell me it came true."

"He couldn't be any closer. Recognize him?" Dyane smiled at the waiter standing next to their table and took his hand in hers. Kate took note of their matching rings.

"Kate." The waiter called her name before she realized who he was. "You're back?"

"Good God, Toni?" Kate stood and hugged the tall man with his dark goatee and brown eyes. "I'm back, for a few weeks only." She released him and shot a glance at Dyane. "I knew you two would end up tying the knot. How long you've been married?"

Dyane cast her husband a wide smile. "About a month."

Kate jerked her head back in disbelief. "Congrats are in order then. You've been together since the high school. What took you so long?"

Dyane's smile disappeared. "My mother passed away last year. You know she always thought I could do much better than Toni. She couldn't be more wrong. I can't live without him."

The memories of all the lies Kate had come up with to give Dyane's mom when Dyane was on a date with Toni stabbed her mind. "I'm glad you two are finally together, but it is sad your mom kept you apart all these years."

"She died believing she did the right thing by keeping us apart. All the years we'll never get back." Dyane drew a strange symbol in the air with her finger and chanted.

Kate frowned. "What are you doing?"

Dyane broke her chant. "This will protect us from the evil spirits."

Evil spirits. After what Kate just witnessed at the *Donatus*, anything was possible. "So which god or goddess are you worshiping now?"

Toni cleared his throat and hugged his wife. "I hope she worships me, as I'm worshiping my only goddess."

"Who else, baby." Dyane tapped her finger on his nose.

Kate observed the two lovers. A lump formed in her throat. She and Matthias could never be anything more than an employee and employer. Nonetheless, she'd allowed her imagination to run wild and now, well she'd gotten what she deserved.

"Amazing. You two picked up exactly where you left off. Cappuccino?" Toni's voice snapped her back to the present.

"Please, and double Cherry Brandy."

"You are having a real drink?" Toni flipped the towel over his shoulder. "The world must be coming to an end."

"I need something strong." Kate sighed. Her often-ridiculed sobriety kept her out of trouble, but not letting lose all these years did her little good.

Toni disappeared inside the bar. She turned to Dyane. "I'm so happy for you, and I see the honeymoon isn't over."

Dyane nodded. "And I hope it never ends." A peculiar smile played on her lips. "Hey, do you remember what we did in high school?"

"What? The fortune telling?" Kate waved her hand. "That was balderdash."

Dyane closed her honey-brown eyes and swayed in the chair, snapping her fingers to the rhythm of a smooth jazz song coming through the speakers. "No it wasn't. We were good."

Kate gave her friend a mocking smile. "Please, we were good at fooling everyone. The tarot cards, coffee sediments, palm readings—it was all for fun, and if we 'predicted' anything it was a pure guess. Or we quoted lines from *Abba* songs. "

Toni brought their cappuccinos.

"Thank you, baby." Dyane smiled, giving him a wink, then turned back to her. "Kate, you know as well as I, we both have a special gift." Her head dropped when she inhaled. "My seeing gift is real and so is yours." She grabbed Kate's forearm. "Why did you let go of your *Dancing Queen?*"

Kate shrugged, throwing her hands up in the air. "I had to grow up and put the nonsense away. I had to earn a living." Doubt crept into her mind about the incident at the *Saint Donatus.* Maybe Dyane's words held some weight. The strange events that had happened since she took on the employment with Matthias pointed to the paranormal. Did she really possess the sensitivity?

"Look, I earn a decent living doing this. People pay me well for the information I can give them about their future. I never have to worry about spending money—" Dyane's gaze traveled over Kate's blouse and shorts, then back up to her face. "On clothes or hair." She leaned closer to Kate. "What happened to you?"

"Why do you ask?" Kate hid her Birkenstocks under the chair. Oh no, Dyane wouldn't start with her famous preaching how women must keep up their appearances?

"When was the last time you took a hard look at yourself?" Dyane cocked her head and looked over Kate's shoulder.

"Boy, am I glad I bumped into you," Kate said through a laugh. Her old friend still let her tongue loose.

"You're so pale and pasty as if you haven't seen the sun in over a century."

Dyane looked over Kate's shoulder again.

"It's the Northern climate. You'd look the same if you had to spend most of the year in a winter coat. Trust me you wouldn't last long in a bikini at thirty below." Kate wrapped her arms around herself and hugged. "Brr."

Dyane groaned. "How anyone puts up with those winters is beyond me." She brightened. "Hey, remember how we helped each other out when one didn't get the exact vision? I need you back. I'll train you."

"I don't know, Dyane. I've got this job I really love." Kate's throat tightened. What if she didn't have the job anymore because of her silly behavior around her boss? The thought of never seeing him again pressed heavily on her mind.

Publishing her book was nice of Matthias, after all. Although, she would've preferred if he had told her of his intentions. He must've meant it as a surprise. And how did she thank him? His sad appearance and the way she had left him standing in the *Saint Donatus* had guilt churning her stomach.

Just how had he managed that vision? The experience wouldn't leave her. Nothing was hurt but her pride, so she would swallow it and apologize to him.

She turned to look in the direction of Dyane's annoying glances but saw nothing. "What are you looking at?"

Dyane sighed. "Tell me one thing."

"What thing?"

"Why do you have an Earth bound spirit attached to you?" Dyane's gaze darted to Kate's left shoulder again.

Kate stared at her and held the air in her cheeks, trying to contain the laughter. She couldn't and burst out in gales of amusement as her back slid down in the chair. "Dyane, it's me you're talking to, and no, you're not fooling me."

Tears formed in the corners of Kate's eyes as she tried to control the merriment. She wiped them away, taking in a long breath.

"Are you done?" Dyane's tight face and folded arms made Kate stop, sit up straight, and reconsider things.

With all the recent events she couldn't find a plausible explanation for, Dyane might be onto something. "So, who is this ghost who's following me?"

"A woman." Dyane leaned back in her seat. "I'd say by her appearance, she's in her mid-thirties, but she's been around this world for centuries."

"Okay, 'Ghost Whisperer', does this woman have a name?" Kate stirred the foam of her cappuccino. Toni must've forgotten about her double order of Cherry Brandy.

Dyane raised her index finger. "Wait, something's coming to me." She closed her eyes. "What?" she whispered, a frown wrinkling her brow. . "E...Em...ina? Does the name Emina mean anything to you?"

Tiny beads of cold sweat broke out on Kate's forehead. She managed to set the cup back on its saucer on the low table before her trembling hands lost their grip. The thumping of her heart replaced the mingled voices of the crowd on the street. Dyane's image blurred as Kate stared at her.

"Kate?" Her fingers wrapped around her arm, snapping her out of a full-blown panic attack. "Kate? Are you okay?"

"No, I'm not." Her vision returned slowly, and Dyane's worried face became clear. "You've gotta help me, Dyane," she moaned. "Help me."

Dyane patted her arm. "I will."

Kate rubbed her sweaty palms on her jeans. "Can, um, can you hear her?"

"There's lots of interference, so I can barely make out what she's trying to say."

"Interference?" Kate had to force the whisper from her tight throat.

"Echoes, like she's talking from inside a well. I'm not getting bad vibes from her, though. She knows she's dead and must go into the light, but she's got unfinished business here."

"What unfinished business?" Kate swallowed hard. "Why is she hanging around me?"

Dyane appeared as if she were straining to listen. "She's fading now. Can't make out what she's trying to say." She levelled her eyes with Kate's. "She is very upset over something."

Kate shivered. "She wants to possess my body to be with her husband, doesn't she?"

Dyane cocked her head. "No, sweetie. Ghosts can't do that. Well, not for longer than a few seconds."

"I think she's done it with me." The mere thought of another soul occupying her body filled Kate with terror, but now at least she could put a person behind the frightening events.

Dyane tapped her fingers on her arms. "Did you feel tingles all over? Hear your own voice from far away? Did you do strange things, things you would never do? Like it wasn't really you?"

Dyane understood, which meant Kate wasn't going nuts. She took a deep breath. Now she knew how the patients whose illness couldn't be diagnosed and were told it was all in their heads must have felt. At least there was an explanation for what she was experiencing. Not that she'd be able to tell anyone without risking some very unpleasant reactions. "How do I get rid of Emina?"

Dyane gave her a sympathetic smile. "You can't. She has a purpose here and when she has accomplished it, she will be the one who leaves you."

Kate pressed her lips together and held her breath, looking up at the night sky dotted with silver stars. God, this couldn't be happening. "So what do I do?"

Dyane raised the cup to her mouth and took a sip then licked the foam from her upper lip. "What Emina wants."

"What does she want?"

"I don't know, yet, but we'll find out." Dyane placed the cup on the saucer. "Sweetie, getting rid of a ghost may take a long time. First, you mentioned this job you love."

"Matthias." Kate sprang to her feet. "God, Dyane. I hurt him. I have to find him and apologize. He was telling the truth and I—I ran away like some scared little kid."

Dyane pointed to the chair, urging her to sit back down. "You will and I'll help you, but first let me make sure I understand." Her voice dropped an octave as Kate lowered herself into the chair. "Years ago, a man's voice appeared in your head. Like an incessant whisper. You were afraid you'd end up on some heavy anti-psychotic drugs and never told a soul but me. And you listened to what he wanted."

"Not quite." Kate leaned forward and raised her finger. "I was up at night trying to get the voice out of my head when a commercial came on TV telling me 'to listen to my inner voice.' They wanted me to order their pizza. Nonetheless, the light went on in my head."

"The voice promised to stop if you would write about his life. So you wrote the book and the story he told you was about Miles and Dobrila."

Kate's eyes widened, she blinked fast when the dryness stung them. "Wow, you're good. How did you know?"

Dyane shot her a mocking glance. "You've been obsessed by their story ever since I have known you."

"I've been obsessed by them long before high school. Ever since I've first read about them, in the fifth grade." Kate sneered. There were so many things she could have poured her energy into, but her mind had been too wrapped around them. "I told him there are books written about them. There's even a stage play."

Dyane nodded. "Yes, but he wanted the story to be written his way. He said this was the true ending." She leaned closer. "That is where my vision stops. I would very much like to find out this alternate ending."

Kate reached in her bag and pulled the hardcover novel out. "Read it, and you'll see."

Dyane arched her eyebrows as she took the novel in her hands. "You did write the book. I can't wait to read it."

Uneasy, Kate played with her spoon. "There's more to this."

Dyane raised her head from the book and glanced at Kate. "Go on."

"Two months ago, I started this live-in nanny job and ever since my first day, strange things have been happening—similar to what you described." Kate pushed the words out of her mouth faster and faster as she went on. "Today, the boys' father told me he's the hero from the book. He's Miles, alive and kicking after three hundred years. Emina was Dobrila, his wife. As far as I know, she died in the childbirth."

"No sweetie." Dyane shook her head. "Emina died a long time ago."

"According to the legend, Dobrila fell ill a few months after her father shot Miles. Some say she died of broken heart, but I don't think anyone can die from disappointment in love. Heck, if that were true, I'd be long gone." Kate swallowed around the lump in her throat. Emina might be listening to their conversation.

"Dobrila's death is written in the legend as such, but she threw herself off a balcony."

Kate straightened. Dyane couldn't know this. She had yet to read the book. "Did Emina tell you this?"

"She tried. I filled in the blanks." Dyane nodded. "And your boss is Miles."

"Crazy isn't it?" Kate sniffed. "He said he is not a vampire."

Dyane raised her hand. "No, it's not crazy. Does he know what he is?"

Kate frowned and shook her head. "Apparently, he doesn't."

"Hmmm, must be still searching for the answers."

"I am dumb struck. How could he still be alive?" Kate pressed her hand over her lips when a few patrons from the neighbouring table gave her strange looks. She lowered her voice to a whisper. "I often imagined what it would be like for them to live their lives the way they should. Could it be, I wished too hard? My wishful thinking brought them to life, allowed them to have children?" Kate winced. "Then I stopped believing and Emina died."

Dyane shrugged. "A lot to think about, isn't it? Maybe they were reborn with Miles and Dobrila's memories."

"No, that doesn't fit with the facts of what's happened. The only thing that makes sense is that he's immortal and so was his wife. If pregnancy and childbirth is dangerous for mortal women then I can imagine she must've put herself at a great risk to have babies." Kate sighed. Her eyes narrowed and she stared into the distance. "Must have been some love. Why did it have to hurt?"

Dyane tsked and reached out to Kate. "Not all is lost. You're now rubbing elbows with an immortal."

Kate squared her shoulders. If Dyane could accept this so easily, maybe it wasn't as farfetched as she'd thought. "You say that as if you come in contact with immortals every day."

"Your guy is the first real one." Dyane lips twitched, her eyes filled with excitement. "I'd love to meet him."

"He's not mine. He just blatantly copied files from my memory stick and published the book." Kate pointed to the volume on the table. "That's the only copy, just for me."

"It is his story, after all. I'll take a good care of it." Dyane flipped the cover and tilted the book towards the patio lights. Her lips moved as she read and she smiled. "Did you see his dedication to you on the flap?"

Kate's throat closed. "No."

She stretched her neck when Dyane turned the book towards her and read, *Without you, Kate, there wouldn't be us. Accept our thanks. ~ Matthias & Emina.* Hot tears stung her eyes. She retold their story the way he wanted. No one would know the ending, however paranormal, was true just like the rest of the legend. All she wanted to do right now was to hold him again. What had she done? "God, Dyane, I don't know what to do."

"I've never seen you like this. Not even after you broke-up with your first boyfriend," Dyane said, cheerfully. "Looks to me you're finally facing your 'Waterloo.' He's got you so miserable."

"What?" Kate sniffed and shot her friend a stern look, shocked at Dyane's bold assumption. "You think I'm in love with him?"

As if on cue, Abba's "Take a Chance on Me" poured out of the speakers.

Dyane gave her a quick smile. "Who's delusional here? Your face lit up when you spoke about him. He is the one, I can tell." She dropped her voice to a whisper and sang along. *"Honey, you're still free. Take a chance on him."*

Fire ignited in Kate's soul and seared her cheeks. Did it show on her face how much she missed him? "No, stop. Please."

Dyane grinned and continued with the song. *"Gotta put him to the test. Take a chance on him."*

"I just want to apologize to him and see if I still have my job." She pressed her feet flat on the ground to stop them from running to him. "He doesn't want me. He wants his Emina. Besides, he's old, ancient in fact." She sighed. "What should I do about his wife's ghost?"

Dyane flipped through the pages of the novel. "It's not like he's taking advantage of senior discounts." She rolled out a low laugh—obviously amused at her own joke—then raised her head. "The ghost, yes. She knows you are aware of her and won't attempt to enter your body again. She must've been desperate and wanted to reach out to her husband."

Kate closed her eyes and exhaled. She had every reason to be afraid. A spirit of a dead woman clung to her. But, Emina wasn't a stranger. Kate knew her under a different name as a historical character, never imagining she was now a spirit and could enter a living person's body. Yet, Kate could sympathize. If it were she who longed to reach out to her loved ones from beyond, she'd probably have done the same.

"Talk to her though. It will open up a channel between you two, and you'll be able to hear her. Take this." Dyane stood, passing a business card to Kate. "I must go help Toni close out the cash, but let's get together again. Promise you'll call me. We'll go shopping, have our hair done, and talk about the old days."

"I promise." Kate stood, too. "People may think I'm crazy if I keep talking to myself, though." She tried to lighten the strange situation with some humour, but her remark didn't help her mood.

Dyane smiled and gave her hand a reassuring squeeze. "I envy you in a way. I have to go now." Kate swung her bag over her shoulder. "Well, Mistress Zrin. I'm off to bed. Hope you find that exciting."

She started home with an easy stroll, convinced she wouldn't get any sleep tonight. Matthias's image, and the feel of his strong arms wrapped around her, returned to haunt her. Without him, an empty, gaping hole ate at her soul. He must've known his wife's ghost clung to her all along. She didn't know whether to be glad of that or to hate him for not explaining it to her. All of this would take some time to process, but right now, it was giving her a mother of a migraine.

CHAPTER 6

With the phone pressed to her ear, Kate tapped her foot on the vinyl floor in her narrow kitchen. The closed blinds prevented the sun from heating the small apartment, but allowed air to flow through the rows of tiny slits.

Dyane sniffed on the other end. "I stayed up all night reading your book. You told the tragic love story so beautifully." Her breath quivered when she exhaled. "If I could go back in time and beat Dobrila's father with my purse—ugh, he was a spiteful man."

A warm feeling swamped Kate. Dyane was an avid reader and from her this was high praise. "I'm glad you liked the story. Did it give you any clue of what Emina wants from me?"

"No." Dyane's answer was broken by her yawn. "The story grabbed me and I forgot to look for clues. I kept on reading and before I knew it I turned the last page as the daylight broke."

Kate groaned in exasperation. "When we went shopping yesterday, it felt like she left me."

"No, you occupied your mind and forgot about her but she's back, isn't she?"

"I think so. I've had the jitters all day, and I'm all thumbs. Even managed to break two glasses. Maybe I should go for a jog." Kate opened the fridge and pulled a bottle of water. "Care to join me?"

"Sorry, I don't have enough energy. I have to go back to bed. Gotta go now."

"Dyane," Kate interrupted before her friend could end the call. "Can I get my book back?"

No answer came from Dyane.

"Still there?" Dread stung Kate. Dyane was up to something. "Hello?"

"I'm here. I, um, passed it onto a friend."

"You didn't?" Kate gasped, heat seared her cheeks. Her book had started to circulate. Others would read it. There would be judgments and criticisms. If Mom found out, she'd have a fit.

"I'll get it back." Dyane dragged her words out. "I thought you wanted people to read it."

Kate searched for a decent reason to give her friend. "It's not ready for everyone's eyes."

"Nonsense, it's perfect. I loved it. My eyes even filled up a few times. The scene when Miles finds Dobrila on the cold floor, dying," Dyane's voice broke. "The fact it's a true story made me want to scream into my pillow."

A realization washed over Kate. "I trust you wouldn't tell anyone just how real all this is. The ending twist was supposed to be fiction. Who knew it wasn't?"

"You know I wouldn't breathe a word of it." Dyane sounded hurt. "I'm a professional."

A professional. Kate exhaled. Dyane might not have trouble speaking her mind but she always knew what not to say. "Good. I'm off for a jog. You get my book back."

"Have a good run and don't worry. I already said I'll get it back."

The late afternoon sun dipped low, easing the summer heat as Kate stepped on to the sidewalk in front of the apartment building. People bustled around her, hurrying to conclude their transactions before the businesses on the street closed in a couple of hours.

She laced up her runners and stretched. High energy music, from the iPod she'd bought on clearance before the trip, suited her jogging mood. *Well, Emina, are you up for five k's?* she asked as she started off.

Kate's pace picked up with each stride, her shoes pounding on the sidewalk.

She crossed the Five Wells Square then passed through the Land Gate bearing the winged lion, the emblem of the Venetian Republic then entered the city's Botanical Gardens. Gravel footpaths replaced the asphalt sidewalk and tree canopies stretched to the sky, providing deep shade.

A newly refurbished high school building loomed on the other side of the cement wall. She slowed down, shivering at the memories of the gossip and mean girls. Knowing all the words to every song of their favorite band earned her and Dyane the status of geeks. As if that wasn't bad enough, their fortune telling put them on the list of resident freaks. How had she ever survived those days?

A steep hill the Phys-Ed teacher had ordered them up, while he'd puffed on a cigarette, came to mind. The foot path in front of her split and she took the one leading to the rise. Maybe now she'd be fit to take on the mound that almost made her fail Gym. Within a few minutes, she faced the incline. It hadn't changed one bit. She charged up, ignoring the pain in her thighs and the stitch in her side.

She pulled the buds out of her ears and punched the air as she reached the top. "Yes! Take that comrade, Kovac."

Crushed rocks crunched under her feet while she walked in circles, catching her breath and waiting for the pain in her side to ease. Beads of sweat raced down her back and disappeared into the waistband of her jogging shorts. From the top of the hill she could see the whole valley spread out below, giving her a perfect view of the city's soccer stadium.

"I knew you'd conquer this hill one day."

She gasped, jerking her head around in the direction of Matthias's voice. He leaned against a tree trunk wearing a black jogger's suit and runners. Sweat glistened on his forehead.

The right words evaded her racing mind when he took two slow steps towards her. With one quick step back, she widened the distance between them.

His eyebrows knitted and disappointment reflected on his face. "You still fear me."

A soft moan escaped her dry lips. She shook her head.

Just one of his deep stares and she forgot the promise she made to herself to keep away from him.

Despite the heat, the rock pressing on her skin was cold when he backed her against the boulder.

Longing flared in his eyes. "Then why do you run away from me?"

She stood rooted, trying to steady her thoughts. Pain pierced her heart. Her crazy mind had dreamed of waking next to him ever since the day they shared the hammock. But who did he expect to find, her or Emina? "I—" She couldn't utter anything coherent in the face of his demanding stare.

His familiar masculine scent enveloped her, melting away her doubts, but her chest and throat still tightened. Tears welled up in her eyes. He had not forgiven her stupid actions. She never should have left him when he told her the truth.

He brushed his hand against her hip. "How's the pain in your side? Easing off?" His fingers closed around her iPod clipped to her waist. The sound from the ear buds ceased.

Darn, she couldn't hide anything from him. "Yes, it's gone."

His bicep flexed as he stroked her bare arm. "Don't fear me, or Emina. We mean you no harm."

She looked up to his face. "I don't fear you," she lied, hoping he wouldn't sense her fear. "What does Emina want from me?" A soft huff slipped out of her mouth when he didn't answer. "What does she want of me, Matthias?"

His chest expanded, brushing against hers. "I wish I knew."

She wiped a tear away. "Can you see her?"

"No," he said and squeezed her shoulders. "But I sense her presence."

"Is she here now?"

He shook his head.

She examined his face. "Why won't she cross over?"

His breathing sped up and his face crumpled.

Kate stared at him, finally understanding. "You can't let go of her," she whispered.

He turned his head away, blowing air out. "We can't let go of each other. You have to understand we had been together for over three centuries."

She forced air into her lungs. What would she know of life-long relationships? Her own marriage lasted six months—nine, until the divorce was finalized. "All these years, I feared I was losing my mind."

His shoulders relaxed with his smile, easing her nerves. "You must've felt as if you were going insane. I'm sorry. When I realized you heard my voice, I couldn't let you go."

"Why me?"

"For centuries I've searched for a soul open to hearing me. No one was receptive, until I found you, but you were still a child when I entered your dreams."

Cold shivers surged through her. That was *him*, all these years? She'd only seen the chaser's hand, never his face. "You—" Dry air choked her throat. "Have no idea how much those dreams scared me."

He brushed a strand of her hair from her face. "I do. It was me who urged you to wake when you fought to draw a breath."

"Why?" she demanded, forcing the word past her gritted teeth. "Did you want to scare me?"

"No. I played tag with you. You interpreted the dream as scary."

Her initial anger calmed by his words, she slapped his arm and said, "Ha. Tag, you're it."

He pressed one hand on the rock above her head then rolled a low belly laugh. "You won."

"As long as you don't do it again. And as for the book—" She averted her eyes to glance at the ground. "I guess I didn't thank you."

"You're welcome." The fingers of his other hand brushed hers, sending butterflies to her stomach. "I wasn't sure about my love life being exposed, but I decided I didn't mind. You made me look like a stud." Pearly whites were exposed with his smile as he pulled back. "But let me tell you, my cheeks blushed for the first time when I read it."

His love life, exposed. She stiffened with realization of others reading all about his skills in bed. "I need a drink—a big one."

He cocked his head, offering his elbow. "Alright, let's get you one then."

Go to him. Go. Her mind screamed, but she halted, reluctant to link her arm with his.

He nudged her. "Come on."

Oh, what the hell? she decided. What did she really have to lose? She knew he was too kind a man to ever cause her harm. With a sigh, she took him up on his offer, her uncertainties slowly dissipating.

Their feet padded on the park's narrow paths as they strolled along without saying a word. She cast him a few glances, hoping he'd break the silence. But he only smiled and squeezed her hand. They reached the park's cement wall. There was not a soul about. The entrance stood a few steps to their left, illuminated by two dim lights. With a hard pull of his hand, he swung her around to face him.

He caressed her hair. She trembled, fearing he would kiss her, terrified he wouldn't.

She stared into his eyes. Deep pools of blue, they held hers captive, weaving a spell of desire. This ancient park, this immortal man, the atmosphere, all combined to surround her heart with magic.

"To hell with the pretences," he growled, cupped her face in his hands, and crushed his lips to hers.

All he could think was thank God, his lips were on Kate's at last. The way they glistened each time she smiled, frowned, or talked had had Matthias on the edge for over two months. Another minute of watching those rosy buds taunt him and he would have exploded. She tasted even better than he'd imagined—minty, yet honey sweet. He didn't want this moment or this night to end. If he let her go, would he ever see her again? Afraid the spell would end with the kiss, he held onto her longer than he had intended to.

He ran his tongue along her lips, parting them enough to slide its tip inside her warm mouth. She surrendered under his coaxing, and he deepened the kiss. Their tongues danced in slow motion. She moaned once, sending a whole new shiver down his spine, straight to his groin. A loud gasp escaped from her throat and echoed among trees when he pulled back.

"Forgive me." He lowered his hands when her flushed skin warmed his palms. Afraid of her reaction to his foolish advance, he held his breath.

She pressed her hand on her chest, drew a long breath, and licked her lips. "Nothing to forgive." The blush in her cheeks intensified.

A load lifted from his mind. Her reaction confirmed his suspicions that she had wanted the kiss as much as he did. The yearning to pull her in his embrace was unbearable, but she squared her shoulders and exhaled loudly.

Caressing her elbow, he turned toward the exit. "Do you still need that drink?"

"I do."

"The place I have in mind is not far—just down this street," he said, taking her hand and leading to a small outdoor café.

"Are you sure we'll get any service here?" she asked as she took a seat on the plastic patio chair next to him and nudged her chin at the only person minding the establishment. "The waiter seems immersed in the soccer game on the television."

"We will, even if I have to get it myself." He stood and crossed the small patio in three longs strides to the waiter seated on the barstool. "What's the score?" The screen flashed *3—2 Croatia* before the young man could answer. Matthias gestured toward Kate. "Can we get some drinks?"

Returning to the table, he smiled brushed his finger over her soft cheek. Delicate as she was, she seemed to have overcome her fear of him and Emina. The old sparkle he'd come to love had returned to her eyes.

She studied him. "What kind of trick was the vision you did in *Donatus*?"

A gaze into her emerald eyes confirmed his suspicions that she had no memory of them sharing visions six years ago. But then how could she? Before he'd left her, he had wiped her mind clean of him, leaving nothing but an awareness of the incessant whisper. At the time, it seemed to be the right thing to do to help her get over her sadness.

With a smile of reassurance, he leaned forward in his chair. "It was a simple memory sharing. I reached into your mind and showed you a small piece of my life. What did you feel?"

He wondered what she'd say. Although he inflicted others with his visions, she was the first one he'd allowed to remember it.

"Joy, pure happiness. I've never been so content. I wanted it to last forever. Then you broke the connection. Can you share your memories again?"

"I can do it any time you want, but—"

"Here you go." A bottle and glass thudded on the table as the waiter dropped the drink in front of them and shoved the bill under the ashtray. "Anything else I can get you?"

Matthias turned to her. "Want something else?"

She wrapped her fingers around the glass "I'm fine with this, thanks."

When Matthias shook his head, the waiter hurried back to the game.

Kate set her glass aside, twisted her hair into a bun, and secured it with a clip. Matthias had to suppress the urge to jump up and kiss her slender neck.

Picking up her drink again, she cradled her chin in the palm of her free hand. "Why did you choose Zrin or Zrinski for your last name? Your family name was Rušinić. I didn't think you'd be related."

"No relation. Dobrila and I—we couldn't keep our identities, not even a single trace." He peeled the label off the bottle. After all these years it felt unnatural to call Emina by her mortal name. The day had come to explain everything, and now he found he wasn't ready. He'd never be. "I was born on the day of Petar's beheading. That's the only connection between me and the Zrinskis."

"I see. Petar, the host of the house you're staying in, he's—"

Matthias leaned closer, bombarding her with his thoughts. "Come on Kate, connect with me the way you did years ago."

Her brow furrowed and she blinked rapidly. "Petar's your son."

"Yes!" he hissed, pumping one fist in the air. "I knew you could hear me in your head. We just needed to re-establish the pathway."

"Emina and you adopted him at birth. He was born on the same day as you, but three hundred years later. You named him Petar to commemorate the anniversary of the viceroy's death." She gulped air. "Try to send your thoughts one at the time."

Tenderness filled his chest. "I'm so sorry, there's so much I want to share with you."

She averted her eyes, shifting her gaze to her drink. "I want to know about the boys. I mean, I didn't think immortals could procreate in the traditional way."

"It all started about ten years ago." He paused and pressed his lips tight. "You can imagine my surprise when I, um—" He shifted in his seat and cleared his throat. How would he bring himself to talk about this issue to her? "The word I'm thinking of, I'd rather not say it in the presence of a lady. You know how old fashioned I am."

"This lady can handle it. Go on and say it."

A loud burst of cheer startled them. Matthias glanced at the screen. Croatian players in their blue jerseys embraced in a group hug.

Within seconds people poured out on the streets, waving the national flags. Small groups of thugs caused trouble, picking fights. Matthias noted the police were present. Armed in riot gear and batons, they reminded him of medieval knights. This night might end ugly if the crowd turned unruly. This wasn't the kind of atmosphere he imagined for them to have an intimate conversation.

Queasiness stirred in his stomach. "Finish your drink. We should get out of the downtown area."

"People are still crazy about their soccer teams, aren't they?" She took a couple of sips. "I can't gulp this down."

"Nothing else to occupy their time, I suppose." He dropped a few small bills on the table. "You don't have to drink it."

With her hand held securely in his, he ploughed through the happy crowd, knowing the euphoria could turn into violence in a flash. Never fond of mass gatherings, his gut urged him to leave the peninsula. She seemed intrigued by the people's celebration. Elbowing his way through the throng, he slowed his stride when he and Kate crossed the bridge.

She squeezed on his hand. He halted. Her palm felt sweaty in his dry one. "My place is two blocks from here," she said. "I'll just go on alone."

He searched his mind to find a way to keep her to himself even if for a short while. "It's not safe for you to be on the streets by yourself tonight. I'll walk you home."

"Let me catch my breath first." She bent over and pressed her hands on her knees, panting.

"I'm sorry, I should've gone slower." Guilt crept over him. Must've been hard for her to keep up with his pace, yet somehow she did.

"I'm fine." She straightened and flashed him a smile. "This was fun. Let's go."

A raucous party was taking place one floor above her apartment. People went in and out of the place, thumping music and boisterous laughter spilled out on the street.

"Oh God." She pressed her hands on her head. "Darn party animals. They're going to keep me up all night. Good thing my mom is away."

This party came at the perfect time. He wasn't ready to say goodnight. He hadn't even begun to tell her his story. "Would you consider staying on my boat?"

"No, no, I couldn't impose on you."

"You're not imposing. We can sit on the deck, continue our conversation and star gaze." He stepped closer and brushed a strand of hair off her cheek, fighting the urge to place a soft kiss on her lips. "What do you say?"

"Remember last time we star gazed?"

"I'm sure by now you've gotten over the jetlag and won't fall asleep in the middle of the conversation," he said with a laugh.

She tilted her head toward the balcony. "May as well. I'm not going to get any sleep here."

"Do you need anything from the apartment?"

"No, I'm staying on your boat for a couple of hours, not the rest of the night."

"These parties don't end till the morning." Or until someone ends in the emergency room in an alcohol induced coma, nonetheless she wouldn't get any sleep here. Still, a couple of hours would be better than bidding goodnight to her right now.

"Maybe I should get a few things and close the windows. You never know how crazy these people could get." She shrugged.

"I'll wait here. You've got ten minutes." He tapped the wrist watch, stretching his lips in a wide smile. "If you're not down by then I'll come to get you."

"Twenty." She stepped inside the foyer.

"What do you need twenty minutes for?"

"I do. Don't rush me," she yelled back half way up the staircase.

"Fine. Twenty, but not a minute over. Go now." He snickered as she took the steps by twos.

The warmth of the building wall seeped in his back while he waited for Kate and watched people pass by him on the street. He tapped his foot to the rhythm of the thumping music coming from the party in the unit above hers.

With a bag in her hand, Kate rushed out the door, her towel dried hair pulled in a low ponytail. The mix of floral hair shampoo and the fresh jasmine scent of her body lotion drifted to him. Her halter-top met her jeans shorts in perfect harmony.

He had never paid much attention to her wardrobe. She could wear anything and have him under her spell. Tonight though, she appeared extra beautiful. "You look nice."

"Thanks. Here, hold this." She handed the bag to him and sat on the step struggling to buckle her sandal. "My friend talked me into buying these, and I like them, but the clasps are so tiny."

He crouched in front of her and caressed her calf, sliding his hand toward her heel. "Let me."

She winced and drew her leg back, but he wrapped his fingers around her ankle and she relaxed, flexing her foot in his hand. "Put it through the first hole."

Had she intended for her whisper to came out so husky? Her scent surrounded him. He revelled in her aura, taking his time to slide the thin belt through the buckle. He noticed goose bumps race up her smooth skin. He moved to her other foot, causing the same reaction.

"All done," he murmured, cradling her ankle in his hands.

She cleared her throat. "What are we waiting for?"

He didn't want to let go of her leg, but he set her foot down and took her hands in his then stood, pulling her up with him.

"How gentlemanly of you," she said and looped her arm around his offered elbow. "Only old couples stroll like this, nowadays."

"Including me?" He'd tried to keep up with the times, but the world seemed to move one step ahead of him.

"No." Her cheeks flushed and she shifted her gaze towards the ground. "I didn't mean you. I'm sorry."

He paused and cupped her cheek. She closed her eyes and leaned into his palm. "You didn't offend me. No need to apologize. Let's talk about something else." A change of subject would smooth this awkward moment, he thought, and continued walking.

"Do you live on the boat?"

"When I'm in town, but I'm rarely here. I stay in the house when on *Aba Vela*." The place that had once echoed with Emina's zestful laughter, now stood silent. Being with Kate seemed to stall his constant thoughts of Emina. Flushed with guilt, he turned away from Kate. He wanted to be with her, but couldn't allow himself to forget about Emina even if for one brief moment.

"Didn't you have a villa in the town?"

"Communists confiscated it." He sighed. "The magnificent place stood neglected for decades. My heart ached each time I saw the walls overgrown with vegetation and the windows broken. I never thought I'd see it in its former glory, but someone has bought the home and restored it."

"Communists took some of my grandfather's property after the Second World War—or during the war, not sure. Either way, our family never got the ships back."

"Many families lost everything. Once they stripped us of our possessions, there wasn't any point for us to stay here. People started to escape the county and settle elsewhere. Emina and I, we—" He paused at the memories of their life. "We went through a few places, before settling down."

"Must've been tough. Trying to make a home everywhere you ended up, only to find out foreigners weren't welcome."

"We had each other. You were alone."

She gasped. "How do you know that?"

"I know you, better than you think." He tapped her hand with his and shivered with the flowery scent of her hair. The magic, that in the past only Emina could awaken, stirred deep inside him.

"We're here." He swiped his membership card and the gate slid open. Kate stood rooted on the spot. Was she uncertain? He reached out to her. "You can trust me."

"I'm not sure if I can trust myself." Her voice trembled while she twirled a strand of her wet, hazel hair around a finger.

CHAPTER 7

The chirping of crickets filled the balmy summer night. Matthias took a step closer to Kate. The marina's wrought iron gate slid back and closed with a click. *She wouldn't change her mind now, would she?* "What are you afraid of?"

A deep crease formed on her forehead. "I don't know."

He reached out, struggling to keep his hand steady. "You must have lots of questions. Ask me anything."

She always appeared nervous in his presence. Tonight, he wanted to reassure her she had nothing to worry about.

A spark of curiosity flashed in her eyes. "Anything?"

"Yes, anything. After helping the boys with their homework and all the school glue and paint on your fingers, I think you've earned it." A long breath seeped out of him when her lips stretched in a wide smile and her warm fingers wrapped around his. He slid the membership card through the reader again and the light changed from red to green. The gate glided opened.

Intoxicated with her essence, he led the way to the yacht docked at the pier.

"The deck is wet from the condensation, best to walk barefoot." His black runners landed on the bow as he kicked them off. "Do you need help with your buckles?"

She shook her head. "It's easier to take my sandals off than put them on."

Disappointment stung him. He wanted to feel those goose bumps rise on her skin again. He held the aluminum steps steady until she climbed onboard then followed her up. The ropes creaked and tightened, causing the yacht to bobble. She grabbed onto his arm. The opportunity to pull her closer and inhale the flowery scent of her freshly washed hair once more was irresistible. He snatched it and the same tremor ran through him again. "How do you like the yacht so far?"

She left her sandals next to his shoes. "It's sleek luxury. What kind of boat is this?"

"This is a Pearl 60 with twin engines and four cabins." He wiped his hand on his shirt after he'd touched the wet steps. "Would you like to see the interior?"

Her face beamed. "Can I?"

"Yes, of course." He opened the door and led her down the four steps. His feet sank into the lush carpet. Her gasp of delight as she examined the navy blue walls and cream seating areas of the boat's belly brought a smile to his face. She liked it. Emina had said the main lounge was too dark for her liking, but he wouldn't change it. "Nice, huh?"

"Wide screen TV, the full kitchen, the lounge areas, luxury with capital L." She spun around in the middle of the salon.

"Would you mind if I hop in the shower? By the way you could've showered here, instead of rushing at your apartment."

"My bag would weigh a ton if I packed my entire toiletry." She giggled and waved her hand. "Go ahead and shower."

"Can I get you a drink before I leave you?" When he opened the small door and pulled out a beer bottle, the cold air from the fridge slithered on his bare feet. "Do you want to sit inside or out?" He grabbed an absorbent cloth from the cupboard.

"Let's enjoy the summer night." She reached her hand out to him. "I'll wipe the seats down, but you're wasting what looks like a good beer on me. Got anything else?"

"Something non-alcoholic I presume?" He faced the fridge again and pulled out a can of soda. He'd kick himself later. How could he forget she refused his offers of wine at every dinner? Except for the few sips she'd taken of the brandy he'd bought her earlier when she'd been shaken, he'd never seen her drink alcohol.

"This will do," she said as she took the tin of ginger ale from his hand. "Can I have a glass?"

"Of course." He turned to the cupboard and slid the glass out from its hole then handed it to her. "I'll be quick. Get comfortable, and I'll join you shortly."

When he stepped back out on the upper deck, Kate was sitting with her legs crossed, gazing at the night sky. "I see you found where the cushions are stored," he said as he plopped himself down next to her.

"I'm not a stranger to boats, luxury or not." She squirmed to the edge. "Feeling human again?"

"What?" He blinked, taken aback by her question. The results were still preliminary, the professor couldn't be certain. Had her heightened senses pick the changes in him?

She tensed, staring at her hands. "You know, when you shower you feel clean and, ah, and refreshed." Strands of her ponytail came loose when she turned away from him and covered her face. "You wouldn't, by any chance, have a hole in your deck where I could vanish in? I apologize for the stupid human-analogy."

He wrapped his arm around her, exhaling. A mistake, nothing more. "No need for embarrassment. I did say you can ask me anything, didn't I? Yes, I'm feeling human again." Not because he showered. Certainly, her presence here tonight had everything to do with him feeling alive. He had hoped he'd find a friend in Kate, someone who'd understand. Never could he have imagined his heart, soul, and body would react to her this way. "What else would you like to know?"

"You were about to explain how the boys were conceived before we got interrupted."

A lump formed in his throat and a tight bend constricted his chest. He stood and walked to the stern. The glow of harbour lights and the steady rhythm of the lighthouse reflected on the calm surface. To answer her question meant to bring back memories of Emina. "I'll never forget her. I'll never let her out of my heart."

"She'll stay in my heart forever, too." Kate's voice jerked him back from his reverie. "I knew the characters were real and I even played in my head what would it be like meeting one of them someday. Why didn't you show your true self years ago?"

He cast her a glance and turned toward the harbour again. Just how much did she remember? "I couldn't, you weren't ready to see me and you found someone else."

"Craig." A hint of disappointment crept in her voice. "I don't want to talk about him."

"Then we won't." Matthias went back and sat next to her. She appeared shaken and in need of comforting. He wrapped his arm around her shoulders and pulled her closer. The urge to press his lips to hers again had his stomach in a knot. But, he couldn't be so rash. He must gain her approval for formal courtship first.

"So, how were the boys born?" She squirmed. Perhaps his arm was heavy. He lowered his limb to her waist.

A big gulp of his beer failed to boost his courage. "Well." He sighed. "I still cannot bring myself to say the dreaded word in your presence."

"Then act it out, maybe I'll guess."

He grimaced. "That would be worse, much worse."

She cocked her head. "If you're to whisper it in my ear, would that make it easier?"

"Maybe." Her jasmine lotion enticed his senses and stirred the need in him when he leaned closer. "I started." He drew in a long breath. "To...ejaculate." Then he sat straight and took another sip. "There, I said it."

She burst out laughing. "That's it? I'm sorry. You're a doctor, why would you be embarrassed to say it? I'm sure you must've heard worse."

"I have, but I'm very old school."

"I noticed." She brought the glass to her lips. "Besides, I had no idea you couldn't before."

"Once I became immortal, some of my bodily functions ceased. Only true love evoked the feelings inside me that could cause my body to respond. While I could please a woman, I couldn't father a child." He paused. What possessed him to explain these things to her? He never discussed them with Emina.

"So, yes." He cleared his throat. "Small amounts at first, but within two years, there was more. I put it through some vigorous tests and each time the results showed the same. Normal." Relief relaxed him when she didn't interrupt him with medical questions. He didn't have the answers himself.

"I couldn't keep it from Emina, for obvious reasons. You know how she was. What was the one thing she wanted more than anything in the world?" His cheeks felt warm. Could it be the beer? He never had more than one on any occasion.

"To give you children."

He nodded and sat in silence for a while. "After Petar moved out she yearned to hold our baby in her arms. We ran tests on her." A loud breath escaped him. "She wasn't fertile, but that didn't stop her. She started to research, spending days on the Internet. Some facility promised this and that. I looked into it. The procedure was experimental at best." Deep pain cut him, slicing his chest. He never told this to a soul, but burying the memory deep hadn't helped the hurt.

"I should've been there for her. Instead, I did nothing but forbid her to think about it." Self-anger built in him. He stood and turned to face the harbour again. "Emina never defied me, until one day she decided to take the drugs in secret."

He looked at Kate. She sat motionless, her eyes wide.

"By the time I found out, she was already twelve weeks pregnant. I was happy of course, but at the back of my mind, I knew this was far too risky. I got involved too late. The medication she injected three times a day fooled her body into thinking she was a mortal woman of child bearing age, but the drugs were slowly killing her."

"The boys are not identical."

Straightening, he turned to face her. "No. Three of Emina's harvested eggs had been viable and fertilized, then implanted. When the first ultrasound revealed three separate amniotic sacs, we were euphoric of course. The doctor explained how dangerous it would be for her and the babies and suggested we remove two. Emina would not hear of it."

"I tried to talk reason with her, but it was no use." What a fool he'd been to let Emina have her way. "Her pregnancy progressed another seventeen weeks. Just when I started to relax about the whole thing, she slipped into a coma."

He swallowed the pain and continued. "Machines kept her heart beating for the babies' sake. She clung to life for another two weeks, but she deteriorated. We had to get the babies out and fast."

His heart racing, he started to tell the most intense part. "We operated in a secret high-tech facility. I didn't want to do it, but the other surgeon couldn't handle it. Every incision on her belly closed before he could clamp it. I managed to get her open and reached my hand in. To this day I couldn't tell you what I grabbed onto but I yanked the first baby out and handed him to the nurse, then the next one. By the time I've got Teo out, he was blue, not breathing. The attending doctor took him from my hands. Emina appeared to be sleeping peacefully, but I knew she was gone." He pressed his elbows on the table and rested his head in his hands. The image of Emina on the surgical table would never leave his mind.

"The doctor kept calling me, but I couldn't leave her side. Then all of a sudden, it hit me. She did this for us, for me. What would she do if it was me who died? She'd help her newborn son who might not make it. I kissed her hand and stepped over to Teo's warmer. A nurse held an oxygen mask over his tiny face and pumped but he was nonresponsive. I urged her to continue, then his body quivered and he let out his first cry."

He glanced at Kate. Tears streaked her face. Her shoulders jerked with sobs as she wiped her eyes on the hem of her top.

"I'll get you a tissue." He stood and went below. Carrying a box, he handed the napkins to her. At least she could cry her sorrow out. Too many times he wished he had tears left.

"Thanks." She wiped her eyes and nose. "You buried her at the top of your island?"

He sat next to her. "She thought it was the most beautiful place in the world. Emina's place is what I called it, but later the boys changed it to Mama's place."

Kate cleared her throat and reached for her glass.

Matthias sighed with relief. She took this all so well, but she was not just anybody, this was Kate, his Kate.

"You took care of three babies all by yourself?" she asked, dabbing at her tears with a crumpled napkin.

"Friends and family helped. I got a nurse, then nannies—basically, paid staff. Teo, he needed his mama. He needed that closeness only a mom could give." The guilt of not being able to give his child what he needed had never stopped eating at him.

She sniffed. "Yes, skin on skin contact is essential to infants, even more so to preemies. We obviously forget all about our entrance into the world, but I can imagine how scared a newborn would be. After spending months in the cozy womb listening to mom's heartbeat, all of a sudden the poor thing is in the cold world with no comforting sound of a heart."

Matthias forced a smile. He knew she didn't mean to lay more guilt on him, but her words stung him nonetheless. The research on newborns was familiar to him, but the way she put it in plain and simple words made more sense than any articles he had read in medical journals.

"I wasn't myself then." He averted his eyes and glanced at the starry sky. "The very sight of the boys reminded me of Emina's death. I put all my strength and time into my work instead of being there for them. While I was busy building my clinic, time passed by and before I knew it, they weren't babies anymore." More guilt washed over him for all the days he missed and would never get back. But, it wasn't his work that had kept his mind occupied. His friendship with Kate had made those early days of Emina's death bearable.

"I've realized I have all the time in the world but they don't. Before I miss another birthday, I have to change my ways and not allow mourning for Emina to consume me. I should spend more time with the boys." He smiled as peace eased some of his guilt. He had told his story to another living being—Kate—and she hadn't run away.

Her soft laugh echoed through the summer night. "You already took the first step by dedicating this vacation to them. The rest should follow."

He squeezed her shoulder. "All thanks to you."

A passing boat caused the yacht to sway on its waves. She grabbed the side of the table and stopped her glass from sliding off. "Are you sure it's thanks to me?"

"Yes. I'd like to make a toast to you and to the beginning to our wonderful friendship."

She cocked her head. "I'll drink to that." Her glass and his bottle clinked together. "Where did I hear it before?"

He winked. "Some good, old movie, I suppose."

She pressed the heel of her hand on her stomach, suppressing a growl.

"I apologize for being such a bad host," he said. They'd both jogged earlier, he had dragged her out of the city's core, and now they'd been talking for hours without food. Not good, the doctor in him scolded. "You must be hungry. Shall we eat?"

"I thought you'd never ask. You have food here?"

"No." He should've filled the fridge with more than just drinks. "But the marina has a good restaurant. Are you up to it?"

"Would it still be open?"

He glanced over his shoulder at the glass restaurant building. "Look, the lights are on and there are people sitting at the tables. I think it's open all night."

She stood. "Let's eat, then."

"I almost forgot." He pulled a folded paper from the pocket of his shorts. "I've got a surprise for you."

Her brows rose. "What kind of surprise?"

"Well, I called the agency since Mr. Wilkins is on vacation. They faxed me your release papers. So, now you're my full time employee." He passed the sheet of paper to her.

She took it in her hand. "How did you know Wilkins is on vacation?"

"I bumped into him the other day."

She lifted her glance from the paper, her expression sharp. "What? He's vacationing here? Of all the places in the world, he chose this city?"

Matthias shrugged. "It's a free country. No one can stop him from coming here."

"Did you speak to him?"

Matthias shook his head. "No, I barely recognized him. He's grown a beard and long hair. As if he's hiding from someone."

Her eyes narrowed. "I don't trust him,. He's up to something."

She might be right. Matthias had had a hard time convincing the replacement clerk Kate's starting day was over two months ago. But what did it matter now. Wilkins couldn't hurt them. "Come on, Kate. Let's not spoil this night with Wilkins. Who cares about him? You now work for me, not the agency."

Her shoulders relaxed and she let out a breath. "All right, boss. I guess you're right. But I wouldn't lower my guard. That man's creepy."

"He is history. Let's go, I'm starving. And please, call me anything but boss."

"I'll need to bother you to help me with the sandals again."

"It's no bother. It would be my pleasure." Matthias's voice came out huskier than he intended.

A warm summer breeze played with the lose wisps of Kate's ponytail as Matthias led her out of the restaurant.

She pressed her hand to her stomach and exhaled. "I don't normally pig out like that in the middle of the night. Or day."

"Your plate was still full when the waiter took it away." He leaned toward her, glad she hadn't mentioned Wilkins again. This night was just for the two of them—the first of many.

"I was hungry but then my appetite shut down. I guess it's just too late to eat. What time do you think it might be?"

She climbed on board and he followed. "The sun will soon come out and the heat will rise." He nodded towards the horizon where the first light broke the darkness and flexed his wrist. His eyes focused on his watch. "It's twenty to five."

"We talked the whole night?" Her eyes looked tired. She sat at the same table on the upper deck, leaned her head on her hand, and closed her eyes.

"Time flies when you're in good company." He was tired, too. If she insisted on going home now he'd have a hard time walking her there.

"Can I ask you one more question?" she said with her eyes closed.

He stifled the yawn. "I believe you already did, but go ahead."

Her eyes fluttered open. "Do the boys know?"

"Emina said the truth will set us free and lies and secrets hurt everyone. So, yes, they know in their own way." He drew in a long breath and revelled in her jasmine scent.

She smiled "She was so wise."

"Yes, she was," he said, allowing emotions to take over him for one brief moment.

Kate slouched over the table and laid her head on her folded arms. "I have to rest for a minute."

"You'll wake with a hell of a cramp if you sleep slouched over." He stood and squeezed her shoulder. Eyes closed, she replied with an incoherent whisper.

"Kate?" The only response was the sound of her slow, steady breathing. He scooped her up in his arms and carried her below. "You'll sleep well here."

A soft moan escaped her when he lowered her on the double berth of the boat's master cabin and placed a kiss on her temple. Her eyes opened to thin slits. She lowered her lids again as her head rolled to the side. Exposed to him, her carotid artery pulsed under her skin.

He waited, but nothing happened. He grinned in relief. His lack of response was a good indication the infection was leaving his body. He couldn't remember the last time the sharp pain pierced his gums at the sight of an inviting vein. Soon, he might be living a mortal life.

The light cover rustled when he pulled it over her, and the empty half of the bed tempted him, but he decided against lying next to her and left, closing the door behind him. He groaned and rubbed his neck on his way to his temporary cabin.

His feet dangled over the edge of child size bunk amidships. Metal springs poked his back through the thin mattress. He rolled to his side and yawned. Was this what mortal men meant when they said they were in the doghouse? Was he?

Emina smiled softly at him from the picture frame. He took the photo in his hand.

"I sense it too, my dove." The coldness of the frame and picture glass pierced his skin when he pressed the photo to his chest. "Your spirit has calmed down."

Deep inside him guilt mixed with pain. Life was supposed go on with him and Emina forever, raising their little family. Now, he was a widower, an outcome he never thought he would have to face. Kate didn't kiss like Emina used to kiss him. When Kate called his name it didn't sound the same. Was kissing Kate better or was he unable to recall what it felt like to kiss Emina? While he was with Kate he felt alive. He wished to hell there were some clear cut guidelines, a protocol. One thing was for certain, he must not forget Emina. Could he share his devotion enough to love Kate?

CHAPTER 8

The sound of roaring engines jerked Kate from sleep. Matthias's yacht bobbed on the waves and thudded against the pier. She sat up. Through the small, round window she watched a neighboring craft slowly reverse from its spot.

She scanned the spacious cabin where she'd slept, nestled under the yacht's bow. The firm mattress of the queen size bed had given her a restful sleep. But how had she ended up here?

The last thing she remembered was the two of them returning to the deck from the restaurant and talking till dawn. Oh, yeah, she'd closed her eyes for a moment. A vague memory of him scooping her in his arms and holding her against his hard chest made the blood rush to her head.

The bag she brought with her belongings waited by the foot of the bed, her nighty still folded inside. With a quick peek under the blanket, she checked her clothes. She still wore the pair of jeans shorts and the halter top she'd worn last night, though they were badly wrinkled. So Matthias had been discreet enough not to undress her or change her into the pjs she'd brought. Fingers laced, she stretched her arms over her head, leaning from side to side.

Although she must have slept alone last night, there was no doubt he enjoyed her company. But did he also desire her? His conduct had been very gentlemanly, but the kiss in the Botanical Gardens still caused a slight tickle in the core between her legs.

She wondered if it was Emina's constant presence that kept him from taking her. The guilt must eat at him, knowing his dead wife could see him if he romanced another woman.

Though Kate didn't feel the spirit's presence when she was alone with Matthias. And she didn't feel her now. Where could Emina have gone?

She climbed out of bed and put on her sandals. Then with her bag swung over her shoulder, she left the cabin.

She found Matthias asleep on the child size bunk in the cabin next door. Should she wake him? His contented expression and his long feet dangling over the edge coaxed a smile to her lips.

The buzzing of her cell phone made her cringe. She slipped out of the cabin, dug into her bag, and pulled out the phone. Dyane's name flashed on the display. Shoot. They were supposed to meet last night. After replying to her with a text message to meet at Toni's, Kate scribbled a note for Matthias and left it on the galley's sink.

The late afternoon sun cast the long shadows as she ran to the jetty on the mainland side of the footbridge. A handful of tourists clutched the sides of the little red ferry as the boat rocked on the wakes of passing craft. She jumped in and paid the fare. Though she wished the old man could row faster, a hundred meter trip across the bay saved her a twenty-minute walk to the Old Town.

The patio of Toni's café was engulfed in shade when Kate arrived, but she didn't dare remove the sunglasses hiding the dark circles under her tired eyes. Dyane was already going to blast her for standing her up. What was it about Matthias's presence that turned her brain into a mushroom?

Dyane plopped down on a cushion and set a tall glass of ice water with a floating slice of lemon in front of Kate. "You missed a great party here last night, but something tells me you had a good time of your own."

Kate smiled, lowering her head.

"Out with it." Dyane demanded.

Kate leaned over the table then paused. Her friend's grin confirmed her anticipation. Dyane would burst if Kate didn't tell her soon.

She smiled and said, "I spent the whole night with him."

"I knew it," Dyane hissed. "I want details."

"Well, I, um—" Kate took a sip of water and licked her lips. "I ran into Matthias at the park."

Dyane sat up straight. "Matthias, is it? Are we now on the first name bases?"

Kate's remembered their first day in Zadar and the gentle sway of the hammock. "He insisted on it as soon as we arrived here." She couldn't keep the dreaminess out of her voice. "But, there really isn't much to say. We stayed up all night, talking. That's all."

"Then why are you wearing black sunglasses in the deep shade?" Dyane reached for a pack of sugar when the waitress delivered their espressos.

"I'm not used to staying up all night and not getting a shower in the morning," Kate retorted, sticking her tongue out.

"So, what did you guys talk about during the night that you didn't get any sleep?" Dyane demanded.

The story of the boys' birth and their mother's death pressed on Kate's mind. "He explained everything. The boys are mortal, thank God. I didn't ask but I assumed he couldn't save Emina from dying this time. Maybe you don't get an infinite number of chances to be immortal."

"It's only fair. We mortals can only die once." Dyane leaned back. "I can't believe you didn't at least kiss."

"There was a kiss." Kate stared at the table. Her kiss must have been different from Emina's and he had not liked it because he had not even attempted to kiss her again.

"Looks like that kiss knocked your socks off." Dyane poured sugar into her coffee, stirred, and took a sip. "I knew you were with him, but I wanted to hear it from you."

Kate's eyes widened. "How did you know?"

Dyane blew a strand of her hair. "The ghost's been hanging around my store. I don't mind her now that she's calmed down and hums a soft tune."

Kate's soul rippled with sympathy. Poor Emina's spirit, reduced to something of a stray ally cat. "She's back with me now, right? I can feel her but she's not making me jittery like before."

Dyane nodded, shifting in her seat. "Let's see what's in your cup. Espresso is not the best for reading but we don't have anything else. Drink up and turn your cup upside-down."

Kate glanced at Dyane and raised the cup to her lips, but her friend's words twisted her stomach. "Emina wouldn't want me to take her place. Would she?" Frowning, she imagined herself in Emina's situation. She doubted she could stand to watch her widowed husband make love to another woman.

"We'll see." Dyane gestured with her hand. "Drink up."

Kate ignored the burn on her tongue and gulped the bitter, black beverage down in a few long sips. She flipped the cup on its saucer and pushed it toward Dyane. "Should I read yours?"

"My only future is to lose ten pounds." Dyane tapped her finger on the bottom of Kate's cup and picked it up in her hand.

"I wish I only had your problem." Kate watched her friend spin the cup in her fingers.

"I'm having a hard time reading this. It could be because we didn't drink proper coffee. Anyway, there are too many paths and all of them broken, except one that leads home." Dyane tilted the cup and levelled her eyes with Kate's. "See, he's got you messed up. I'll have to try some other time."

Kate lowered the sunglasses and leaned closer. One thick line ran from the rim of the cup straight down to the bottom. If her memory served her right, the symbol meant her heart found love. She'd had similar if not the same forecasts before.

"*Messed up* doesn't begin to explain it. Yes, my heart is broken. Seems Matthias is trying to piece it back together, but I'm afraid it's too late." The warmth in Kate's chest faded a little. The effect of last night's events still pumped her up with joy, but this conversation was putting a dumper on it.

"Sweetie," Dyane sighed. "Past is past. You have to let it go."

"How do you let go of the past?" Kate asked, pushing her sunglasses up her nose. "Is there a secret formula? I'd like to know. Especially if the past repeats itself."

"Now, now, you sound just like your mother."

Kate cringed. Those were Mom's exact words. She'd never thought she'd hear herself saying them. "Still, I'd like to know how to forget."

"You stay busy, don't think about the pain, and one day it doesn't bother you as much. Yes, the past could repeat itself, but we learn and don't make the same mistakes." Dyane opened her purse. "I have two guest passes for that new gym. The rumour has it they have a great yoga class. Let's get busy right now."

Kate moaned. She didn't have the energy for a workout, but she could at least keep her friend company and check out the facilities. "I'd have to stop by my place and change. By the way, did you get my book back?"

Dyane stood. "My friend's sister wanted to read it."

"Please make sure she's the last one." Kate wanted to hold the book in her hands. It represented a dear gift from a dear man.

"Don't worry. It won't get lost. Matthias could get you another copy." Dyane put a stress on his name, leaning forward.

No doubt he could, but Kate wouldn't ask him. This copy was supposed to be for her and she shared it without his consent. It was his story after all. "Still, it's special to me and another copy wouldn't feel the same. Ready to go?"

Matthias brought the water bottle to his lips and leaned over the counter. He read Kate's note for the fifth time. She didn't want to wake him but she had to go and would call him, later. He scratched the back of his head. For the first time in six years he slept so deep and peacefully, he didn't hear her leave.

He raised his head to the ceiling of the cabin with the sound of footsteps on the deck. The whole yacht bobbed. Only one person he knew walked with such heavy step.

"You had a woman here last night, my friend?" Fortuno's voice thundered. His bald head almost touched the low ceiling when he straightened up at the foot of the stairs. "I can still smell her sweet perfume."

Matthias nodded. Yes, the faint jasmine scent of Kate's lotion still lingered in the air. He smiled and jerked his head toward the couch. "What brings you here, old friend?"

"You've been in town for a week and didn't stop by. Not like you." Fortuno stroked his blond goatee and took a seat on the cream-colored sofa. "Are my godsons here? Adriana would love to see them. And so would I."

"The boys are with Petar. They are itching to see their cool aunt and uncle." Matthias sighed. "And the woman who was with me last night wasn't just anyone, but Kate."

Fortuno's thick brows knitted. A peculiar smile bloomed on his face. "Hmmm, that explains you ignoring me."

"You know I would never ignore you, old man, but I've been busy." Matthias joined him on the couch. Though Matthias was a century older he knew Fortuno liked it when he referred to him as old.

"It's about time you connected with her." Fortuno ran his thumb over an old scar on his neck. "Does she know?"

"Most of it." Matthias paused. He had failed Emina. Her last wish was simple, find happiness. Instead, he had allowed his grief to make him miserable. To see the sadness in Kate's eyes cut him deep. She had breathed new life into him, and now he would do same for her. "I didn't want to overwhelm her."

Curiosity flashed in Fortuno's pale blue eyes. "What did you leave out?"

"Emina's wish."

"That's all?" Fortuno's voice was laden with irony. "Do I get to meet her?"

"All in good time. First I have to gain her approval to court her." Matthias pulled a t-shirt over his head. The kiss he snatched yesterday in the Botanical Gardens returned to his mind. Not gentlemanly of him to dwell on it, yet the feel of her lips yielding under his and the memory of her sweet scent shot straight to his groin.

Fortuno laughed. "You have much to learn, my friend."

Matthias propped his hands on his hips and studied his minion. Fortuno had only stopped calling him Master in this century yet Matthias had granted him his freedom over a hundred years ago. "What is there to be learned?"

"For starters, men don't court women any more, they date." The stones on Fortuno's rings shimmered as he pointed at Matthias. "You make sure you bring her on a date to my restaurant. I'll even cook."

"I may take you up on your offer—" Matthias spun toward the sound of shattering glass. The water bottle had smashed on the galley floor. "Emina," he whispered. "What is it, my dove?"

Fortuno sprung to his feet. "Can Mistress hear me?"

"I'm sure she can." Matthias raised his finger, straining to listen. "She is trying to warn me of something."

A quick flash of Kate's frightened face appeared in the puddle of water.

"I want to tell Mistress how much I miss her."

"She knows, Fortuno. She knows," Matthias called over his shoulder as he raced for his cabin. "I must go find Kate."

"You go," Fortuno called. "I'll clean up this mess."

Scrambling into a pair of jeans, Matthias hurried back to the galley. "I'll have to take your car."

Fortuno pulled his keys out of his cargo short's pocket and tossed them to Matthias. "Of course, anything for my Master and Mistress."

The sun had gone down by the time Kate pushed open the heavy glass door of the gym. As she stepped out onto the sidewalk, she sighed. The cool darkness surrounding her was a welcome relief.

Dyane followed a few paces behind her. "I'll feel this workout tomorrow."

"I'm feeling it already," Kate said and kneaded her sore bicep. "That girl was no yoga instructor. A drill sergeant, more like. Did you know you had muscles down between..." She trailed off, no need to finish this sentence.

"But you have to admit the gym is great. I loved the yoga studio."

"Expensive place, no doubt."

"Oh, it is. I've got their price list." Dyane squeezed the bag under her elbow. "I'd have to give up one of my spa treatments to take a membership here, but it would be worth it."

Suddenly the color drained from her face and she grabbed Kate's elbow. "Let's go this way."

"Dyane, what's wrong?" Kate had never seen her look this scared.

"Someone is following us," she hissed.

"Another ghost?"

"Ghosts, I can handle," Dyane whispered, pulling her by her arm. "This is a living moron with real anger control problems."

Kate glanced over her shoulder. "What does he look like? I don't see any man behind us."

"He's there. I know it. His girlfriend came to me to read her cards. I told her he cheats on her, and she dumped him. She cheated on him too, but I didn't see the point of bringing it up."

"Where are you dragging me?"

"There's an ally where I managed to escape him the last time."

"Did you try to report him to the police?"

Dyane snorted. "The police are sweet on him, or rather on his dad's money. I have a restraining order against the bull, but a piece of paper won't protect us. Here." She shoved Kate behind a dumpster. "He won't' find us here."

Kate wrinkled her nose at the reek of decomposing garbage and swallowed the bile back down her throat.

Dyane pulled her cell from the pocket and blew a quivering breath. "I'll text Toni," she whispered.

"Forget Toni, dial the police." Fragments of shattered glass scraped the crumbling asphalt under Kate's feet.

"They'll blame the incident on me as always. I can never prove anything against this guy. There, Toni will be here in a few minutes."

Slow footsteps approached. Dyane pressed her finger to her pursed lips.

Panic seared Kate's mind. Beads of sweat trickled down her face. The tip of a black motorcycle boot appeared at the corner of the bin. She stifled a whimper and flattened her back against the rusty dumpster. The chains on the biker's boots clunked then disappeared.

Kate exhaled in relief. "Think he's gone?"

Dyane peaked around the corner. "Yeah, he came close this time. I think we're safe but be on the lookout."

"This is not wise, Dyane. He is stalking you, and one day you'll run out of luck."

"He hasn't acted out his threats. Yet. So the police can't charge him with anything. Toni wants to break his legs, but he can be charged if he harms this idiot. Where's the justice?" Dyane demanded, obviously struggling to keep her voice low.

"There isn't any. Let's get away from here before I throw up." Kate flipped the strap of her gym bag over her shoulder. She stepped out from her hiding place and came face to face with the gloating face of Dyane's pursuer.

Hatred burned in the man's black eyes. "Do you really think I'm that stupid?"

Trembling, Dyane swallowed. "You're not to come anywhere near me. If you leave us alone, I'll forget this."

Muscles on his neck flexed and his jaw ticked as he cut a glance at her. "What's to stop me from getting to you, bitch? The piece of paper you filled against me?"

"That's it." Kate pulled her cell out of her short's pocket. "I'm calling the police."

His nostrils flared and he snatched the phone out of her hand before she could flip it open. It hit the wall and shattered.

Determined not to show fear, Kate glared at him. "What do you want?"

"That witch to close her unholy business." He shoved Dyane's shoulders, knocking her to the ground. Like a frightened spider, she crawled backwards on her behind. Tears flowed down her cheeks as she stared at his face. Each time he took a step toward her, she scooted closer to the cement wall of the run down building.

Kate grabbed the fabric of his shirt and tried to stop him. "Leave her alone."

For Dyane's sake, she would have to be brave enough for both of them. Growing up with boy cousins had provided her with plenty of opportunities for learning how to fight a bully. If this moron attempted to get physical, she wouldn't hesitate to show him just how sensitive his sensitive spot was.

His muscular fist flew at her face. She dodged it. He lunged at her, knocking her back against the opposite wall from where Dyane huddled on the ground, her head clutched in her hands.

"I'm so gonna enjoy your tight ass," he whispered in Kate's ear, pinning her with his torso.

Terror ripped through her. Her efforts to ram her knee into his crotch proved useless. She could barely lift her leg under him. This dog might just succeed, but she'd be dammed if she'd go down without a fight.

His hot breath assaulted her ear as he trailed his tongue down her neck and she cringed in disgust. Wrenching one hand free, she grabbed the bulge between his legs.

"That's it girl," he crowed. "Give up and enjoy me is all you can do."

"In your dreams, pal." Without any hesitation, she squeezed and twisted.

He screamed and tried to pull away. "Let go of my—"

"Giving up so soon? We're just starting to have fun."

His face, contorted in pain, brought Kate a sense of bravado and she let go of him too soon.

Slouched over, he cradled his private parts with one hand and with the other, he threw a punch at her stomach, knocking the wind out of her. She fell backwards, pain ripping through her abdomen.

A large hand landed on the ass's shoulder. Matthias swung him around, his fist making contact with the punk's face. Knocked out cold, the moron hit the ground like a sack of potatoes.

"Kate." Matthias crouched and wrapped his arms around her.

"Matthias." Thank God, he'd come. She didn't know how long she'd have been able to repel the assault. "The guy is not left-handed, couldn't pack much force in his fist," she joked, trying to keep the agony from showing on her face.

"No, you're in pain. We need to x-ray your abdominal area. Make sure you're not bleeding internally."

The police cruiser pulled into the ally with siren's blaring.

Toni rounded the corner and ran straight to his wife.

"He broke my cell." Tears welled Kate's eyes. The threat was gone, and now she couldn't hold her emotions in.

"I'll get you another one." Matthias slid one arm around her waist and helped her up. "But first let's get you to the hospital. I parked on the street. Can you walk?"

She nodded. "Let me see to Dyane, first," she sobbed.

"Just go Kate. I've recorded everything on my phone and will talk to the police."

Kate turned to Matthias. "Are you sure I need x-rays?"

"Yes, doctor's order." He took her bag in his free hand. "I'll get the radiologist to take one photograph and examine the film right away. We'll be done in an hour."

The moron moaned as the officer cuffed him. "You've done it this time." He yanked him to his feet. "Not even your dad's deep pockets won't dispute this evidence."

"He paid me to do it," the buffoon yelled before the officer could shove him in the cruiser.

Matthias's grip on Kate's waist tightened, stopping her in her tracks. "Who paid you to attack this woman?" he demanded.

The punk glanced at him with snide smile. "You can't touch me. I'm in police custody."

CHAPTER 9

Sweat glued Kate's back and thighs to the leather seat of Renault Latitude despite the cold air blowing in from the vents. The scent of pine from an air freshener clipped to the duct filled the interior.

The x-rays showed the punch had not caused her internal damage. The attacker was apprehended and Dyane's quick wits had collected plenty of evidence to put him behind the bars for a long time. His daddy's money would not save him this time. Jail time might do him good.

Matthias's silence made the fifteen-minute drive from the hospital to her apartment building feel twice as long. With skilled precision, he reversed the sleek vehicle into a tight spot, a maneuver she wouldn't dare to attempt. The street, lined with parked cars and trimmed trees, appeared darker through the tinted windows.

He turned the engine off.

Maybe now he'd say *something*. She sank back into the seat when he cast her a soft smile, sending her heart into overdrive.

"Thank you," she said. "I told you I was fine. He caught me by surprise, when I let go of his—ahem—too soon."

Matthias's eyes narrowed. "Kate, you were in pain. I had to make sure." Pushing his knees together, he burst out laughing. "I hope I never experience your iron hold. Ouch."

"Oh, he'll live." She joined in, glad Matthias could joke about it now.

"With a few emotional scars." The leather on the seat creaked under him as he shifted. He leaned closer and caressed her shoulder. She winced with the feel of his cold hand on her hot skin. "Can I invite you to a dinner?"

Her stomach tightened. Another dinner with him might be too soon, but she couldn't resist. "I'm going home to shower and change my clothes first."

"I'll meet you at the bridge in two hours. Is that enough time for you?" The tickle of his breath on her skin sent tingling sensations all throughout her body.

"Plenty. Should I dress in anything special?" she asked. He was used to indulgence, so some fancy place was on his mind no doubt.

"As casual as you can. We'll grab a slice of pizza, sit on the medieval walls, watch the lights of passing boats, and try to guess where they going. How's that sound?"

"Like you read my mind."

"I did." He winked and brushed his thumb over her lips. "In two hours. Don't be late or we'll end up eating cold, leftover pizza."

She smiled. "I'll be there before you."

"Not if I can beat you to it." The engine roared to life when he turned the ignition.

"We'll see." Snatching her purse off the floor, she opened the door and jumped out.

"Is it a race?"

"Yes," she answered as her spirits soared.

The street lights had come on by the time Kate arrived at their meeting place. She scanned the crowd of people in the open area at the front of the footbridge. No sign of Matthias. She relaxed. She'd arrived fifteen minutes early. No way could he beat her.

Her little victory was short lived. He was sitting on the bridge railing. How had he gotten there first? Well, maybe if she hadn't changed six times before settling for a pair of olive-green capris and a sleeveless white top. This was their first real date, after all.

But she had to admit the faded jeans and tight black t-shirt Matthias wore caused a surge of desire to swamp her. She wanted to wrap her arms around him. Tight. "You must've beaten me by half a second," she said as she approached him.

He stood and bowed, clasping her hand. "A whole five seconds to be exact."

She looked around. People went about their business No one paid any attention to them.

She giggled when he placed soft kiss on her knuckles. "No one does that anymore."

"I do." He held her captive with his gaze for a few seconds then looped her hand around his elbow. "Let's stroll like—what did you say?—oh, yeah, an old couple."

Though she longed to slip her arm around his waist, she sauntered forward in step with him. They crossed the bridge to Old Town and got their dinner from a little nook. Then they climbed the zigzagging stairs to the wide fortification that once kept invaders from entering the city. The thumping music from a nearby outdoor nightclub, *The Garden*, bounced off the stone walls.

Matthias scaled the seven foot tall outer wall to place their food on top then jumped back down. "I'll give you the boost."

With his back against the wall, he laced his fingers. "The technique is the same as it was in the medieval times. Grab onto my shoulders and climb. Trust me it's easier if you do it barefoot. Pretend you are a corsair."

Was he serious? He expected her to climb on his shoulders? "They were driven by desperation."

He shrugged. "I'm starving. The smell of pizza makes me desperate enough."

With her sandals in her hand, she scanned the fortification wall. "I haven't climbed like this since I was a kid."

When she hesitated, he said, "I can lift you."

"No, I can do it." She shoved her foot in his hands and took hold of his shoulders. "This is so very romantic."

"It will be once you get up there. Ready?" His muscles flexed when she nodded. "One, two, up you go."

He propelled her upwards so when she neared the top she narrowly avoided shoving her hands in the pizza sauce. This dining experience made her feel like a teenager again. Propped on her elbows, she burst into laughter, her feet dangling above his head. Good thing she decided against wearing the skirt. Though the way the stones scraped her thighs, she'd be lucky if her pants didn't rip.

"Are you stuck?" he called. "Hang on, I'm coming."

Like a cat, he scaled the wall again and grabbed her wrists, pulling her up. The lights of the bridge railing flickered to life and reflected on the surface of the calm sea.

"Look at the view." He raised his arms as if to embrace the entire harbor. "And you doubted our vantage point would be romantic." His fingers wrapped around her hand. "Come, sit next to me."

She lowered to the cold stone wall. Twenty years of living in this city and she'd never seen the harbor lit as beautifully as tonight. "I don't think I can ever get enough of this wonderful view."

"Neither can I." He smiled, yet he was looking at her instead of the harbor.

Her stomach knotted. No one had complimented her in years, and he'd said nice things to her for two nights in a row. She took a bite of pizza, but couldn't pay attention to the taste. "Even after this acrobatic display?"

"Especially after that." The dimples in his cheeks deepened. "How's the pizza?"

"It's good, but I'm not very hungry, I'm afraid." She placed the slice on its carton and wrapped her fingers around the can of soda.

He tossed his crust at the garbage bin on the street. "Besides today's incident, are you having a great vacation?"

"The best." It was the truth. If he had taken his family to anywhere else in the world, she would have had a great time just because of his presence, but being home gave her vacation a nostalgic feeling. When the time to leave came, it would be that much harder. "How about you?"

"Wonderful." He reached for her hand and enclosed it in between his palms. "I was called to hospital only once since we arrived."

Curiosity sparked in her mind. "Why?"

"I work pro bono here, and they needed a plastic surgeon for an emergency facial reconstruction."

She lowered her head. All of a sudden, she felt inadequate. He had worked while she slept in and enjoyed her lazy days of summer. "I planned to write, but I keep getting side-tracked."

"Too many distractions in the city? I have a proposition for you."

No, just one distraction. You. She raised an eyebrow. "I'm listening."

"Would you like to be my guest before the boys' visitation with Petar is over? The house on the island is air-conditioned. I promise I won't bother you, and you'll have the place pretty much to yourself."

Blood rushed to her head. She wanted nothing more than to spend a few days alone with him on his island and forget about the civilization. No matter where in the world she went, thoughts of him would cloud her mind.

"We wouldn't be cut off the world. There's wireless internet connection, and I even have a television."

"It sounds tempting, but I think we should give this dating thing at least one more try."

"All right, how about tomorrow? Would you like to meet my friend?"

His friend? "I'd love to. Is he...like you?"

"Yes, he is immortal." He chuckled. "You'll see."

She picked up a slice of pizza to hide her trembling hands, but she didn't eat it. Tapping her foot to the beat from the club to distract herself proved futile. This city had its secrets, but she never expected them to involve immortals.

"Are you done with it?" He pointed to her food. "If so, do you want to find a place we can dance?"

"I do, but I hope you'd prefer something less notorious than *The Garden*." Her clubbing days were over, thank God.

He tossed the tins of sodas and her half eaten pizza slice in the garbage.

"Since members from U2 bought it and put in such tight security, there haven't been any fights. I don't fancy clubs either. The place I had in mind is on the lower promenade." He stood and jumped down then reached for her. She swung her legs over the side and placed her hands on his shoulders, letting his strong arms wrap around her waist as she slid from the wall. When he kept her body from reaching the ground by tightening his hold, she trembled. Then he spun around with her clinging to him. She laughed as he stopped and let her put her feet down.

"You must have seen a lot more of these defense fortifications," she said, straightening her crumpled top.

"Yes, the walls extended around the entire peninsula at one time. Most of them were pulled down in the nineteenth century, but what's left is put into good use with parks and promenades."

"I wish I could have seen the city back then."

"The layout of Old Town has not changed at all." His hand clasped hers, and he led the way down the stone steps heading away from the fortifications. "But there wasn't much of the city outside these walls, or on the mainland side of today's bridge."

They strolled through the narrow streets of the medieval town and arrived at the old hotel by the sea. Waiters bustled around the tables on the terrace. A few couples twirled on the dance floor as the band played a version of *Save the Last Dance for Me*. Her feet stopped, and she stared at the dance floor, longing to be in his embrace and move her body in sync with his.

As if on cue, he cocked his head toward the patio. "Shall we?"

She wrapped her hand around his bicep. Thrilled as she was he wanted to dance with her, she was nervous, sure that she would be clumsy and awkward. Suddenly, scaling the medieval wall had seemed easier.

He led her though the maze of tables and chairs on the hotel's terrace. When they reached the clear area in front of the small stage, he slipped his arm around her waist. "We can do better than these other couples. Come on, let's us show them how dancing is done. Just relax and follow my steps."

His left hand pressed on her hip, pulling her close as the fingers of his right hand wrapped around her left. When she placed her free hand on his solid shoulder, her fingers fumbled, but his warm, reassuring smile eased her tension. Her feet wouldn't cooperate for the first few swings. A funny frown appeared on his face when she stepped on his foot for the third time. She glanced at her feet. God, he must think she was terribly uncoordinated.

He squeezed her hand. "Look at me."

Their eyes met. Lost in his mesmerizing gaze, she forgot what her feet were doing and her nervousness disappeared, replaced by a sense of peace as she picked up his rhythm, following him with ease. Even when he twirled her under his arm, her feet didn't falter. Before she knew it, the song had come to an end.

"We were good," she said, joy and wonder filling her voice.

He hugged her. "We were."

The band leader strummed the guitar and stepped up to the microphone. "And now, it's ladies' choice."

He turned back to the band and they joined in with his song. Many left the dance area with the slow melody. But Matthias wrapped his arm around her waist.

"I hope I'm your choice," he murmured

When the vocalist joined in with the three guys from the group, Kate turned her attention to the lyrics. Every single word of the song "I'll Leave the Light On" struck a nerve. Memories she had suppressed for years flooded to the surface as the band played on. Her chest tightened, constricting her breath. Tears stung her eyes. Matthias stopped his feet, but kept his body swaying. Kate stared at his shoes. Sobs spasmed her shoulders, betraying her attempts to hide her emotions from him. Four hours earlier, she had boldly stood up to an enraged bull, but the words of this song reduced her to a wimp.

His hand inched behind her neck and pulled her head onto his chest. She prayed the tune would end, but the band kept playing.

When the beat of the next song sped up, and people poured back onto the dance floor, Matthias kissed her hair and led her away from the loud music. "We should sit this one out."

She collapsed on the edge of a bench and pushed her palms into the splintered wood. "Thank you for not asking."

"This is but the tip of the ice berg," he said. "I suspect there's a whole mountain in there."

"It's not fair for you to see this. You didn't cause me to break down." She turned to him. His shirt stained with her tears. Last night, he told her his life story on his boat. She had to share hers with him. She owed it to him. "I committed a great sin, Matthias, the greatest a mother can commit. I'm afraid I'll go straight to Hell for what I've done."

CHAPTER 10

Humiliated, Kate shifted on the wooden bench, while Matthias stared at her. Averting her eyes in shame, she glanced at the sea side of the promenade where people strolled happily along, enjoying the balmy summer night.

"I know you couldn't commit such a deadly sin," he said, his voice so serious, her heart trembled with fear.

"I killed my baby," she choked out, burying her face in her hands.

Dread and grief churned her stomach as she imagined what he must think of her. He didn't speak, just stared at her, his eyes piercing and unreadable. Terrified the worst would happen and Matthias would hate her for the loss of her child, she hurried on with her story. After all, Emina had stopped at nothing to have children.

"When I found out I was pregnant, Craig—" The words caught in her throat and she wasn't sure she could get them out. "He did the right thing. He married me, but he was unhappy. He was hardly ever home."

She tucked her trembling hands under her legs. Mom would be proud of her. For years she had been pressuring Kate to open up and talk about this. Kate pushed through the pain as Matthias's face softened. The gentle touch of his hand on her back lessened the terrible ache in her heart.

"A week after the ultrasound my doctor's office called me in. I nearly freaked out. All the way there I prayed my baby was all right and it was only a routine thing they wanted to check on. But it wasn't routine. The doctor said the baby's heart and lungs weren't developing properly."

Tears spilled from her eyes, burned her cheeks. She accepted a tissue from Matthias and wiped the droplets away. Even though the memory threatened to crack open a slowly healing wound, his warm look gave her the strength to continue.

"The doctor suggested I terminate. He said there was hardly a chance for my baby to even survive the pregnancy, and it would endanger my life, too." She swallowed hard. "I let him talk me into an abortion. Craig was relieved, and he left a few weeks after the procedure. Selfish bastard couldn't stick around till I recovered physically and emotionally." Her voice trailed off and she stared into the distance a long time, seeing nothing but the face of an unborn child.

Matthias remained silent, but his hand rested softly on her back. She knew he watched her. She could feel his compassionate stare. It was time to tell him the full extent of her cruel actions.

"Before the abortion, my mom suggested I get a second opinion, have more tests, just to be sure. But without doctor's referral we'd have to pay for one. I didn't have much money at the time and the doctor seemed so certain. Besides, I had reconciled myself to it, and I was afraid to get my hopes up, just to have them dashed again. So I just went ahead with it. Then a few months after the procedure, the doctor's office called me in again. He was all apologetic, saying a big mistake had been made and there had been nothing wrong with my baby." Her voice broke and she struggled to steady it. "He'd made me kill a perfectly healthy baby. My baby. I still cannot believe I agreed." She turned her head to face him, pleading with his eyes. "I should have done like my mother suggested and sought a second opinion. He was a doctor, Matthias, I believed him. How could he make such mistake?"

"The lab mixed up the labels on the forms," Matthias said gently, but even his soft voice couldn't calm her raging heart. "The diagnosis your doctor made from the ultrasound pictures he saw was correct. That fetus didn't make it. The other couple in the waiting room at the imaging place you went to was grief stricken when they lost their baby after they were told it was healthy. They investigated and discovered the mistake."

She remembered the ecstatic couple in the waiting room holding hands, anxious to see their baby on the screen for the first time. Craig, of course, couldn't have been bothered to accompany her to the appointment and see his child growing in her belly. She had accepted the rotten marriage deal with Craig, just to give her baby a father and that father didn't give a damn if his child lived or died. "How do you know the details?" she asked Matthias.

He didn't respond.

"My God," she whispered. "The voice in my head stopped, but you never really left, did you?"

He held her stare for an immeasurable moment then shook his head slowly.

"You promised," she breathed.

"No, I said the voice would stop. I cared too much to leave you. I tried to reach for you after your husband left, but you had created a prison of solitude and didn't allow anyone in—or yourself to escape." He pulled her into his embrace. Her tears poured out, soaking into his shirt and melting the ice in her heart.

"You're a clover with four leafs, there's always room for you in my heart. Welcome to my life, my happiness, that's what you are..." He sang the words of a love song in her ear along with the band. His chest rose and fell with each breath.

She'd calmed down by the time the song ended. At this perfect moment, she was closer to him than to anyone in the world. The steady beat of his heart spoke to hers, telling her he understood her turmoil.

With his fingers, he brushed her hair back from her face and placed a kiss on her brow. "None of this was your fault. You couldn't have known," he said, wiping away a tear that escaped from her eye. "There now. Are you feeling better?"

"Yes." She sniffed. The knot in her chest had loosened. For the first time in three years she took in a real deep breath and let the air seep out all the way without the pain. A realization washed over her—she could let go of the sad memories and get on with her life, but she didn't have to forget her child.

"The loss of the baby left me desperate to pour my love onto any children. I volunteered in family centers, but the sights and cries of cherubs tore at my soul. The new mommies' gazes turned sharp, slashing at me in some imagined self-defense when I seemed too eager to hold their little bundles of joy."

Matthias tucked a stray wisp of her hair behind her ear. She closed her eyes and allowed herself to surrender to his caress. His silence spoke to her louder than words.

"Let's go for a walk. You choose where." He grabbed her by the hand and pulled her with him.

The crushed pebbles crunched under her feet "I'd like to see the famous *Greeting to the Sun*."

"You haven't seen the solar circle yet?"

She gave a weak smile. "Only on YouTube."

"Then let's go."

They walked hand in hand along the promenade. Silver moonlight washed over the calm water surface, soothing her soul. She drew in a deep breath. The salty smell of the sea filled her nostrils.

They arrived at the point on the promenade, where the people gathered to sit on the marble steps of the Sea Organ. Matthias stepped on the thick glass panels of the circle. An array of flickering fluorescent lights raced across the surface of the floor. "The panes absorb the energy from the sun and at night they create this colorful show," he said.

She elbowed her way through the crowd. Cameras flashed all around her. "The circle is packed."

"You must visit in the middle of the winter when the solar circle is empty." He pointed to the wide marble stairs, leading straight into the sea. "Too bad the sea is calm tonight. When the waves push air through the pipes underneath those steps, chords are played by the world's first sea organ."

Calm water lazily hugged the steps. She smiled at the thought of how much she had longed to see this and now she was here. "Quite someth—"

A shove on her back propelled her toward the sea. Matthias caught her and wrapped his arms protectively around her.

"I beg your pardon." The tourist spoke with a thick British accent.

"Please mind your step." Matthias snapped. His sweet scent filled her lungs when he pulled her close.

"Will do mate." The man said and turned back to his friends.

"Do you want to go somewhere else?" he asked, his arms surrounding her like a protective wall.

"No."

She slipped her arms around him, and he tightened his hold. With a sigh, she shut her eyes and melted into him. Soft music drifted to them from the distance. Somewhere, someone played a piano. Matthias swayed with her to the melody. She nestled her head under his chin, her weight supported by his arms. Seconds later, she realized the song she heard was meant for her alone. No piano player sat nearby caressing a melody from ivory keys. The music was in her head, as beautiful as a bird's song on a spring morning.

He cradled her face with both his hands and pressed his forehead to her brow. His lips touched hers. She parted them, and his tongue plunged into her mouth. Butterflies had stirred in her stomach all night, but now they spread through her entire body. Since their first kiss at the Botanical Gardens, she'd thought of little else. Now she was like wax under his hungry mouth and gentle hands. With a soft nip on her lower lip, he ended the kiss and ran his lips along her jaw, leaving a trail of fire on her skin

She frowned when his body shuddered. Did he have an allergic reaction to her lip gloss? When he buried his face in the crook of her neck, his gentle swaying reassured her. The song came to an end, and he stopped the dance.

"I must apologize. I got carried away." His husky whisper sent another wave of shivers down her spine. "Please forgive me. My behaviour was inappropriate."

"No, it wasn't," she whispered in hopes he'd kiss her again.

He took her hand in his and led her away from the circle. "We should enjoy these last few hours of the night."

The lazy stroll back to her apartment building was excruciating. Her mind searched for some appropriate words to break the silence, but found none.

He paused at the front entrance. "Stay on the boat with me tonight," he whispered, his voice husky with need.

She bit her lip and shook her head.

"Are you sure?" He gave her a smile but she could see the disappointment in his eyes.

"Right now, I'm not sure of anything except that I'll change my mind the second I step in my apartment." She looked up at the second floor balcony. "If the sleeping arrangements stayed the same, maybe I..."

She hoped he would understand. He should. After all, he came from a time when gentlemen were bound to respect a maiden's honor, and ladies protected their virtue like treasured gold.

"I'll gladly suffer another night on the child-sized bunk, as long as I have you near."

"Okay, come up while I pack a few things." She led the way to the second floor. Her parents' flat was small and plain, in comparison to the luxury he was used to, but maybe the modesty would tell him something about her.

"As you can see, the apartment is very basic." She flipped a switch and soft light illuminated the narrow hallway. The tiny unit appeared even smaller with him filling most of the front room. There was no breeze tonight, the sheer curtains over the open windows hung still.

"I want to see the place where you grew up and your toddler pictures." He pointed to an old framed photograph of her standing on the chair, chocolate stains on her little green dress. The sincerity in his smile and voice convinced her she'd made the right decision.

"Make yourself comfortable." She disappeared into the bedroom and packed her laptop, nighty, and a change of clothes, along with her comb, toothbrush and other necessities.

"I'm ready." She beamed at him and swung the backpack over her shoulder.

The old kitchen chair creaked when he stood. "Let me carry the bag for you."

She handed him her cloth drawstring sack without hesitation and they left the sweltering apartment.

When they arrived at the yacht, he bid her goodnight with a quick kiss on the cheek and left her alone in the master cabin. She breathed a quiet sigh of relief. As much as she wanted him, she wasn't ready for anything physical. Yet.

She hoped she'd be able to fall asleep. Talking through the nights and sleeping the days away had started to grow on her. Even though her crying jag earlier and reliving the painful memories had worn her out, she was grateful for the ease it had given her soul. Mom was right, opening up about the loss of the baby to someone else had helped.

The crisp linen sheets rustled around Kate when she crawled into the comfortable bed. A hint of guilt nagged at her. He gave up this spacious cabin for her. Would he be able to sleep in that small berth? She yawned and hugged the pillow. Her thoughts drifted to the solar circle where he showed her how tender and sweet he could be. Dreams mixed with reality. She saw Matthias's angry, disappointed face and heard her own heartbroken sobs and jolted back into the world of the awake. The ropes of the yacht creaked as she lay on her back, trying to make some sense of the short dream, but sleep took her again.

The laptop warmed Kate's skin through the thin bed sheet. Her fingers flew over the keys and words filled the pages. For the past hour since, she woke this afternoon, she'd been steadily writing. The first chapter of her new book was almost finished.

She paused and glanced at door of the master suite—no sound or sight of Matthias. Was he still asleep? She'd check on him in a few minutes.

A long yawn escaped her. As she started to return to her writing, the shrill ring of the cell phone made her jump. Getting used to the new phone would take her some time. She flipped it open, her finger hovering over the dial pad until she found the talk button.

With the mobile pressed to her ear, she continued typing. "Hi Mama."

"Kate, where are you?" her mom demanded sternly. "I called the apartment a few times but no one answered."

"I'm on Mr. Zrin's boat in the marina." Too late Kate realized what she had just said. Her fingers stopped. Would Mom think the worse as usual?

"I thought your vacation isn't over for another week. Kate—is there something you're not telling me?"

"Mama, I'm not a teenager." Kate snapped, slapping her free hand on the bed. Would her mom ever stop treating her like a little girl?

"No, but you jump into things without thinking."

"It's not like that. I'm happy for the first time in—"

"Happiness has nothing to do with what you're doing," her mother growled, irritation snapping in her voice.

"Don't you want me to be happy?" Kate's own voice rose to a near shout.

"Of course I do, but please, think with your head and not with your—"

"Mama," Kate snapped. "I know what I'm doing."

"And what is this I hear about a book you wrote. Apparently there are dirty words in it."

Kate's heart jumped to her throat. Oh, no, here we go. Once again she would have to justify her actions to the only woman who should understand her even without words. "It's a love story and there aren't any dirty words. The words are sensual."

"You can call it whatever but the implication is there. I'll say a prayer for the salvation of your soul."

"You do that, Mama."

The phone went dead before Kate even finished her sentence. She pressed the end button and closed the mobile. Well, now Mom knew she was alone with a man on a boat and about the book. Good. No Kate didn't have to tell her. And whether Mom liked it or not, she returned to the story. The urge to write overpowered her. How could any of this be wrong?

A few minutes later Matthias knocked on the door. "Kate, you awake?"

"Yes, come in." She lowered the lid and put the laptop to the side. The first draft was not yet ready for anyone's eyes.

Opening the door, he cocked his head in. "Can I get you a cup of coffee?"

The smell of fresh brew enthralled her. "Yes, God bless you."

"You stay put. I'll bring it to you."

He disappeared into the galley. Despite his order, she jumped from the bed. Her muscles rebelled, reminding her of yesterday's yoga practice. She pushed against her tight legs and moaned her way to the bathroom to check on her appearance. The last thing she wanted was to look like she just rolled out of bed, even if she had.

"Black and bitter is how you like it, right?" He placed the cup on the nightstand and reached for her when she limped out of the bathroom. "Why are you up?"

"I can't lie around all day. The tightness will loosen if I keep moving." She sat on the bed, took a long sip from the big mug and moaned. "This is my kind of coffee."

Matthias smiled. "Glad you like it. Was that your mama on the phone?"

"You heard that? Yes, that was her. She's too worried about me."

"She's your mother. She has a right to worry." His eyes filled with sadness, and Kate understood. Just like his boys, he had never experienced a mother's love. The *Rose of Crimson* novel wasn't only "dirty words."

"She can be overbearing sometimes," Kate said and drank the coffee. She set her empty mug on the night stand. "To her, I'm still a kid."

"I'm afraid I can't comment." He smiled and took her cup. "More?"

Her back sank into the fluffy pillows while she watched him through the opened suite door, as he poured her another delicious cup.

"Would it set your mom at ease if she met me?" he asked, returning with a refill and a big pastry on a plate.

Kate took a sip but the hot liquid went down hard. He'd be willing to meet her crazy family? The sight of this yacht alone would provoke some wild imagination among them. "You'd do that?"

"Are they three headed monsters?" He reached for her leg and kneaded his fingers on her sore calf muscles.

God, his arched eyebrows and smirk made him irresistible. Kate suppressed the desire to wrap her arms around him and kiss his lips. His massaging fingers caused her to wince in pain. "No, ah," she said as her leg jerked. "Though sometimes it feels like they are."

He moved to her other leg. "Hurts?"

She moaned, sliding down the pillow. Would he get bold enough to move up her legs and caress her thighs? He did. "Everything does. I could use a full body massage."

To her relief, he ceased his rubbing an inch away from her panties. His intense stare ignited a blaze in her. If he pulled off her underwear, she would crumble in his arms and surrender to him. He cleared his throat and sat up straight, a soft smile replacing his ardent expression. "Unfortunately, I'm not a masseur."

"You were doing just fine."

"I think your idea to keep moving is better." He pointed to the pastry on the plate. "Eat your croissant."

She picked up the pastry. "You went shopping?"

"Me? No." The coils on the mattress sprang back when he stood. "Petar dropped off some food. He says the boys miss us, but are excited about going to the amusement park."

Her throat closed. "I miss them too." Soon, she'd be tickling their bellies while they tried to squirm away. "You were a sleepy head today. I thought you'd never wake."

"I was up a few times to see if you were still here. You slept in peace."

"Matthias, I wouldn't leave." Guilt stung her. Had her sneaking away the last time caused him to distrust her already?

He leaned over her. "I know."

His fingertips brushed her cheek, causing her breath to quiver. She sank deeper into the pillows and closed her eyes. Would he kiss her again? *Please.*

"Have you heard of *Fortuno's*?" His voice shattered her fantasies.

"How can one not hear of that restaurant? It's advertised everywhere." The place must be very fancy from what she gathered.

He chuckled. "Yes, Fortuno is very eccentric."

His shifting eyes didn't escape her when her bunched up nighty exposed her thighs as she sat up straight.

"You mean there's someone named Fortuno?" she asked.

"I'm not sure if he knows his real name. He always went by Fortuno. For two centuries."

"He's that friend you mentioned?"

"No. I'm his Master, he's my minion, but I granted him his freedom long ago."

Matthias was the Master of a person? No, not him. When she described him as a Master she meant he owned houses, lands, but not another being. But that had obvious been what he meant. She sighed. How little she knew of his world.

"From your expression I think I should tell you his story. To bring the tale to life we must return to the peninsula. I'll leave you now to get ready." He bowed to her, left the suite, and closed the door.

Curiosity had her throwing on her clothes, despite her sore muscles. She opted for a dress this time. The way his eyebrow arched when she stepped out of the cabin a few minutes later made her very glad she had. As they left the marina and headed for Old Town, her excitement mounted. Whatever tale he was about to tell her would be thrilling, knowing this ancient place.

They walked across the familiar bridge, through the gates of medieval walls, and down the cobblestone paved road, where Matthias stopped by the large stone building housing the antique store. "What do you know of this place?"

"Not much. The dedication on the wall says the building and the court yard were a naval infirmary." She had often wondered about it, but couldn't find much about the massive building with its large, stone-paved courtyard recorded in the history books. "Did this part ever have a roof?"

"No this was always the courtyard."

He led her in through the narrow doorway. An image of the yard littered with wounded soldiers in naval uniforms lying on stretchers replaced the scene of today and the courtyard packed with stands selling trinkets. Was Matthias inflicting another vision on her?

"I found Fortuno here." Matthias pointed to the cobblestone ground. "He was just a poor cook in the service of His Majesty, Francis the Second."

A man with a bald head and blond goatee, his face contorted in pain, appeared before her eyes. A sudden surge of electricity ran down her legs. "Naval battle of Geona," she whispered.

"That's right." He nodded, his gaze still fixed at the spot under the tree. "Despite his wounded leg, his spirits remained high. I checked on him every day and prayed, but when a raging fever took his body, I knew gangrene had settled in. We had to amputate." Matthias's forehead creased as he exhaled as if he were remembering details, perhaps even reliving them.

"If a soldier was moved from this courtyard inside the building, the physician thought he had a chance of surviving, but it also meant amputation." Matthias continued and turned around. "All we could do."

"We operated for weeks without ether. Two bottles of rum before the surgery became the norm. The soldiers knew we didn't have any sedation. Alcohol saturated their blood and caused them to hemorrhage. Many bled out on the table. I struggled to keep my feet steady on the slippery floor."

Her heart sped up as an image of Matthias in a blood-soaked apron and shirt entered her mind. A sudden panic struck her. She felt as if the orderly would whisk her inside where they'd amputate her limb without any anaesthetics.

"Blood permeated the air and attracted vampires. I'd let them in at night to help ease the dying. Fortuno had seen everything through his delusional fever. Every man pleaded, grabbed my arm before the surgery, but there was a desperation in Fortuno's pleas I couldn't ignore. He wanted to live."

The coldness of the stone seeped into her back when she leaned against the wall to steady her shaky legs. Cries of desperation rang through her head while the metallic smell of blood assaulted her senses. Her dress clung to her as sweat popped from every pore.

"I asked him to write a letter to himself. Then I opened the door to the vampire."

Matthias paused for a long moment, and Kate imagined Fortuno must've felt like her at that moment— Nausea swept through her and acid burned in her throat. She scanned the yard for a trash bin. Not finding any, she forced the bile back down.

"His maker didn't have a need for a minion. Since I initiated his transition, he belonged to me. I gave him that letter when he woke with his memories wiped. Now it hangs on the wall of his restaurant. His patrons eat and drink there, but no one as much as glances at it."

The nausea passed and her breath slowed down. Wounded soldiers vanished. The stands appeared before her. The clock chimed in the tower of the City Sentinel at the nearby square, announcing the seventh hour of the evening. "What did he write?"

"Let's see if you can read it. So far no one was able to decipher the words." The nod of his head indicated the direction of the place.

She frowned. "Why? Did he write it in Morse code? I mean, he was a sailor."

"Morse code could be easily read, his words, not so much. Let's eat now."

He could hardly expect her to eat after this gory experience. "Did I tell you, you're crazy?" Yet her feet followed him when he turned for the exit with her hand in his.

He chuckled. "You might have mentioned it once."

She tried to compose the burning question in her head then decided to just ask. "Is Fortuno a vampire now?"

"No, Fortuno is like me. I sucked the poisonous saliva out of his blood after a few minutes. He was exposed to it long enough to turn him immortal but without other side effects."

"How were you able to do it?"

"I'm immune to the poison. No more questions now. We're here." He pointed to a long line extending around the corner of the restaurant a short walk away from where a hospital once stood. They wouldn't be eating any time soon, she thought, but he led her in through the employee's entrance. The bustling staff greeted him on their way through the packed dining room and bar. As her feet tread on the rich terracotta tiles, she decided to leave the questions for later.

"Here it is."

Matthias stopped by the wall with the framed letter. The handwriting resembled a chicken scratch. Understandable, Fortuno had faced death. She cocked her head this way and that, but words didn't seem to form. Maybe Fortuno hung the reminder of the last hour of his short human existence upside down.

"Can you read this?" She squinted and struggled to make the words out and soon gave up.

"No one can."

With a laugh and a gentle tug on her hand, he led her to the stone patio. Had Fortuno hidden something in a plain sight? she wondered.

The legs of the cast iron chair scraped along the hard surface as he pulled the seat out from the reserved table for two. The firm cushion caressed her back. "But you must know what the letter says."

"Sorry, but I don't. Fortuno says the writing makes perfect sense to those who are desperate. My guess is no one who looked at it was firm against the wall. Let's enjoy the dinner now."

Upbeat dinner music came through the speakers. She scanned over the veranda. Good, while the restaurant was fancy, the guests seemed to be dressed casually. She didn't feel out of place in her low-cut, knee-length dress. The smells of local cuisine wafting from the kitchen enthralled her senses, reminding her of her hunger. A waiter lit the candle on the table and nodded to Matthias's order of a bottle of most expensive Dubrovnik's Malvasia vine.

Matthias took her hand in his and planted a kiss on the back. "You look nice tonight as always."

"Thanks." The heat rising in her cheeks made her lower her head. Would she ever get used to his compliments? She searched for another topic to ease her embarrassment. "So, which one is Fortuno? Is that him?" She nodded at a tall waiter who brought the bottle of wine to their table.

The young server popped the cork and poured a tiny amount of the golden liquid to Matthias's glass. Matthias swirled the sample around the tumbler and drank. After swallowing, he nodded to the guy and the waiter filled her glass, then his.

"Enjoy," he said, leaving the bottle on the table.

Matthias raised his glass. "That wasn't Fortuno. I know you don't drink anything alcoholic, but tonight is special."

Their glasses clinked, and she took a sip. Sweet nectar tantalized her taste buds. Matthias certainly knew how to choose a vintage. "Is that him over there?" She pointed to another guy, bringing the beverage to her mouth.

"No. Be patient and you'll see." His wide smile melted her heart.

A tall, bald man with a blond goatee approached their table. Plates balanced on his arm. His very presence caused

Kate to shiver. She rubbed her sweaty palms on her trembling knees under the table.

"Isn't this first class service?" Matthias said with a wink at Kate. "What are you cooking tonight?" The casual tone in his voice suggested the relationship between the two men was that of old friends, not a Master and his minion.

"My best friend reserves the table for two—this I got to see." The waiter placed the dishes in front of them. "I only cooked for you and your lovely guest."

"But, I didn't even see your menu." She stared at her favourite grilled squid dish. Matthias must've told him. How else could this man know?

"The menu?" The man chuckled and turned to Matthias. The deep throttle in his laugh suggested she had yet to learn the rules.

"Kate, this is Fortuno."

The man extended his hand.

"P—pleased to meet you." Of all times, she had to stutter now. She got to meet Matthias's friend, something of a vampire, and this was all that came to her?

"The pleasure is all mine." Fortuno took her shaky hand and placed a soft kiss on her knuckles. His dry lips couldn't compare to Matthias's soft ones. Although Matthias had already acquainted her with this gesture of acknowledgment, she swallowed hard. Fortuno's icy hand raised goose bumps all over her. She couldn't peel her eyes away from the golden glow around his hazel pupils.

"I'll let you two enjoy your dinner. Leave room for the desert." Fortuno strutted through the patio and stopped to shake hands with other patrons.

A sudden shiver ran down her spine urging her to take another sip. "How many immortals are here? Besides you."

"Two." He answered after a short pause then refilled her glass. "Don't worry, you're safe." Matthias unrolled his napkin and placed the cloth on his lap. "As long as you don't ask Fortuno for ketchup—he doesn't like that." With a fork in his hand, he motion to his plate. "Our food is getting cold."

Chewing the first mouthful, she moaned, "Fortuno can cook."

"That, he can. Try this." With a piece of steak speared on his fork, he extended his hand to her lips. She couldn't believe her eyes. He wanted to feed her. Although the meat was a bit too rare for her liking, she closed her mouth over the cutlery and pulled the piece inside. Flavors exploded in her mouth. She might have to confiscate his dish, she decided, and she wasn't that big on steaks.

"Good?" His voice snapped her from almost reaching ecstasy.

"I'm speechless." Suddenly grilled squid seemed less appealing, but she returned to her own plate. As she savoured the last bite, her earlier question rekindled in her mind. Two immortals resided here in this small city. How would people react if they knew? This was surreal and yet it seemed so normal now that she was used to it. "Who's the second..." not wanting to use an improper word, she searched for the right one but nothing came to her.

"Adriana is his lifelong companion," Matthias answered before she could finish her question. "When the tourist season winds down, they close the restaurant and return to Canada. They have a place not far from us." He lifted her hand and kissed the tips of her fingers.

"Unreal." She'd need a good night's sleep to process all of this. The second glass of wine went straight to her head, and she began to slur her words. "If I have this right, one must be bitten by a vampire in order for you to turn him immortal but not a total vampire."

He cut her a stern glance. "Don't you even think about it."

She snorted. "Please, where would someone like me find a vampire?"

"They are secretive but chances are you could come across one. With all the new inventions they can mingle among mortals unnoticed."

She winced in fear. "What inventions?"

He played with her fingers. "Like the spray-on tan."

Her hand tensed in his. "Something tells me you can spot them."

"And smell them." He leaned over the table. "Relax, there aren't any around."

"What would you do if there were?"

He frowned. "Acknowledge him or her with a nod."

She slapped her shoulder at a sudden pierce, crushing a mosquito between her fingers. "You are wrong. Blood suckers *are* out. Fortuno should put some citronella repellent around the patio."

"Mosquitos don't bother me," he said through his laugh. "But I'll mention it to him. He wouldn't want his guest to be slapping themselves senseless."

His chuckles coaxed a laugh out of her. She stopped and licked her lips, contemplating her next question. "Is that how you became immortal? Were you bitten? And I don't mean by a mosquito."

His smile vanished. He grew quiet and gripped her fingers. "I don't have all of the answers yet."

Their conversation had turned serious, all because she got too curious. Her dinner threatened to come back up. She swallowed the acid. The ladies' room? Yes she'd retreat there and pull herself together.

"I'll be back in a minute." She yanked her hand out of his and stood. He followed suit. "Are you going somewhere, too?"

"I can't read all your thoughts. You should have told me you wanted to get up so I could hold the chair for you."

"That's right, the olden ways." She snapped her fingers. "I'll try to remember."

He chuckled and sat. "The ladies' room is that way."

With her eyes focused straight ahead, she scurried to the bathroom. She scanned the huge powder room in the large mirror while cold water poured out of the faucet onto her forearms. Not even her thoughts were hers anymore.

Dread filled her. What was she doing? Fortuno and Matthias, they co-existed with her world. She put herself in danger by mingling with them. A quick departure would be in order right about now, and she should forget she had ever met them. But Matthias had a knack for finding her anywhere she was. Maybe, if she explained how scared she was about all of this he'd leave her alone. But could she live without him? No. Not after the last night's kiss.

Outbursts of laughter and loud talking overwhelmed her as soon as she stepped into the main hall of the restaurant. The smells of grilled fish wafted from the kitchen. Guests occupied every high stool around the bar. A man in a trench coat and wide brim hat sat at the corner. How strange to wear rain gear on such a hot summer night. Fortuno must have a big heart if he fed the local homeless.

The man raised his head from the plate of food he was consuming with gusto and looked at her. Beady eyes stared out from his bearded face. She dug her fingernails into her palms, forcing herself to stay calm and silent. *Barry Wilkins.*

CHAPTER 11

Wilkins? It couldn't be. Kate was sure her nerves must be frazzled if she was seeing things. Maybe she should return to the ladies' room. No, she'd left Matthias alone at the table long enough. Tearing her eyes away from the man in trench coat, she hurried towards the patio.

At the first glance the man had resembled the Nannies' Care agent, but it couldn't have been him. Though Matthias had been positive the man he'd seen was Wilkins, she couldn't believe he wouldn't travel to places where people hardly spoke English.

Fortuno sat in her chair and talked to Matthias. When she approached the table, both men stood. This would be another of the "old day's" gestures she'd have to get used to.

"I bid you good night." Fortuno bowed his head.

"Are you ready to go?" Matthias's brows knitted at the sight of her. He took a hold of her elbow. "Is everything all right?"

"I'm fine." Would he see through her quick smile and trembling limbs? "I just need to sit for a minute."

He lowered himself onto the chair and reached for her hand. "What's wrong, love? Tell me."

His endearment made her giggle. She put her free hand on her trembling knees to steady them. She shouldn't have drunk so much wine. "For a second there, I thought I saw Barry Wilkins sitting at the bar."

With his lips pressed together, Matthias cocked his head and gave her hand a reassuring squeeze. "He's not worth you getting all upset like this."

"I know." She gave a dismissive wave of her hand. "I won't bring him up again. It's just the man I saw, gave me a creepy look."

"Let's find him and put this to rest." He stood, placing the napkin on the table.

"No need. Really." Kate attempted to stand too, but lowered herself remembering his olden ways.

He stepped behind her and held the chair as she stood. Not noticing the hem of her dress snagged on the zipper of the cover, she pulled the cushion from the seat, causing the cast iron chair to tip over. His quick hand grabbed the frame before the piece of furniture hit her back.

"Maybe I'm not cut out for this ladylike treatment." She shook her head and smiled. "Just let me get up whenever I want."

"Fine, have it your way." He righted the seat and looped her arm around his. "As long as we get to keep strolling like this."

"I can live with that."

He led her from the restaurant patio. "I've spent more time in the city than I intended to. We are on our 'second date' as I promised. Have you made a decision on my proposition to be my guest?"

His guest. Kate stared at her feet, walking in step with him. On the uninhabited islet, there would be just the two of them. No other souls. No way of getting away. He kept his promise and his distance. She should give him a chance. "When are the boys arriving?"

"In a week. Fortuno will drop them off." His quirked brows didn't fit with his half curled lips.

"You're an islander. How can you stand the sweltering city?"

"Good question. I never spent more than a day or two in the city during the summer and then only if I had to." His warm hand squeezed hers. "So, what are you waiting for?"

Away from the heat of the city, a tranquil islet, and only him and her. The offer was too good to refuse. "I accept."

He grinned and tucked a strand of her hair behind her ear. "Good. We'll be happy there."

"Do you still want to meet my family? I must warn you, they are a bunch of crazies." Her stomach tightened. She could just see the scene—Mom bombarding him with questions about his true intentions with her only daughter.

"In that case, I'll fit right in." His quiet chuckle brought a smile to her lips. "Your description has given me a funny visual."

She hoped he didn't get the same visual as her. The memory of her research on him surfaced, reminding her of the fact that Emina's mother had not liked him. Maybe instant dislike to the man a daughter brought home was inborn here. "When do you want to leave?"

"In an hour. Does that give you enough time to pack all your stuff? The closest store is in the port of Sali on Long Island in case you forget something."

"You don't want to stop by Esa tonight?" Her mom would be in bed by now and the rest of her small family scattered in the bars. Besides, she must alert her cousin to prepare everyone for this.

"No, *Esa* is out of our way. If you want, we'll go there tomorrow at sunset. I have a smaller boat for island hopping. I don't intend to take *The Pearl.*"

"I hope your other boat is nothing more than an inflatable zodiac." Her family would get all kind of currency signs in their eyes if they smelled the money on him.

"Why?"

"Islanders get curious about the speedboats." And being the center of attention wasn't her thing.

A soft laugh escaped him and he looked adorable scratching his sideburn with his thumb. "I could get the boys' row boat if that would be better."

"Not a bad idea." An image of his pecks and biceps flexing with each stroke of the rows entered her mind. Heat started to build in the pit of her stomach. Time to talk about something else. "There were some old fishermen's tales going on around about your piece of rock. Any of them true?"

He winked. "Of course, the sea monsters and all."

"No mermaids?" After all the talk about vampires, anything was possible.

"No, but you can pretend to be one. I'd like that." His nudge stirred butterflies in her stomach and she giggled again.

"The boys would like to see the famous donkey race in Sali. Would you care to join us?" With his gentle squeeze on her hand and the soft plea in his voice, she couldn't refuse him.

"It's my job, Mr. Zrin." She stopped, realizing they were in front of her apartment building.

"I forgot you work for me."

He brushed his thumb down her jaw and circled her lips. The street was quiet, except for a single car that passed by and left a pungent smell of burnt gasoline behind. She closed her eyes, her legs liquefying with his touch.

"One hour," he whispered and brushed a soft kiss over her lips.

Would he pull her against his chest and wrap his arms around her? Would he bring the same enchantment of the other night? No. To her dismay, he moved away from her and stepped back.

"Won't you come up?" Her voice trembled with anticipation.

"No, I'll bring the boat by the bridge and return to carry your suitcases. Now, go pack." He gave her a little peck on the cheek and stood on the sidewalk till she got inside.

She scurried up the stairs and fumbled with the keys in front of the door. The metal slid in the hole and she unlocked the latch. Her mind raced. No, this was not a time to doubt her decision. She'd go with him. He seemed determined to leave, and the city wouldn't be the same without him.

The clothes sprawled over the floor, bed, and chair inside the apartment reminded her of her promise to tidy the mess when she returned from their first date. It seemed the date had never ended. She sighed. Packing might take longer than an hour.

After Craig, she had vowed not to give her love to anyone, but it seemed God had thrown the dice. The attraction she had felt for Matthias had grown into something stronger. She could no longer fight the feeling.

The summer night air was thick with moisture. The harbour lights reflected on the calm sea. The salty smell filled her nostrils, and Kate's anticipation soared. A few late night partygoers went about their business as she and Matthias approached the yacht. He had carried her suitcases the two blocks without any effort. His smiles, each time she asked him if she could take one of her bags, eased her guilt over it.

With a dull thump, her suitcases landed in the corner of the deck. "The boat will glide through the calm sea like a knife," he said.

"I'll get the lines." Kate removed her flip-flops and threw them onto the deck then untied the knots at the bow and stern. When she tossed the lines onto the deck, the thick braiding of the rope scratched her palm. But the engines purred as she jumped on board and she quickly forgot the minor pain.

"You know your way around a boat pretty well." The iron chain clanked and the sleeves of his tight fitting t-shirt bunched up with muscles on his arms when he retrieved the heavy anchor.

"Islanders cannot forget."

His hand clasped hers and he led the way up the stairs to the navigation deck. "Come, sit with me. Once we get out of the harbor, I'll teach you how to be a skipper."

"Looks complicated. What are all those lights?" The coolness of the leather seat seeped into her thighs as she sat next to him. She smiled, but her stomach tightened with the thought of the two of them alone for days.

"It's easy." He shifted and pushed the metal bar forward. The boat gained speed. "As you can see, this is the accelerator. Just turn the wheel in the direction you want to go. Don't worry about the lights. I'll keep my eye on them. You can take over now."

The engines roared and the yacht's bow rose when he pushed the handle to the top. With hands gripping the wheel so hard her knuckles turned white, she concentrated on keeping the boat headed in the right direction. The speed was reckless. She'd never dare drive this fast on land and this was the sea—even more need for caution here. There might be smaller boats around that wouldn't have time to move out of the way. Not to mention the wind in her face obscured her vision and made her hair a tangled mess.

He must've read her terrified expression because he pulled the lever back. The boat slowed and the bow lowered.

"We shouldn't go this fast here. I just wanted to show you what she can do."

"Show off." She punched his shoulder, but his smooth chuckles coupled with his arm around her made her wish he'd set the auto pilot so he could pay all his attention to her, instead of the navigation controls. Her self-confidence rose as she realized being around him didn't turn her into a giggling teenage girl anymore.

The islands in the distance loomed through the veil of darkness, and the outline of a giant whale head appeared after an hour of comfortable cruising speed. He slowed the yacht then cut the engines, allowing the craft to coast on the water. The white rock rose straight from the sea to pierce the night sky. Kate stood on the bow with the line in her hands. The moment the boat bumped the pier, she pounced on the cement jetty and wrapped the line tightly around the iron peg. Matthias secured the line on the stern and got the luggage out.

"There're a few stairs to the house, I'm afraid," he said, starting up the winding stone staircase.

A little confused, Kate followed. Where was the house? The stairs seemed to go straight up to into the cliffs above. Then in the dim lights that illuminated their surroundings, she saw they had arrived on an open terrace with covered patio furniture. There still was no sign of a building, but the dark glass of a sliding door reflected the crescent moon.

His face beamed as he opened the door. "Welcome to my house."

"It's carved into the face of the rock," Kate said with a gasp. "This is some feat of engineering."

"I planned to build on the other side where the islet slopes, but Emina wanted to preserve the little beach there. So we compromised."

Pain reflected in his eyes for a brief moment, then he seemed to shake it off. Kate shivered when a sudden drift of cold air brushed her bare arms. But instead of fear, serenity washed over her. Probably just Emina's spirit setting her at ease. "Let's pay Emina a visit," she said suddenly inspired.

The moon provided an ample, if dim, light on the dirt footpath as he led the way up the hill in silence. He stopped by a single, marble grave marker carved as an open book. Kate stared at the engraved letters. Tears stung her eyes as the melody of a long forgotten song played in her head. She knelt and brushed her finger over the words. "'Twas grace that led us safe thus far and grace will lead us home.'" Her whisper echoed through the silent night.

"Emina liked that." Matthias's deep voice and the soft brush of his hand on her cheek brought Kate back to the moment. "Let's go back to the house."

He wrapped his fingers around her wrists and pulled her to her feet. She glanced over her shoulder at the burial site and offered a silent prayer—May Emina's soul rest in peace.

"First things first." Matthias said, leading her inside the open-concept living space. "Here's the guest room. My room is right next door." He opened the door to the guest chamber. "It has a big window overlooking the channel. You can watch sunsets from here."

"I believe you, but any room will do." Through a window the length of the wall, she saw the calm, moon washed surface of the Adriatic Sea. The sleigh style double bed, with a matching nightstand on each side, and a wardrobe against the inner wall spread out in front of her.

"I'll leave you for now. If you wake before me, feel free to explore. Sleep well." He gave her a little peck on her cheek and left, closing the door behind him with a soft thud.

Separate bedrooms and a single peck on a cheek. Twice now, after he'd given her such a wonderful kiss last night. She yanked her nightgown from the suitcase. Maybe somehow she'd misread his affection and he didn't desire her. She must've been an idiot to think otherwise.

She changed into her nighty. The mattress sank beneath her when she plopped herself down, and she inhaled the faint scent of fresh linen.

No, she scolded herself. It was foolish of her to think he didn't desire her. He promised he wouldn't harm her in any way and he was a man of his word. For him to jump in bed with her would mean forgetting his gentleman's honor. He was probably suffering as much as she, fighting the urge to come to her.

She eased her head into the downy pillow and curled into a ball. The hum of the generator indicated the central air-conditioner was set on high. Within minutes, she shivered under the thin covers. The urge to sneak into his room and snuggle up next to him assailed her, but she resisted. He was the one who read her mind. It should be him who came to her. Her eyelids started to droop and she yawned, but sleep wouldn't take her. She needed him to chase the darkness away and take her through to the break of the dawn. Her mind was hovering somewhere between sleep and wakefulness when the door to her bedroom opened.

She opened her eyes and saw him standing beside the bed. It had to be a dream. Then he lifted the covers and slid in beside her. His arms scooped her up and spooned her against him. No, this all felt too real, too right, to be a dream. He really had come to her.

"Matthias, I—"

"I'm here, love. Go to sleep." The breath of his whisper tickled her neck. He laced her fingers with his.

Her heart soared. He wanted her. With her face against his chest, she inhaled his musky scent. Words were not necessary for this perfect moment. Her eyes closed, but her mind couldn't settle. She squirmed and sighed.

"Can't you sleep?" he whispered, smoothing her hair.

"No, no I can't."

"Me neither."

The air around them charged with sexual tension. His face took on a predatory look and his eyes narrowed. Her pulse quickened as he took her mouth with his, his lips hungry and demanding. The same soft piano melody she had heard on the solar circle just last night played in her head.

His teasing tongue coupled with his hands exploring her body coaxed a loud moan out of her. He tucked his fingers under the thin straps of her nighty and slid them down her shoulders. His hands continued down, pulling the fabric with them. When her pebbled nipples pressed against his bare chest, he let out a low hiss. His sensual kisses on her neck and breasts raised goose bumps all over her skin.

"You're beautiful," he whispered softly.

She was like putty in his hands. She barely heard his murmurs of endearment over the drumming of her heart and the sound of her rapid breathing. For days her body had tingled in anticipation. She wanted this, needed this. She was ready to give herself to him, body and soul.

His hand wrapped around her crumpled gown and pulled it down her hips. When his fingers brushed against her thighs, she cried out his name. Ecstasy slammed into her as his fingers explored her body, teasing and tantalizing her senses.

His warm body covered hers. She grabbed a hold of his shorts and pulled them over his tight butt. After sliding the boxers down, he kicked them to the floor. She moaned at the size of his erection pressing down on her lower belly. As he poised himself at her entrance, she wrapped her legs around his hips and opened herself to him. With his gaze locked to hers, she gave him an encouraging nod. Anticipation was over, she was ready for him.

Her back arched as he glided inside her bit by bit, spreading her legs wider. She grabbed onto his shoulders and pulled him to her. His tongue and lips massaged hers, sending her body into overdrive. The feel of his thrusts inside her pushed her over the edge. Euphoria claimed her and sent her hovering above the world.

His fingers brushed her cheek as her shudders ceased. She opened her eyes to his gentle caress. Love was reflected on his face when his gaze met hers.

His deeper and deeper thrusts pushed her legs farther apart, positioning her to take all of him. The crescendo of arousal poured over her again. One more lunge like that and she'd—

She ruptured again, stronger, harder, and the waves of bliss propelled her into orbit. A scream tore from her throat. She dug her fingers into his mane of hair, and pulled his head to her breasts as her body shuddered.

With her body still trembling, he pulled her up with him, sat her on his muscular thighs, and buried his face in the crook of her neck. His big hands seized her hips while she lowered herself onto his erection. She clung to his shoulders, kneading his muscles.

"Matthias," she whispered, her mouth searching his, her body shaking like a twig.

"I'm yours, Kate. Forever." His husky whisper sent another rush of bliss through her. "Will you be mine?"

"Yes," she uttered through her moans as she rolled her head back in total surrender. His tongue trailed down her neck.

He wrapped his arms around her. Pressed against his chest, blissful waves rocked her in unison with him. He let out a slow hiss as he went rigid then collapsed under her.

He laced his fingers with hers. Sweat glistened on their bodies while the scent of their coupling filled the air.

He traced her eyebrows with his thumb. "Have I told you how beautiful you are?"

She raked her fingers through his hair and planted a kiss on his lips. "And so are you." Their first intimate joining had been beautiful, much more so than she had imagined it would be. He kissed her again and nestled her next to him.

She brushed her fingertips over his torso and he sucked in a breath.

The slippery feeling between her legs blasted her with a cold realization. He must know that the poorly handled abortion had left her barren. Between the two of them, she was the mortal, infertile, one. Before he could hear her thoughts, she forced them away and laid her head on his chest until sleep claimed her.

Golden sunrays bathed the room when Kate woke. Matthias's bare chest rose and fell with his even breaths. A blaze ignited inside her and tensed her body. He had loved her at the break of the new day. She wanted his hands to caress her every curve again, his lips to sear her skin wherever they touched her, his body to cover hers—Hell, she couldn't stay in this bed another second.

A rigorous swim would do her good, but she didn't want to rummage through her suitcase, trying to dig out her swim suit, and wake him in the process.

The soft fibres of a colorful Persian rug caressed her fingers when she pulled her nighty off the floor. Kate slipped her nightgown on and set out on a small exploration.

Her phone sat on the dining table, next to his pager. She should call Dyane to make sure she was okay after the attack, she thought, but when she called, she got Dyane's voice mail. Kate's fingers worked fast typing the text message, "*Waterloo*—the total surrender." Dyane would call her as soon as she read it.

On the lower level of the house she found the exercise room and tried the cross trainer, but working out barefoot and in her nighty felt odd. She continued down the spacious corridor. The door at the very end drew her attention, as if a voice told her to enter. Her hand hovered above the knob.

'*Do not be afraid*,' the whisper echoed. Kate turned her head in all directions but saw no one. Maybe what she heard was the howl of the wind. Or was it Emina?

She grabbed the handle and turned, not expecting the door would open. But it did. A small room containing a tall piece of furniture covered by a dusty sheet faced her. An armoire, perhaps. She stepped in and the door closed behind her. Must be the draught, she reached for the knob and the door opened. A breath of relief escaped her. Good. The door hadn't locked when it slammed shut. With both hands, she lifted the cloth and stared at the mahogany wardrobe. The doors of the chest creaked on their hinges when she opened them. Six vacuum sealed white dresses from different time periods hung neatly on the rod. She ran her fingers over them. Emina's essence still resided in each one. Brief scenes from their wedding days flashed into Kate's mind. Matthias's face beamed as he bent to kiss his bride.

"They married twice in each century," she whispered.

Her gaze lowered to the stack of books at the bottom of the wardrobe. She took one and examined the rich leather binding. After untying the thin strap, she opened it to the first page of handwritten calligraphy.

> *"January 1ˢᵗ, 1700, the turn of the century found us in sorrow. Today we buried our beloved Rahela. She prayed to raise our bairns. I betrayed her."*

Kate gasped. The ten books were Emina's diaries. She closed the one in her hand and replaced it. Matthias had said to feel free to explore, but she was snooping. These were private thoughts, and she should respect them. Her fingers curled. One page, she'd read the first page and not a word more. Nothing bad could come from reading a book. It wasn't as if she tried to raise the dead. Then again, the way the events unfolded over the last few weeks, she might.

She took another volume and opened the cover.

"May 15, 1873 – The morn of my 200ᵗʰ birthday I am about to wed Matthias for the third time. His tender love is what keeps me going. We should have been dead long ago, buried next to one another. Not a soul suspects our graves lay empty."

Kate, engrossed in reading, forgot about her one page promise. Before long, she flipped to the last page of the volume. "No, Emina, don't. God, no. Why?" she whispered through her tight throat, chewing her nails and inhaling every word.

Matthias's voice snapped her back to the present. "Kate, are you in there?"

The door shook with his attempt to open it. She gasped and scrambled to her feet. "I am."

After placing the diary back in the armoire, she closed the doors and pulled the sheet down.

"Don't panic. I've got the key." His voice, although muffled, reflected worry.

"It's not locked." She stepped to the door and turned the knob, but it wouldn't open. She tried again with the same result. Was Emina trying to lock her in?

CHAPTER 12

Matthias's voice and the muffled clicking of the key in the lock came through the wooden door. Kate's sweaty palms slid off the knob as she tried to grip the round handle. Her heart drummed. Why wouldn't the door open? The room was not sealed when she came inside. She had made sure by trying the door twice. Was Emina doing this? With the fabric of her nighty wrapped around her slippery hands, Kate tried once more. The wooden door swung open and she stared at Matthias's bewildered face. She shivered as the cool air enveloped her bare arms and shoulders and seeped through the thin fabric of her nightgown.

"You didn't hear me when I told you to let go of the knob? You kept turning the handle the other way." His voice sounded deeper among the stone walls.

"I couldn't make out what you said." A breath of relief burst out of her. Emina wouldn't scare her, not after leading her down here.

His confusion was reflected in his face. "I locked the room the same day I buried Emina. No one has ventured down here in over six years."

"It wasn't locked." A hint of fear rippled through Kate. She never should have snooped. "I heard a whisper telling me not to be afraid then the door opened."

"The door opened on its own?"

She nodded. "I felt the cold air brush my shoulders when I entered the room, but when I touched the gowns I had a vision." Cold seeped in her soles from ceramic tiles and spread to her knees.

His big hands caressed her back infusing her with heat. "I don't know why I kept the wedding gowns and the diaries. I can't bear to look at them."

Emina's written words appeared before Kate's eyes. Emina loved him so much she chose to end her life to be with him in immortality. Had he known she carried his child he wouldn't have allowed her to. She hid her secret, knowing he wouldn't be able to bring himself to read her personal thoughts.

Four short beeps from the kitchen above pierced the silence between them.

"Come." He took Kate's hand. "You can read the diaries any time, but now join me."

She nodded. As much as she wanted to engross herself in Emina's writings again, right now she'd rather enjoy his company.

"I'd like to discuss a matter with you."

"What matter?" she asked as she followed him. The fresh brewed coffee tantalized her senses.

"A small one." His nod toward the white sectional facing the large window overlooking the vast sea indicated where he'd like to discuss this matter. "I know how you take your coffee, go get comfortable."

She laughed and strutted to the couch. "You're spoiling me."

"Well." A few long seconds later, he placed the mug in front of her on a low table and sat in the chair facing her. "There's something I haven't told you yet."

Her stomach clenched at his words. Her few scarce affairs had ended with words like these. She held her breath, expecting to hear how she was a nice girl, and he liked her very much, and how it wasn't her, it was him, and last night never should have happened.

His fingers wrapped around her hand and brought her gaze back to him. He closed his eyes. His soft lips brushed over her knuckles, setting her at ease and lighting a different kind of fire in her belly.

"What 'matter' do you want to discuss?" Her voice came out huskier than she intended.

He lowered his arm never letting go of her hand. "Emina's last words." He moved next to Kate. "She told me to find you."

"Why?" Kate whispered, feeling her stomach drop. He had employed her for her credentials, hadn't he?

"She said I'd find love and happiness with you. I refused to believe her. With her passing all my hopes died, too, but now I know Emina was right."

Kate exhaled loudly. Dyane's guess had been right. Emina wanted for Kate to be with Matthias. She wasn't trying to drive her away.

"I'd like us to be more than just friends." The longing in his whisper sent goose bumps rushing along her skin.

She took a deep breath. "We're way passed the friendship boundary."

"I want you to raise my boys and someday, God willing, children of our own."

"Matthias, I—" She choked. What had he just said? Of course, she would want to be more to him and the boys, but she wouldn't be able to give him children. Her child bearing years had been cut short. The fact she couldn't have children devastated her, but no matter how hard she tried not to think about it, the truth remained.

He squeezed her hand. "There's a fire deep inside you I never thought I'd see again. The same flame Emina carried. Yours has ebbed to a few smouldering embers, but I know it can be rekindled."

His words resonated with the truth. Yes, life had beat her down and the zest inside her had died along with her spirit. But maybe not all was lost.

"Your boys are special to me. I fell in love with them as soon as I saw them." The image of the three cute boys surfaced in her mind. She longed to shower them with love as Emina would have.

"It shows. They love you, too." His irresistible smile melted her heart. He fell silent and stared into the space. "Two years ago at Christmas I found a letter on my desk written in large letters addressed to Santa." His solemn voice broke the dead air. "What the boys asked for broke my heart."

More silence followed. She squeezed his hand. He jerked and looked at her.

"They wanted their mom." She shared the same disappointment about Christmas. Hers had been filled with cheap presents from Craig meant to shut her up for the rest of the year.

Matthias sighed. "They know they can't have their mama, but yes, they want a mother." His frozen yet soft stare was familiar to her by now. He was preparing for something big.

Her mind went blank, nothing came to her but hope.

He laced his fingers with hers. "I came to you last night because my intentions are noble and although our courtship is short, I hope you know me well enough by now."

"It feels like I've known you all my life." Now she understood the recurring childhood dream. Later in life whenever the world asked too much of her, she had found comfort in "'talking" to her imaginary friend. He had always been there for her.

"But, the immortality fact is hanging heavy in your mind. It shouldn't." His fingers played on her palm. "Every five years I undergo extensive physical tests. They show a steady acceleration in my aging process. According to the professor who is studying my phenomena, as of now I'm a forty year old human."

"Rosalia said forty-four." A very good-looking forty-something. Kate raised the mug to her lips in an attempt to cover the smirk on her face brought on by the thought.

"You could imagine the reaction I'd get if I'm to show my driver's licence, dating back to last century, to a cop. I think I'd end up in a lock up."

His solemn expression confirmed her suspicion—he didn't want infinite life. "So are you turning mortal?"

A grin replaced his serious expression. "It is too early to tell, but all tests indicated this as a possibility."

"Does this professor have a hypothesis on what you might've been?" She felt an overwhelming burst of joy, he could be a normal-human. There could be a chance for them.

Matthias nodded and sighed. "Yes, and now that he has ruled out a post hoc fallacy assumption it's safe to tell you." Couch cushions depressed under him as he shifted. "I was bitten by a vampire. Everything about me is similar to a vampire, yet different. My last x-rays confirmed the buds in my gums where the fangs would've formed have disappeared. I'd say I'm becoming human again."

"You were bitten? So after the bite you didn't feel any different?" If he had told her of a vampire bite before, she would've run off screaming, but now she was certain he would not harm her.

"Not at first." He looked away and stilled like a carved marble statue. "No one noticed anything different about me. Though the process of transitioning had not completed, the beast still entered my body and overtook my mind, but I fought to control its demands." With a loud sigh he turned to her. "In a moment of desperation, I jumped off the cliff into the sea."

She caressed his hand. He had been through so much. His pained expression ripped through her soul.

"The waves trashed my body against the sharp rocks. When my lungs filled with salt water, the darkness engulfed me, and my heart stopped beating. The next thing I knew, I woke washed up on the beach."

A weight pressed down on her chest. He moved closer to her and continued.

"The demon revived my body after every suicide attempt. Then I noticed each time I came back the beast had less of a grip on my mind. I could control its impulses. Nonetheless, I feared I'd harm Emina. But I hurt her the most by avoiding her. Until she came to me one night and the fiend calmed down."

The turmoil he had gone through reflected in Kate's head, causing her to clutch at his hand. An ancient saying crossed her mind. *"Cogi qui potest nescit mori."* She dragged the words out, struggling to remember the exact pronunciation.

He breathed a smile. "You are smart, even when you mispronounce the Latin, or use the quotes in the wrong context. Though what you said is not too far off."

Snickers shook her chest, while she made a mental note not to speak Latin again in front of a doctor. "What did I say?"

"He who can be forced has not learned how to die." Circling of his thumb tickled her palm, he leaned toward her. "What did you want to say?"

"There's an old saying that goes something like 'who lives well, lives twice.'" She shrugged, feeling the heat in her cheeks. "Or in your case, more."

He winked. "Then you say *'Bis vivit qui bene vivit'*."

"God, what I said sounded totally different." She chuckled. "I'd like to know—" She paused, contemplating how to ask him about what seemed difficult for him to discuss. "The bite. How did it happen?"

He drew a long breath and lowered his gaze. "I have a vague memory. I couldn't have been more than fifteen years old. My father re-married. His new wife and her daughter were odd. Kept to themselves. One night, I stumbled across them feasting on my father. He appeared in a trance. I tried to escape but one of them caught me. I remember spasms as every nerve in my body throbbed in excruciating pain. An entity materialized and set the two of them on fire. Afterwards, all I recalled was the melody this angel-like lady hummed till the dawn. To this day I believe the angel was my mother." Matthias's voice trailed off. He sat motionless for a few minutes.

"Did the melody sound like this?" Kate hummed the first few cords of the piano song she had heard last night and on the solar circle while he had held her in his arms.

His eyes widened. "That's it. Where did you hear it?"

"Last night when you came to my bed and while we danced on the circle, only no one hummed the sonata. The way I heard the melody was as if someone played the piano. I thought you made me hear the music."

"No," he whispered. "But I heard the piano, too."

She nudged him. Somehow, the conversation had taken a serious turn and she needed to change the atmosphere. "So you're ten years older than me. I like older men."

"Older men? I could be your great, great, great, grandfather." His chuckles echoed in the spacious room. The mischievous sparkle in his eyes had returned, and it sent tremors down her spine.

He took the cup from her hand, placed the mug on the table and knelt in front of her.

Her eyes narrowed. He was up to something.

"I don't know how much time I have left on this Earth." If she didn't know him better, she'd say his eyes filled with fear.

She snorted. "No one does. Welcome to the finite club."

He stared at her without blinking. "However short or long, I want to share my days with you. I meant to ask you in front of the boys, but decided against that. I didn't want to put you on the spot."

He wouldn't pop the big question, would he?

"Will you take me as your husband?"

The sound of thousand bells chimed in her ears. Enchanted, she stood, her heart pounding madly. She would have given a kidney and a part of her lung to hear him ask this. *Yes, say yes,* her mind screamed, but the word couldn't form in her dry mouth. Instead, she stared over his shoulder out of the large window at the sparkling sea surface tinted with the last rays of sun.

"You don't have to give me an answer right now, but please don't say no before you at least give my proposal some thought." His voice jerked her back, and she returned her gaze to him. Love was reflected in his eyes. "I want to be the greatest man of your life."

She wanted, needed this. The truth was she had drowned in the complicated dating scene and had hit rock bottom until he pulled her back and pieced her heart together. He made her whole again and without him, she'd crumble like a long forgotten clay statue. She had always been a good girl, playing it safe with her life, and not risking anything. What had that gotten her? It was time for her to take a chance and break away.

His remark about raising their children one day sprang to her mind. She thought he knew everything about her, but his words now made her believe he, in fact, didn't. He was a doctor, he may know of a treatment that would reverse the damage done to her.

His soft expression slowly changed to puzzled as she contemplated her reply.

"I won't say no now or tomorrow or any other day. My answer is—" She drew a long breath and exhaled. "Yes."

A wide grin lit his face. "Say it. You know I'm old fashioned. Give me the full answer."

"It would make me the happiest girl in the world to be your wife and the mother of your children." And it would, it so would. Her heart soared with the realization and her eyes watered, but she pushed the tears away. She fought the urge to throw her arms around him. Her life would change, for better or for worse. Whatever the case, there would be no more loneliness and cold leftover pizza nights. A family to raise and a man to love was now at the top of her things to do. "But, there's someth—"

He stood and stifled her words with his lips, causing her to forget her concern. Gentle strokes of his hands coaxed a soft moan out of her. Her knees buckled. Would he take her again tonight or must she wait until their wedding night?

She tried to pull away from him, but he wrapped his arms around her. "I should change into something more appropriate," she said. "After all, it's our engagement day."

"No. Don't. Stay like this." The husky tone of his whisper caused her to rub her bare thighs together. She squeezed her buttocks tight and moved her hips closer to him.

"You want me to stay in this nighty?"

"Is there anything underneath?" His hands glided over her belly.

"No." Her answer quivered with her breath and he hissed.

"Will you show me?" He took a step back.

Her hands crumpled the thin fabric, but she didn't raise her gown.

"Won't you show yourself to your husband?" His hands covered hers and he raised them over her head, pulling her gown along.

She gasped. Was he role playing? Or trying to get her used to the idea? Either way, she liked this husband-wife name calling.

"Is this more to your liking, husband?" She sucked her belly in to ease the tension in her midriff as his eyes devoured her nakedness. To call him "husband" for the first time seemed so strange. She didn't think she'd even pronounced the word right. She had never addressed her ex like this.

The cloth of her nightgown dropped from her hand onto the floor. The throbbing of her heart filled her ears. If it beat louder or faster, she would probably suffer a coronary. She wrapped her arms around him and pressed her naked body to his. As her hips rubbed on his pelvis, his groin hardened under his shorts. She dragged his pants down and he stepped out of them.

"My wife." He cradled her neck. His mouth sought hers.

Yes, she'd be his wife.

How would she explain all of this to her mom? Her family had already written her off as an old maid.

Her hands slid down his torso, stopping at his hips. The size of his erection sent shivers through her and flooded her with wetness. He cupped her buttocks, pressing her against him. Her nipples rubbed against his chest, igniting a fire in her.

She pressed her lips together, struggling to keep her moans quiet while his finger explored her innermost core and infused her with a powerful arousal.

"You're so ripe for me." With his arm wrapped around her waist, he lowered them onto the couch. She straddled him. The tip of his manhood teased her opening, causing her to squeeze her muscles in response to the rhythm of his hips.

Sensual friction created even higher libido as she slid down his shaft. Unable to stifle her moans any longer, she screamed. The crescendo of exhilaration cascaded over her. Their eyes met as their bodies rocked in unison. His soft gaze showed all the love he had for her now and always. His expression of enjoyment ripped another wave of blissful shivers through her, bringing her to the brink of climax. The orgasm mounted in her despite the efforts to push back the yearning and delight in his thrusts.

Matthias's soft tongue trailed along her neck and fuelled her passion further. The tension in her ruptured, flooding her with immense ecstasy. She screamed out her release.

With his foot, he pushed the coffee table away from the couch and lowered her to the lush carpet. The fibres caressed her back as he covered her body with his.

She wrapped her legs around him and arched her hips in time with his thrusts. As his body stiffened, she sucked in air then held her breath, surrendering to the ripples of pleasure. He stopped for one brief moment and let out a loud groan then held her tighter with each thrust until his body collapsed on hers.

"Wife," he panted, placing soft kisses on her cheek and neck.

With a loud sigh, she threw her head back and dug her fingers in his hair as he fondled her breasts. His hands caressed her naked form while she lay snuggled against him.

He stretched his arm over his head and reached under the couch cushion in front of them. A cool metal ring slid down her finger.

"Well, future Mrs. Zrin, how do you like this one?" He held her hand against his opened palm. The three diamonds set in platinum took her breath away, closing her throat.

"I love it." She stared at her ring. What a wild turn, just when she thought he was about to dump her. Instead, he gave her a whole new future.

"I knew you would."

Kate raised her head and covered his lips with hers.

He hissed at her little nibble. "Don't do this to me, wife, unless you're looking for trouble." His hand tugged on her hair. He pulled her head back then planted another hot kiss on her neck. "Hungry?"

"For you," she whispered and an unexpected ripple of passion rushed through her.

"And me for you. How about food?" He rubbed her belly.

"If we must." His hands ignited a new blaze in her.

"I'll order pizza, but it takes forty minutes to deliver considering we're so far out." He stood and pulled her to her feet. Like an eagle grabbing its prey, he swooped her in his arms. "In the meantime, I'm going to kidnap you to my bed."

Kate woke in a spacious bed surrounded by Matthias's arms and tangled sheets. Her bursting bladder urged her to run for the bathroom, but his leg wrapped around her as soon as she attempted to creep out of his hold.

"Are you trying to escape me, Kate?" His muffled laughter came from under the pillow.

"To the bathroom and back, I promise." Her stomach fluttered with excitement. Just a short time ago, her definition of happiness had been paring all the socks in a load of laundry.

His head emerged from under the pillow. "Okay, I'll let you."

She scrambled to her feet as soon as his arms released her. As she scurried to the bathroom, the soreness between her legs reminded her of the last night's marathon.

"Are you up for a swim?" he called through the closed door.

"Sure, let me dig out my swim suit from my luggage."

"You don't need that here. Who'll see you, besides me?"

She opened the bathroom door and faced his grin. "According to the tourist brochure there're five hundred and seventy six fish species in the Adriatic. That's a lot of eyes."

He threw his head back and roared with laughter. "Have you ever gone in naked?" he asked when he could talk again.

"A long time ago, a bunch of us girls removed our bikini tops." God, how pathetic. She hadn't lived until now. "You're going to get me in some serious trouble."

"I thought I already had." He winked. There it was again, the mischievous sparkle in his eyes that spun her mind and raised goose bumps all over her. He scooped her up with one arm and gave her a little pat on her behind. "Put your swim suit on if it makes you feel better."

After wrapping her naked form in a beach towel, she placed her hand in his. "No, you're right. Let's live a little."

The late afternoon sun dipped low, but hot moisture in the air remained. The stony steps to the shore felt easier on her legs going down. The yacht bobbed on the gentle waves. She dropped the towel and dove in, her body gliding through the water without the restraint of swimwear. Coming up for air, she submerged again and tried to follow

Matthias, but the current pushed her back so she didn't get far. She propelled herself to the surface and flipped on her back.

For a moment, she closed her eyes and spread her limbs, allowing the current to carry her. The smell of the sea filled the air. As she licked her salty lips a loud splash broke her serenity. She opened her eyes and straightened. Dread filled her. A boat about the size of Matthias's had dropped anchor. How had she missed the roar of the engines?

"Matthias." She spun around, wiping her eyes and searching for him. He surfaced behind her and wrapped his arms around her. "There's another boat at the pier," she whispered, her voice trembling with fear.

Matthias turned his head, his brows knitted. Then he cursed. "It's Fortuno. What's he doing here?"

Fortuno stood on the deck with his arms out. "Did you forget to charge your phone?" he shouted across the water, irritation reflected in his voice. "I've been calling you for the past two days."

"What for?" Matthias swam to the jetty and stood waist deep. Water beads rolled down his torso.

"I brought your troop down. No need to thank me."

"Papa. Katie." Ivan and Luka ran out and appeared eager to jump in, while Teo stood hesitantly on the deck.

CHAPTER 13

The last rays of sun stretched the shadows of pine trees over the small bay. Her back turned to the jetty, Kate stood knee-deep in the water, trying to keep the ends of the beach towel from dipping into the sea as she wrapped the warm terry cloth around her naked body. With the corner securely tucked in between her breasts, she gathered the wet curls of hair stuck to her back and wrung the water out. It would take Fortuno one look at her to figure out what she'd been doing with his Master.

She glanced over her shoulder. Matthias stood behind her. His broad shoulders blocked the view from the three pairs of little eyes. "Remind me to pinch your butt for this later," she whispered.

He caressed her shoulders. "I am already looking forward to it." The feel of his soft lips on her skin tensed her back. "Thanks to Fortuno's fast thinking, no one saw more than they should." His sweet laughter eased her embarrassment, and she couldn't help but chuckle.

She took his offered hand. Her feet slipped over the pebbles on the bottom and she clutched her improvised outfit before it could come undone. As they approached the jetty, Fortuno crouched with his arm extended. She tucked the towel tighter and placed her hand in his.

He grinned as he examined her ring. "Congrats are in order, I see. No wonder Master ignored my summons. When is the big day?"

Pride reflected on Matthias's face. "We have not had a chance to set the date yet."

Kate was sure the heat in her cheeks exceeded the air temperature. After her acceptance of his proposal neither of them had uttered anything coherent—other than whispered declarations of love. The image of Matthias's firm body covering hers formed in her head and she pressed her lips together to stifle a moan.

Fortuno twitched his eyebrows at her. "I see." Then he pulled her up onto the jetty.

Could he read her thoughts like Matthias? No, it had to be her flushed cheeks that gave her away. One didn't need to be mind-reading immortal to figure what was on her mind.

"Sorry I spoiled your time alone. I would have kept the boys for a day or two, but Petar and Ana had to cut their vacation time short."

Matthias climbed onto the dry land and tightened the towel around his waist. "Is everything all right with them?"

"Yes. Work called them in early. I'll get the boys luggage for you."

The boys' unexpected arrival meant the time to announce their love to the world was here. Kate wondered how they'd react. Until last night Matthias was her boss. After all, most people were under the impression she had only met him three months ago. No one but she knew he'd been a part of her life for years. Even before he came to her under the guise of Miles, he'd intruded on her dreams.

In addition to her concerns over how the boys would take the news, Fortuno's possible reaction to Matthias marrying below his class had her worried. In his world, Matthias probably deserved someone better than her.

During the old days, aristocrats just didn't marry commoners. But, Fortuno seemed happy for his friend and Master.

The three boys came running and embraced Kate first. With one hand holding onto the towel, she crouched and kissed their faces. "I missed you so much. Did you have fun visiting Petar and Ana?"

"We did, but we missed you more," Ivan was quick to inform her.

She hoped that was true and her engagement to their dad wouldn't come as too much of a shock. The little guys had expressed their wish for her to be their mother on a few occasions, but sometimes reality didn't measure up to fantasy. She had always changed the subject, when they mentioned it, not wanting to raise their hopes, or her own.

"Boys." Matthias crouched next to her. "Kate and I have wonderful news. Come to the house, and we'll tell you."

Their eyes widened.

"Is Katie going to be our mommy?" Luka burst out.

She couldn't contain her laughter. She knew that from here and all the way up thirty six steps to the house on the top of the hill the boys would stop to ask her after every stair they climbed. She needed to tell them right here, on the jetty. With a smile and creased forehead, she cast a "can I please" glance at Matthias.

He wrapped his arm around her shoulders. "Go ahead."

She had to resist the urge to perform a somersault out of pure joy—even if there was nothing under her towel. Instead, she nodded and bit her lip. "Yes, I am."

The boys' faces beamed.

"Yay!" Luka was the first one to throw his arm around her. "We have a mommy now."

Ivan followed his brother, while Teo seemed uncertain until she reached out to him. He gently hugged her, placing his head on her shoulder.

"Mama," he whispered.

A lump formed in her throat. She kissed his forehead, forcing her tears away.

Matthias pulled them all into a bear hug.

The realization this was her family now sank in and for a moment, she forgot about the fear when she had to break the news to her mother.

A slender lady in a black sarong walked onto the jetty, stopping beside Fortuno.

Matthias nodded to her. "Adriana, thank you for being so patient with the boys."

The light caught Adriana's long raven hair. "They caused no trouble, Master. You know how much we love our godsons." She turned to Kate, a soft smile revealing pearly white teeth. Her heavy rose scent overpowered the smell of the ocean. "I see our Master chose wisely."

Kate gasped and gave the woman a smile of gratitude.

"No 'Master,' Adriana." Matthias stepped up to her. "You're to call me Matthias. How many times must I tell you?"

"Just once more, for a good measure." The woman's voice had a hypnotic quality that seemed to thicken the air, making everyone's movements appear in slow motion.

"Let's go for a swim, Kat—Mommy. Before the sun goes away."

Ivan tugged on Kate's arm, snapping her out of Adriana's spell. Still, it took a second to realise he'd addressed her as his mommy. Yes, this was her son now, and he wanted his mom to go swimming with him. Overcome with love, she knelt in front of him and tenderly cupped his cheek. "Honey, you need to get your swim trunks on."

"These are our swim trunks." Luka giggled, jerking his t-shirt over his head and cannonballed into the water.

"Fun." Ivan seized Kate's arm and pulled her towards the edge of the pier. "Come in with us. Let's see who'd make the biggest splash."

She cast an embarrassed glance toward the house where her bathing suite sat neatly folded in the luggage.

The oak dining table provided enough space to seat eight people, but coloring books and markers covered most of the surface. Kate had barely enough room to squeeze in her laptop.

Three little heads hovered over the pages, absorbed in their busy coloring. No matter what she tried, Luka still clutched the crayon in his fist. She smiled. Who else but a mom or a teacher would obsess over how her child held the marking tool? Now she was both.

At the chime of her laptop, she opened her email. Ten new messages waited, none important. She frowned in disgust at the sight of an email from that low-life Craig. Where did he get her address? This was absolutely like him to contact her on some off chance, hoping she'd be eager to correspond. His latest fling must have ended, and he figured if he'd come crawling back, she'd take him in. Never again. Select the message, hmm, the only way to stop him from contacting her was to label his email as spam. Oh well, she never blocked anyone before, hopefully this would do it. Delete forever. Yes. Goodbye Craig and don't come back. Done.

She glanced over at the boys again. Ivan, his tongue stuck out, colored the picture on the page with zeal. Luka hummed some made-up tune and doodled. Teo propped his head in his hands and scrunched up his lips, reading his book—little genius that he was. Kate was both excited and sorry for the teacher who would have him in her classroom this fall. Teo would make quite a pupil.

Everyone seemed content at the moment, so she grabbed the opportunity to read more of Emina's diary.

> *"May, 1942 – Three weeks since we arrived at the underground hospital of Petrova Gora and Matthias immersed himself in the work. I am yet to get used to him carrying that blasted gun holstered to his belt. He is exhausted, and although he hides it well, I can see the sorrow on his face from the lost lives of those in his care. The supplies are running short, forcing him to relive the horror of when he had to operate without sedation. This war has made animals of the best of men, with brothers, willing to kill each other. What for, I ask? When will all this needless dying end?"*

Kate shivered at the horrors of war and flipped to the next page. Matthias stared at her from a sepia photograph. She smiled and ran her finger over his image captured in time. Two large golden stars on the epaulets of his jacket indicated his rank of Lieutenant-Colonel. The five point star was displayed on the tilted wedge cap nestled in his thick hair.

Then Emina's diary took Kate to a different world once again, and she lost any sense of time until Matthias's hand caressed her neck, sending sensuous shivers down her spine. She placed the diary on the table and looked up at his face. He held the phone pressed to his ear.

Over sixty years ago, during the Second World War when her parents were children, the man she was about to marry fought as a *Partisan*. Would she ever get used to his real age?

"I see...and you can't get another surgeon?" An apologetic expression flashed on his face. "Do you have an OR booked?...All right. I'll be there. Have the patient prepped and ready." He flexed his wrist to glance at his watch. "In about an hour," he said, flipping the phone closed.

"You have to go?" Disappointment slithered through her. Since the day he surprised her at the Botanical Gardens, they've hardly been apart.

He sighed. "Yes, I do. Would you and the boys like a short break from the islet to come to the city?"

The three small faces looked up at him.

"No, we want to go for a swim," Ivan said.

Kate chuckled at his frown, so resembling Matthias's "I promised to take them to the beach on the other side." She took Matthias's hand in hers, feeling a hint of anxiety.

"All right, have fun and, guys, listen to Mama." He turned to her. "I should be back by dinner time, if not earlier." A soft kiss and a brush of his feathery hair on her neck made her stomach clench, increasing her feeling of unease at them being apart even if only for a few hours.

"Don't be late. We're having guests for dinner. Remember, it's our engagement celebration."

"How can I forget? You must be looking forward to see Dyane again. The two of you certainly chat up a storm over the phone." He paused, arching an eyebrow. "Did you invite your mother?"

Under his demanding stare, Kate lowered her gaze to Emina's diary. He should have been an interrogator not a surgeon. "Not yet, but I will."

"Kate, does she still think you are my employee?"

"I'll tell her when I am in the mood to listen to her preaching." Which would be never, but the pressure of his stare was unbearable. Her mom meant no harm with her lectures about life.

"We've been engaged for a month now. The longer you wait, the more she'll be disappointed. She should have been the first person you told." With another feathery touch he tugged on the thin bra strap hanging lose over her shoulder and pulled her closer. "Do it for me."

"Yes, she would have been the first person I told." Kate slipped her arms around his neck. "If she could be happy for me."

His embrace enveloped her, stirring her desire. "Will you bake another batch of your cookies?"

"Of course." Chuckles escaped her. He may not come with fangs, but one big sweet tooth more than made up for two sharp cuspids. With him and the boys around, she could never bake enough cookies.

After another quick peck on her cheek, he hurried out and dashed down the stony steps to the jetty then waved to her from the yacht. She waved back, her nose pressed to the glass of the large kitchen window.

"When can we go to the beach, Mama?" At Luka's voice, she tilted her head toward the boys seated at the table.

"In a little while, honey. The sun is still too hot."

The roar of the engines drew her attention back to the window. Matthias was gone. She sighed, but the tightness in her chest remained.

Her stomach rumbled. "We should have a snack first. I don't want to hear any of you complain you're hungry as soon as we get there. Can you clean off the table now, please?" She opened the fridge and, remembering each boy's food preferences, pulled out cold cuts.

The boys' self-help skills had improved tremendously during the time she'd been with them, but they still struggled with cutlery. Petar and Ana must have caved in and indulged them. But Kate couldn't spend the rest of the afternoon cleaning after them if they wanted to go to the beach.

"After our snack, can we go?" Impatience got the best of Ivan and he jumped to his feet.

"We should wait half an hour before we go swimming after the meal." Teo said, putting his two cents in.

Luka flapped his arms, adding a little drama to his complaints. "We've been waiting for hundreds of hours."

"Goodness me, hundreds of hours?" She giggled as she poured juice into their cups. With any luck, there would be no spills today. "And just how long is that?"

"Since we got up." Luka stored the crayons in the box.

Kate took the coloring books from the table and set the stack inside the cupboard. "Look who's talking, Mr. Sleepy Head. You were the last one out of bed and still in your pyjamas." She placed the plate with sandwiches on the table. "Eat now then you can get changed into your swim trunks."

After wiping the crumbs off the counters, she joined them at the table with a bowl of salad. Fortuno had promised to make his famous gnocchi tonight. Her mouth watered at the thought of potato dumplings in rose sauce. "Guys, don't shove food in your mouths just so you can finish faster. Take small bites, please. When we get back, I want you to tidy your rooms. Papa will be impressed."

Her eyes travelled from one boy to the next, waiting on their response, which wasn't forthcoming. Maybe they communicated among each other in some way unknown to her. Multiples could do that and considering their lineage, she wasn't surprised.

She might be asking too much too soon. They weren't used to chores. But the fact they really were of noble birth didn't excuse them from tidying their toys. "I'll help. What do you say?"

Three pairs of curious eyes blinked at her. Those puppy dog looks would get them whatever they wanted from her. Much to Matthias's annoyance, they'd gotten Fortuno to load them with toys, sweets, and even cash, but he was their cool uncle. She was someone they looked at for guidance, and she must learn how to set limits and say no. Their sweet faces lit with mischievous smiles. They were up to something. How would she learn to resist them and hold her ground?

"Okay, I'll do it and you can help me. How's that?" Darn, so much for her pep talk.

"I'll help you, Mama." Teo was the first one to promise, and he won her over.

"Thank you, Teo." She stood and kissed his head.

"I'll help too." Ivan and Luka nodded.

She hugged them both and her heart soared. Just when it seemed she couldn't love them more, she did.

"Did you finish your snack? What do we do with our dirty dishes?" She watched in delight as they brought their plates and cups to the sink. "Thank you. Go get ready now."

They scurried to their rooms, but came back out, not in their swimwear. The long string of complaints followed. They couldn't find their trunks, or towels, or flip-flops. Their shirts wouldn't go over their heads. Unable to resist the opportunity, she wiggled her fingers as she stood. "Here comes the tickle monster."

They screamed and scurried away, giggling. She chased them through the house and caught them one by one until each squirmed in her arms, receiving a dose of tickles. They toppled her down to the floor, and she pulled them to her for a group hug.

"Okay, enough goofing around. Let's get ready for the beach." She stood, remembering their first "Tickle Monster" play. They'd come a long way since then.

After slathering the boys and herself with the sunscreen and placing wide brimmed hats over their heads, she held the side door open, and the four of them stepped onto the stone terrace. "We'll take the Zodiac, so it will feel like we're on a real excursion."

The sea glistened in the golden glow of the dipping sun. The strap of the beach bag dug into her shoulder so she adjusted the sack then took Teo's hand in hers. Ivan and Luka skipped down the stones stairs a few steps in front of her as they descended to the jetty and boarded the small boat.

After a short cruise around the islet, she turned the boat toward a small, sandy beach nestled in between sharp rocks. She pulled up to the dock and shut down the small engine.

The boys removed their life jackets and jumped out. With the boat tied to a peg, she joined in on the splashing match between Ivan and Luka. Teo turned towards the shore.

"Come on, Teo," she called, throwing water over the two other boys. "Help me get your brothers wet."

No reply came from him. "Teo?"

She swung around and caught a glimpse of him running among the pine trees.

"Teo," she shouted. "Come back."

A few seconds later, his shrill scream ripped through the thick air.

She gasped and her blood iced over as his cries continued. At least he was alive. Her mind worked fast. Teo was hurt and needed her, but she couldn't leave Ivan and Luka alone in the water.

She ushered the two boys to the beach. "You're to stay here. Do you understand?" Before they could answer, she took off along the dirt path. "I'm coming, Teo."

Sharp rocks cut into the soles of her feet as they pounded the ground, but she couldn't stop. She had heard him cry before, but never like this. Terror was reflected in his voice. *God, don't let him be badly hurt.*

"Teo." She searched the low bushes on each side of the narrow footpath, calling his name. There was no sign of him, though his cries grew closer. Climbing over some thick tree roots that stuck out of the soil, she found him at the bottom of a deep hole.

"Teo, honey, are you hurt?" The dry soil crumbled under her feet as she approached the edge. She flipped her wet hair out of her face as she peered down at him.

How had a hole like this gotten here? Had it been dug? She couldn't see a reason for it. But it hadn't rained in a long while, so maybe the drought caused the dirt to cave in like this.

She didn't think the dry roots would be strong enough to hold her weight as she lowered herself down to him, but there wasn't anything else to hold on to.

"Mama, get me out of here." His tear-streaked cheeks broke her heart. The only way to get him out was for her to descend some ten feet.

Taking a deep breath, she tugged on the exposed roots, searching for the one that would bear her weight.

"I thought I saw our kitty," he said.

She grabbed onto the thick piece of root and descended a few inches. "Darling, you know your kitty isn't here."

The dry root she clung to ripped at the top. She scanned for another one she could grab a hold of. There weren't any thick vines within reach, so she clutched onto the one in her hand until it tore away completely.

The fall was quick and ended with a painful stab in her ankle, but she didn't care. She hugged Teo's little frame and planted kisses all over his face.

The blood smeared on his forehead worried her. She wiped the wound with her hand and exhaled in relief. Teo's skin was scratched, but it was nothing a large bandage wouldn't cover. "You'll be fine. Now, let's get you out of here. Remember when we played knapsacks?"

He nodded.

"You hold on to my shoulders and wrap your legs around me."

"Like my school bag?"

"Yes, pretend you're my knapsack." She crouched in front of him and he climbed on her back. His thin legs wrapped around her waist.

"Slow and easy," she whispered as she stood, contemplating her next move.

The dirt crumbled under her feet with each step she climbed, but inch by inch they neared the top. As light as Teo was, his weight pressed on her back after a while and she feared she wouldn't make it. It was a great relief when they got close enough to the rim that she thought she could boost the boy over it and onto the ground.

"Crawl over my shoulders to get out," she told him.

His toes dug into her as he obeyed. Once he was safely on the firm ground, she started to climb out. The root she clutched snapped, catching her by surprise. She plunged to the bottom again, her head hitting a flat rock. The image of Teo standing at the top was the last thing she saw before the darkness closed in on her.

Hidden by the thick brush, Barry Wilkins leaned on the shovel and lit a cigarette. It had taken him days to dig the ten feet down into the lithic soil. A long drag on his smoke scorched his throat and chest and made him hack. What the hell did they put in this cheap tobacco? Another swig of Slivovitz added to the burn. The folks here distilled a marvellous plum brandy that even he could appreciate.

He glanced at the tub with the outboard engine he'd bought second hand. More like stole, even with non-existing knowledge of Croatian, he still managed to negotiate the bargain to his advantage. The two indigenous rocks provided the perfect seclusion for the little boat. No one could see the vessel from the sea. The summers spent as a camp counsellor in Muskoka Lakes in his late teens had finally paid off.

The roar of a white yacht approaching the shore caught his attention. A few minutes later, the three boys led a tall, bald man to the hole. It was that cook from the fancy and grossly overpriced restaurant. The guy jumped in as if he were a cat. He brought the nanny out on his shoulder, seemingly without any effort. The boys called her mommy and broke into tears. Tall guy stroked his goatee as he spoke to the boys in their native tongue then they all scurried to the luxury cruiser.

Barry lifted the binoculars to his eyes and inspected the yacht closer. The intricate letters on the stern spelled *Adriana*. The engines roared to life and the cruiser disappeared into the distance. They were probably headed to the hospital in the city.

That bitch of a nanny was too damn resilient. So far, nothing had worked to get rid of her. He *had* to place another nanny in the Zrin's household—someone who could be easily manipulated. Canada wasn't big enough for Barry to hide from the loan shark's henchmen. The trip here had maxed out his credit cards, but once he gained the info needed to embezzle the funds from Zrin's clinic, he'd steal someone's identity and start a new life. Someplace down south with one hand wrapped around margarita and the other around a senorita.

It was unfortunate that little boy almost got hurt. But desperation had driven Barry to this. Doctor Zrin had a soft spot for the nanny, but his days with her were numbered. Why should Zrin get to enjoy his family? The late Mrs. Zrin's desire for children had cost Barry his wife and daughter. His bastard of a boss had had the audacity to look Barry in the eye and lie through his teeth—downsizing, don't take it personally, he had said. What did management care of Barry's sick child? His medical benefits had gone with his job and the waiting list to get on the sponsorship for leukemia patients had been extensive. His wife had left him the day after they buried Lily.

Barry flicked the cigarette butt toward the sea and scurried up the path covered with pine needles. Late summer had settled in and the darkness fell earlier now.

The sliding door to the house was unlocked. He tsked. Miss Rokov should know better.

He pulled on the latex gloves he'd brought and they snapped around his wrist. He stepped inside, scanning the spacious living area. Damn, wasn't the huge mansion in Canada enough? No, of course not. Zrin had to show off here, too. How many luxury places could one man enjoy at any given time?

The fan of the nanny's laptop buzzed. He looked around and, spotting it on the table, tapped the mouse. The screen lit up. Three programs still ran. The email would be the obvious place to start. Kate's Inbox popped up on the screen as he clicked the icon on the taskbar.

No drama here, the girl must lack any excitement in her life. But, no one was without a flaw. He'd just have to dig deeper. Where would be a good place to look?

A click on the arrow down displayed the list of six more folders. He opened the Spam folder. "Let's see what little Kate has in here."

His eyes scanned the messages of special promotions. "You should empty this trash more often, girl. Speaking of garbage, let's see what you have deleted."

With a left mouse click, the Trash folder popped up. Wait, what was this? Displayed in bold letters, the only unread email caught his attention. Someone named Craig. He leaned forward and opened the message. A delighted smile stretched his lips, chuckles shaking him as he read the content.

He clicked on the reply button. "Bingo. Thank you Craig. You just made my life a whole lot easier."

CHAPTER 14

The halogen lamp of the surgical light dissipated most of its heat into the warm air rising to the high ceiling, leaving the air down near the operating table fairly cool. But the sweat under Matthias's scrubs stuck to his skin all the same. The strings of the cap tickled the nape of his neck each time he turned his head, a distracting annoyance he tried to ignore without much success. He knew he should pause and ask the nurse to tuck the loose ends under his cap, but he wanted to keep going. The steady beeping of the life monitor mixed with the whoosh of the suction machine served as a reminder that the patient had already been in surgery for several hours since the cleft palate reconstruction had taken longer than expected.

He peered over his mask at the x-rays displayed on the computer screen. "May I have the next slide, please?"

The gray picture of the upper palate provided little new information. He had closed the cleft by careful repositioning of muscles and tissue so there was nothing more he could do for this child on the table—at least not with the limited equipment in this hospital. He'd improvised enough already as it was. It was time to stitch the repair closed.

He turned to the intern. "Doctor Roman, would you do me the honor?"

The young surgeon stepped to the head of the table. "The honor would be all mine. Excellent work as usual, Doctor Zrin."

"Thank you. Now, apply the absorbable sutures through the midline of the roof of the mouth." Matthias observed the recent medical school graduate follow his directions with shaky hands. "Take your time. You have scrubbed in on a few surgeries with me, and you should know by now this work takes patience and immense concentration. You can't be thinking of anything else."

"I know." Doctor Roman threaded another stich. "Medicine has advanced in the three centuries since my great, great, great, uncle lived, but I think he would be proud of me today."

"I'm sure he would." Matthias smiled under his mask as the memories of the old doctor surfaced. The young intern mentioned his distant relative often. What would have become of Matthias and Emina had this man not taken them under his wing and bequeathed Matthias all of his possessions? To take a new Doctor-Roman-in-the-making under his wing was the least Matthias could do to repay such kindness.

"All done."

Doctor Roman's soft voice snapped Matthias back from his musing and he stepped forward to inspect the stitches. "Excellent. Your suturing has improved."

"Thanks to you, Doctor Zrin."

Matthias raised his head. "Team, we are finished here. Great work, all, as always. The patient can go to the recovery room."

Nods of approval and thanks came from the surgical nurses and anaesthesiologist.

"I'll inform the parents." Dr. Roman's rubber gloves snapped as he removed them. "They will be ecstatic with the results."

"Thank you, Doctor Roman."

Matthias held still while a nurse untied the strings at the back of his cap. He removed the cap, tossed it into the bin, and stepped into the scrub room, exhaling in relief as a blast of cold air enveloped him.

For a brief moment, he contemplated hopping in the shower to wash away the sweat, but decided to wait and take a plunge in the sea. Fortuno and Adriana must be on the island by now. And so would the rest of their guests, Dyane and Toni, Petar and Ana. And if Kate had mustered enough courage she'd have invited her mother, too.

Matthias shook his head. He couldn't let himself push Kate too hard to repair the damaged relationship with her family. As far as he could tell, they'd never had a healthy bond. The thought of Kate dancing around Fortuno in an attempt to discover his well-protected culinary secrets chased the gloomy thoughts away and coaxed a low laugh from his chest. Yes, a quick washing of his hands and face would suffice. He'd change his clothes and head straight back to Aba.

A nurse with a clipboard in her hand waylaid him as soon as he stepped into the hall. "Doctor Zrin."

"Yes?"

"I'm from Emergency."

He put his hands up. "I can't perform another surgery today."

"It's about your fiancée." She hesitated, the frown lines in her forehead deepening. "And your son."

He grabbed the clipboard from her and scanned the forms. His heart drummed as he flipped through the papers. The words fall, head injury, unconscious, concussion, contusions, abrasions and lacerations stuck out.

"Lead the way," he ordered, returning her clipboard.

"They were brought in an hour ago by your friend." The nurse led him through the maze of corridors. "Doctor

Leone preformed a CT scan on her and will inform you of the results. One boy was kept for observation. The other two were not involved in the accident so your friend took them home."

The panes of the automatic door slid opened on the ground floor and he followed the nurse into the emergency ward.

She pointed to the two small examination areas. "They are in the adjacent rooms."

Teo sat on the bed, dirty streaks left by dried tears on his cheeks. Another nurse tended to the scratches on his forehead, arms and legs. Matthias looked over his chart, patted him on the shoulder, and slipped back into the hall.

In the room next door, Kate lay on the bed silent and pale, with lacerations on her beautiful skin and her hair a tangled mess. The thought of both his son and fiancée injured broke his heart.

A round man in scrubs came in. "I'm Doctor Leone," he said, shaking Matthias's hand. "The boy only suffered some contusions and abrasions. I expect to discharge him today." He hesitated and shifted his feet. "CT scan showed the woman suffered a concussion. I'm expecting a full recovery, although prolonged dizziness, memory loss, decreased mental functioning, irritability, and headaches may occur."

"Has she gained consciousness yet?" Matthias asked, forcing his words out through his tight throat.

"Yes, she slips in and out. It is hard to say at this point how much she'll remember."

Matthias pressed two fingers to his forehead and exhaled. "Thank you, Doctor."

As Matthias stepped back into the hall, the nurse came out of Teo's room pushing a cart with supplies in front of her. Matthias went in to see him.

He examined the boy's face. The laceration on his forehead appeared superficial. With a proper care there wouldn't be any scaring. "Can you tell me what happened?"

Teo's chin shook and his eyes welled up. Matthias sat on the low stool next to the bed. "Son, don't be afraid. Just tell me in your own words."

Teo broke into sobs. "It's all my fault, Papa."

The sight of his little boy in such distress tore at Matthias's soul. What was he to do? What would Kate do in a situation like this? Maybe if he held him, the boy would calm down. A gentle touch helped to calm Kate when she cried. Only, he had never held his boys in his arms. Teo especially.

But it wasn't the boy's fault he resembled his mother. He shook his head in self-disgust. His son needed him and all he could do was to sit and watch the six-year-old child blame himself for the accident. That was all that Matthias knew how to do. His father wouldn't have done anything different. But fatherhood had changed since then. Nowadays being a provider wasn't enough.

He got up and sat on the bed next to Teo. "Don't cry, child. It wasn't your fault." The boy's small shoulders shook as Matthias pulled him onto his lap. "There, there, now. It was never your fault." He rocked Teo in his arms. Fear his children were growing up with the guilt that their mother had died because of them gripped his mind. This was not a feeling a child should have to bear. He knew this only too well.

"I thought—" As Teo's voice calmed, Matthias lowered his gaze to meet his son's eyes. "I saw my kitty in the woods, and I ran to catch him. Mommy called me to come back, but I didn't listen. Then my foot crashed through something and I fell in a hole. I lay there and cried until Mommy carried me out on her back."

That darn cat. Matthias never should have caved in and allowed the boys to keep the stray kitten. "You know we gave Hades away last summer before we left. A kitty can't survive on the island by himself."

Teo placed his little hands on Matthias's cheeks and melted his heart. "I miss him so much. I'm sorry, I disobeyed, Papa."

"I know. Let's go see Mommy." Matthias placed Teo on his feet and took his hand in his. "She must rest so you have to be quiet."

Teo nodded, his expression too serious for a little boy.

Matthias led him to Kate's bed. "We'll sit with Mommy until Uncle Fortuno comes for you."

Tenderly, Teo stroked Kate's hair with his small hands. "Mommy? Can you hear me?"

The corner of Kate's lips twitched.

"She can hear you, son. Talk to her."

Teo nodded again. "I'm sorry I didn't listen."

Matthias pulled the stool closer to Kate's bed and sat on it and put Teo on his lap. "See, she'll be fine, but for now she has to sleep."

"When will she wake?"

Matthias gave his son a cheerful smile. "Soon."

Doctor Leone entered the room with papers in his hand. "There you are. I need your signature on Teo's discharge papers then he can be on his way. Providing he promises me he'll be careful." He tapped the top of Teo's head, stressing his last word.

Matthias took the clipboard and signed. "What do you say, Teo?"

"I'll be careful, I promise." Teo's solemn voice and face coaxed a laugh from both doctors.

Doctor Leone patted Matthias on the shoulder. "She's in good hands, Doctor Zrin. If you want to get some rest, feel free to leave."

"I'll sit with her for a while. My friend is on his way to get Teo."

"My little man is all right?" Fortuno's voice thundered from the doorway.

"I'll leave you then." Doctor Leone tore the top copy of Teo's discharge form and handed the sheet to Matthias. "This is for your records."

"Thank you for all your help, Doctor Leone."

"Don't mention it. It's our job." The pudgy doctor nodded once and left.

Matthias shot Fortuno a sideways look. "How big was this hole?"

Fortuno shrugged, his eyes scanning the room. "It was deep, I'd say nine maybe ten feet, and about—" He stretched his arms out. "This wide. That's about six feet, I'd say."

Matthias sprang to his feet. "How the hell can such hole exist there?"

"Drought, the dry soil caved in."

With one hand shoved into his pocket and the other scratching the back of his head, Matthias paced the small room. "We'll need to investigate this. In all the years I've owned the island there has never been anything of the sort."

"Of course we'll examine it," Fortuno hissed. "But if we discover it's something deliberate, what are we going to do?"

"Deal with it." Matthias stopped pacing and took Kate's cold hand in his. "Before worse things happen. Both Teo and Kate could've been killed." The thought of losing his loved ones stirred snakes in his stomach.

Fortuno pulled the boy into his arms. "I'll take Teo now. He looks tired after his ordeal."

"Yes, put him to bed. I'll try to be there by the morning to reapply the ointment on his scratches."

Matthias handed the tube of antibiotic cream to Fortuno. "In case I'm not there."

"I'll do it." Fortuno stored the cylinder in his jeans' pocket and left with Teo half-asleep on his shoulder.

Matthias placed a soft kiss on Kate's fingers and pressed her palm to his cheek. He sat down on the stool in silence, staring at her and trying to calm his mind. Her chest rose and fell with even breaths. She'd be fine, he told himself, but what danger lurked around her? Could it be his presence? Why hadn't Emina warned him this time? He supposed it was possible she had tried but couldn't break through his deep concentration in surgery.

Kate drew a deep breath and coughed.

"Kate, love, can you hear me?" he asked.

Her eyes opened to thin slits. "Matthias," she rasped. "Where am I?"

"You're in the hospital. Do you remember anything?"

She licked her cracked lips and her face contorted in pain. "A hole. I remember falling. Teo?"

"He is fine, love."

"My head hurts so much, I want to die."

Matthias kissed her forehead. "No, you don't. Pain, as tough as it is, is a good sign. We can handle pain. Numbness would worry me more."

"Then handle it." The urgency in her voice and the tears that spilled onto her cheeks had him springing from his seat.

"I'll get you a shot of Demerol." He stroked her hair. "I'll need to stick your rump with a needle. Can you roll to your side?"

The hospital bed creaked under her as she obeyed him.

"Good. I'll be right back."

After filling out the request form for the drug, he got a nurse to unlock the fridge and retrieve the ampule. She gave him a sterile syringe and needle in the plastic wrapper. "Do you want me to do it, doctor?"

"I think I can handle giving one simple shot. But you can prepare the syringe for me."

The nurse did as he asked then followed him as he went back to Kate's room.

He caressed Kate's shoulder. "The pain will go away in a few minutes." The nurse handed him the syringe and he lifted Kate's hospital gown. "Try to relax your buttocks. The muscle is too tense."

"I can't relax anything," she cried. "Does it have to go there?"

"Look at me, Kate." His hand massaged her backside. She turned her head and gazed into his eyes. "This won't hurt."

Though the tension in her muscles slowly eased off, she yelped as he stabbed the needle into her flesh. He depressed the plunger. He had to work fast and not allow her to tense up again.

"There, all done." With an alcohol pad pressed to the puncture site, he handed the empty syringe to the nurse. "The pain will alleviate in a minute."

He reached for her hand and her fingers instantly wrapped around his, so he raised them to his lips. Warmth and color returned to her skin

She raised her eyebrows as his chin brushed her knuckles. "When was the last time you shaved?"

"I've never shaved." Perplexed, he sat up straight, ran a hand over his face, and gasped. "I had not had a chance to grow any facial hair before my bite."

"Mmmm," she said, caressing his cheek. "Seems you sprouted some stubble."

The feel of sandpaper against his palm made him smile with delight. "You're right," he whispered as he leaned over her ear. "You're turning me more mortal with each day."

"And you're turning me on. Are you sure it was Demerol you gave me?"

"I'm positive," he whispered before sealing her lips with his.

"Oh, oh, I apologize."

Matthias straightened, coughed into his fist, and smiled at the nurse who stood in the doorway. "No, no. Come in."

She hummed while she strapped a blood pressure cuff around Kate's arm. "Have you experienced another episode of nausea, dear?"

"No, I haven't."

Kate's blood shot and tired eyes stung Matthias to the core.

The machine beeped. "The blood pressure is back to normal. How's the pain?"

Kate yawned. "It's going, aw..." Her eyelids drooped as her voice trailed off.

"Go to sleep." Matthias stroked her hair. "I'll stay with you."

"Doctor Leone will assess her in the morning, but she seems on the right track to recovery." The nurse pulled the covers over Kate's shoulders, cast Matthias a cheerful smile, and left.

Hours ticked away as he sat at Kate's bedside, though his eyes closed on a few occasions.

The same nurse came to take Kate's vitals again. "Doctor Zrin, I'll take a good care of her. You should go get some rest. The night shift is hard."

He stood and stretched his aching muscles. "You're right. Is there an empty bed I can use?"

"The staff room is down that corridor." She pointed to her left. "At this time of the night it should be empty. You can crash on the couch."

"Thank you. Take a good care of her," he said on a yawn. "She's very special to me and my boys."

"You know I will, Doctor Zrin." She waved her hand at Kate. "But I'm jealous of her. Every girl deserves a man like you. Unfortunately, there aren't many out there."

He let out a quiet laugh. She had no idea just how few of men like him there were. Soon, it seemed even he wouldn't be one of them.

The staff room stood quiet and empty. The sectional couch smelled of spilled coffee but he couldn't be too picky. Stretched out on the cushions with his head braced on his arm, he let his thoughts focus on the hole. Had anyone else known of his and Fortuno's existence? In the past three centuries, he had been careful not to give out his secret, but maybe somehow he had slipped. If he had an enemy, it wouldn't be anyone of his kind. They had secrets of their own to protect. That meant it had to be a mortal.

What would a human want from him? Money. What else?

CHAPTER 15

Matthias's yacht glided through the sea. Seated next to him, Kate clutched her book to her chest. Dyane had finally returned the novel to her—in fairly good condition. The corners of a few pages were folded but at least none were missing.

"There's your home island." Matthias tilted his chin toward the horizon. "We'll be docking in a few minutes."

"Good, the boys won't wait for long," she replied.

The sight of Esa's outline rising from the sea tightened her stomach. The pain of her mother's sobs over the phone was still fresh in her mind. Kate wasn't sure if her mom had been more upset with her because of falling or because she'd kept her engagement a secret. Matthias had been right of course. She shouldn't have waited to tell her mom that she had accepted his proposal and of the family she had gained, along with the man she loved so much.

She let out a heavy sigh. No more secrets from now on. Emina's words resonated in her mind. *'No matter how difficult truth may be, it was still better than a lie.'*

Kate glanced over her shoulder at her little guys seated around the same table where she and Matthias had sat the first night they spent on the boat.

"Lucky for us, your cousin's cat had a litter of three," he said, casting her a glance before returning his attention to the water in front of them. "Are you sure she'll be willing to take them back when we leave for Canada?"

"Yes, she said she would." Kate pushed the loose strands of her ponytail off her face, but the high wind of the speeding boat on the open sea blew them right back. "Don't you know cats can fend for themselves?"

"On the bigger, inhabited islands, yes, but not on our small chunk of rock." The bow lowered as he pulled the accelerator back. "Want to get the ropes?"

"Of course."

The sun had set behind the hills by the time they docked and disembarked on the long jetty. Except for a few locals, relaxing before supper, the sleepy port, with its fishing nets heaped along the shoreline, stood quiet.

A waitress nodded at her as they passed by the patio of a café awaiting tonight's business. "Hey, Kate, how are you feeling?"

Kate smiled at the skinny girl. "Fine, thanks."

The news around these parts travelled faster than any Internet provider could deliver. The people here didn't need Facebook when God had equipped them with mouths. But they all meant well.

"Whoa," Matthias gasped, staring at the number of stairs they faced. "I can't see where they end. Tell me your house is at the foot of this hill."

She gave him a sympathetic gaze. "I wish. Once we reach the top of these, you'll have even more stairs to climb."

Ivan stood transfixed at the bottom. "Do these stairs lead to Heaven, Mommy?"

Kate chuckled. "No honey, it only looks like they do."

"Well, to climb a few stairs will do us all good after the feast Rosalia put out for us." Matthias patted his stomach and put his foot on the first step.

"I'm sure my mom will have food on the table, too," Kate told him. She took Ivan and Teo's hands in hers and followed Matthias. "I'm happy for Rosalia. She deserved to spend her golden years here, surrounded by her family. But at the same time, I'm sad she won't be returning with us."

"Me, too." Matthias glanced over his shoulder. "We'll find another maid."

"No, Matthias. I'll take care of my family."

Kate forced a smile when more islanders greeted her. Yes, Rosalia was irreplaceable, but this was Kate's family now and she was determined to show Matthias they didn't need a maid.

"Fortuno will cook for us." A hint of disappointment resonated in Matthias's voice. "Not all the time though."

A smidgeon of frustration stirred in Kate. She had to prove to him, she could take care of him, the boys, and the huge house. "I admit my cooking isn't anything like Fortuno's, or Rosalia's, but we won't starve. We don't need a maid or a cook."

He paused and turned to her. "Okay, how's this? We'll get a cleaning service once, twice per week. At least until you recover fully, then you can decide if you want to take over all the household duties."

A smile tugged on the corners of her lips. This might be the first time in his life he would live without a hired maid. And while his aristocratic lifestyle demanded he have a servant, she was taught not to be frivolous.

"Come on, love." The strap of her top slid down her arm as he caressed her bare shoulder. "I don't expect you to clean such big house."

"Rosalia did it, all by herself."

"She was a maid all her life and she did her job well. I'll set her up with a good pension." With a shrug, he faced the hill again and continued up the stairs nestled between the houses.

Kate followed in silence for a short time. She shouldn't get miffed at him for wanting to help her with the housework. His heart was in the right place. With a loud sigh, she said, "I'll go with the cleaning service then, if the offer still stands."

Glancing over his shoulder again, he shot her a winning smile, but she felt like the real winner.

With a frilly apron around her waist, Kate's mom appeared at the top of the hill and clasped her hands. "There you are. I waited and waited."

Tears stung Kate's eyes. She ran up the stairs two at the time and threw her arms around the frail frame of the older woman. "I'm so sorry, Mama."

Her mom hugged her back. "Kate, it's so good to have you home. I was so worried."

Kate stepped back, taking Matthias by his hand. "Mama, this is—"

"I know, my future son-in-law." After wiping her hands on her apron, she took Matthias's hand.

He pulled her into his embrace. "Glad to finally meet you, Mama. Do you mind if I too call you Mama like Kate does?"

"Not at all." Mom patted his shoulder then turned to the boys huddled around Kate. "My grandsons."

Their puzzled looks made Kate snicker. She lowered her head and whispered, "Go hug your nana. She's nice. You'll see."

One by one, they all wrapped their little arms around the old school teacher. She planted a kiss on each boy's head. "Now let's go to the house. Your cousins can't wait to meet you."

"We want to see our kittens," Ivan burst out.

"Yes, cats." Matthias stopped to ogle the canopy of a large fig tree hanging over the stone paved path.

Kate grabbed his elbow and pulled him away. "If the owner sees you picking a fruit he'll have a fit. Come, there's one at our house, too."

The entire family, all ten members, waited in the courtyard in front of the stone building. Kate swallowed a lump but couldn't stop from grinning.

"Everyone," her mom announced, pointing at Matthias. "This is my future son-in-law, Doctor Matthias Zrin."

"Hi there," Kate's blonde cousin leaned over the railing at the top of the stairs. "Nice catch, Kate. Got any brothers? Single or married doesn't matter, as long as they look like you."

Matthias laughed. "Sorry to disappoint you."

Kate rolled her eyes. The best way to survive her family was to sit back and enjoy the show, but tonight they'd put her on the spot.

"See, I told you they'd approve of me," Matthias whispered in her ear.

Kate cast him a smile. If her family ever discovered his secret, what on Earth would they make of him? Or her. She averted her eyes and glanced at her boys making friends with two young cousins. With a cheerful face, her mom served them ice cream.

"The boys have a grandma now and cousins," Matthias said softly from behind her. "An extended family."

"Yes." She nodded towards the table where the boys giggled as their nana showed them how to handle the kittens. "The old school teacher. She revels in being around the kids."

"Hey, Kate"

She turned to her left and faced a young man, another cousin. "Hey, what's up?"

"You singlehandedly raised our numbers."

Kate burst into a laugh. "Oh, Simeon, you've always been such joker."

Simeon took two beers from the table and handed one to Matthias. "Can we call you Matt? Matthias is kind of— old fashioned. I thought you'd be a hundred years old?"

Mischief in Matthias's eyes as he took the bottle from Simeon. "Three hundred, to be exact."

Kate froze. What had Matthias just said?

Simeon snorted. "Yeah, I hear you. Sometimes, I feel like I'm hundreds of years old, myself, especially after partying hard."

Matthias patted Simeon's shoulder. "I know what you mean. But, yeah, you can call me Matt."

Kate grabbed Matthias's arm and jerked him to the side. "What the heck are you doing, *Matt*?"

He took a sip of beer. "Just testing this theory I had. If I tell the truth, mortals won't take me seriously, and as you saw, I'm right."

"Someday someone may believe you. I did."

"Not exactly, the way I recall." He tapped his finger on her nose. "Well, if anything the remark was a good ice breaker."

"Hey, Matt," Simeon called. "Another beer?"

Matthias tilted the full bottle and shook his head. He seemed in his element, becoming one of the guys as he strolled away to join them.

Kate wandered over to a low wall and sat down, watching Matthias joke and laugh with her family.

"He loves you," her mother said, as she sat down beside Kate.

Kate gave her a dreamy smile. "And I love him."

Her mom stared at the ground. "Kate, I know you and I never saw eye to eye."

Kate sighed. "Mama, let's not talk about this now."

"As a teacher, I saw many children on the destructive life-path. Their parents didn't care, but I wanted to protect you from the world. Instead, I suffocated you and we grew more apart."

"Mama." Kate's throat closed and she took her mother's hand in hers. "I understand now. I'm a mom, too."

Her mother hugged her. "Don't make the same mistake I did." She pulled back and smiled at Kate. "I'm happy for you."

Unable to utter anything through her tight throat, Kate nodded while pushing the tears away.

"We have ton of stories about Kate." With a mischievous smile, Simeon turned to her then back to Matthias. "And all of them embarrassing."

"No, you don't." Kate's cheeks burned as she growled at him. Every member of her family seemed to be itching to fill Matthias in on her awkward teenage years. Yep, she was in the hot seat tonight.

The late summer breeze shoved small waves toward the shore. Seated on the beach, Kate reveled in the smell of pine and the soft chirping of the cicadas. The sight of her boys cooperating in the building of a sand castle while she instructed them from the deep shade sent a hint of guilt through her. Matthias had forbidden her from staying in the sun for too long. He was right, though. The dizziness spun her head after a few minutes, despite the wide brimmed hat. The pain killers she was prescribed turned her into a real zombie and she'd rather listen to her doctor's orders so she didn't need the pills.

One of Doctor Leone's recommendations was to have sex and lots of it. Apparently, releasing the oxytocin during climax rejuvenated the brain cells and helped in healing. Matthias was happy to oblige and, two weeks later, aside from dizziness when staying out in the sun too long, she hardly suffered from any symptoms of her concussion.

Still, sadness nibbled at her mind. They would leave this enchanted islet next week. But, the summer had come to an end. She'd have to take the boys shopping for back to school as soon as they returned. At least they'd be in the same classroom and she wouldn't need to meet with three different teachers.

The rustling in the bush drew her attention. Matthias approached, digital camera in his hands, and crouched in front of her. "Well, the police officers agree with me. The hole was dug by someone on purpose. I took more pictures."

She caressed his handsome face. "The hole is becoming your obsession. Just let it go."

"I can't. There are shovel markings in the soil and on the rocks. I intend to find out who did this and why."

With both her hands cupping his cheeks, she tilted his head down so their eyes met. "How are you going to find out? Why would anyone go through the trouble of digging it?"

"Too many unanswered questions." He raised his finger. "But once I find who did it, let God help him."

She shot him a stern glance. "Matthias, promise you won't do anything rash. I don't want any trouble with the law."

"Don't worry." He took her hand in his, reassuring her with a smile. "I won't do what you are thinking."

She grabbed onto the brim of her hat as a gust of wind threatened to blow the sombrero off her head. "What am I thinking?"

He exhaled loudly. "I can read your thoughts loud and clear. You are afraid I'll kill the person, but you're wrong. I'll turn him into the police."

"We're leaving in a week's time. The trail will go cold." She stood, adjusting her bikini top. "In the meantime, I want to grab as many swims in the Adriatic as I can and put the incident behind me."

He glanced at the boys, immersed in their sand play. "We should sneak down here tonight and give another healing boost to your brain cells."

"Doctor's orders? I can hardly wait."

Maybe it was the head injury, but she hadn't heard the sad, longing piano melody since her accident. Or could it be Emina had crossed over and had taken the sweet sounds with her?

Cool water surrounded her, reaching as high as her knees. She splashed some at Matthias. He groaned and sprang to his feet. Scrambling out of his black t-shirt, he took two steps to her and scooped her into his arms. His mouth seized hers. Their tongues collided in a demanding union. A moan escaped her as he pulled on the string, releasing her breasts from the constraints of her bikini top.

"Hey, not in front of the kids," Fortuno hissed, his words shattering the lustful moment.

Kate panted against Matthias's chest, retying her swimsuit. What was she thinking? Had Fortuno not interrupted them, she'd have let Matthias have his way with her right in front of the boys.

"I brought your friends here," Fortuno continued as Dyane and Toni emerging from the tree line.

Kate gave a yelp of joy and ran to them. "Guys, it's so good to have you here. We'll party tonight."

"Well, you'll leave next week and we never did celebrate your engagement, so—" Dyane pulled a bottle of vodka out of her bag. "I figured, why not surprise you?"

"Great, but I can't have any booze." Kate darted a quick glance at Matthias. "I am to regenerate my brain cells, not fry them."

"This is for the guys." Dyane pushed the bottle down in her purse. "There are few more people coming."

The scar on Kate's head itched. This was not a good sign. It usually meant a headache would follow. "Who else did you invite?"

"Your cousins from Esa and a few people from our old high school. Party, baby." Dyane wiggled her hips.

"Please excuse me a minute." Kate stepped aside, motioning for Matthias to join her. "I know how these guys party. There may be drugs involved."

"No one leaves the islet until they are sober. Fortuno and I will police them and seize any illegal substances." The feel of his hand on her wet hair sent another surge of tingles down her spine.

"Let's party then." Kate said and turned back to Dyane.

"Come boys," Matthias called. "We're going back to the house."

"Oh," Dyane gasped opening her bag. "I brought the boys a little something. I hope you don't mind. My nephew loves dinosaurs so I got them each a book."

"Books are allowed." Matthias narrowed his eyes at Fortuno. "Expensive toys that require batteries and make annoying noises are not."

They climbed up the hill on the narrow path, winding through the pines and low brush. Kate followed Matthias with Dyane and Toni in tow. The soft melody Dyane hummed stopped Kate in her tracks.

"Where did you hear that song?"

"The ghost hums it all the time." Dyane said then finished the song. "It's a catchy tune."

Kate's eyes widened. "Emina crossed over. It's over. She's gone."

Dyane frowned. "What gave you that idea? She's still here."

Chills spread down Kate's spine. "What else could she want?"

"I don't know, Kate." Exasperation edged Dyane's voice. "She's not telling me."

"Maybe she disapproves of me as the future Mrs. Zrin, but she held the position for three hundred years. Me, I just started."

"I don't think so," Dyane said. "You still haven't set the date for the big day."

"We haven't set the date yet." Kate dropped her chin onto her chest and exhaled. Everyone seemed in a hurry to dance at their wedding. So was she, but Matthias didn't seem preoccupied with getting married again. He had done it many times, but to her this was her first real one. Tying the knot with her ex didn't count.

The roar of the boat engines drew their attention toward the sea. Dyane cocked an eyebrow. "Guests are arriving."

Suitcases waited by the front entrance as Matthias scanned the large open-concept living area. The summer he had just spent here was the best since Emina's death. He stared at the sectional couch facing the large window overlooking the sea. The night of his proposal to Kate came to mind. The way her face lit up when he'd asked for her hand would forever warm his soul.

Her acceptance had made him very happy. The boys adored their new mom. No more nannies. They even had a grandmother and a few cousins. God willing, he and Kate would be blessed with a child of their own.

"Ready?" Kate said from behind him.

He whirled around to face her. He wasn't ready to leave. This islet held many fond memories for him, and Emina's presence was the strongest here. "I suppose."

"I know," she croaked. "I don't want to leave either."

"Let me check on the surveillance camera once more." All attempts to find out who could have dug the hole had come up empty and with them gone for the winter, installing the cameras around the property was his last hope. Criminals always returned to the scene of the crime.

With two long strides, Kate closed the distance between them and wrapped her arms around him. "Don't obsess. I don't think whoever dug the hole will return."

He kissed the top of her head. "I'm not obsessing, love, but house *will* be empty until we return."

Ivan kicked the beach ball into the kitchen. "Are we coming again next summer, Papa."

"Yes, son. We are." With his foot, Matthias stopped the colorful ball from rolling. "No balls indoors."

"I asked him to put the ball away for the summer." Kate stepped to Ivan. "And I also said to let the air out."

Matthias sighed. "Well, are we ready to go? As much as we don't want to."

"We'll be back." Her soft smile warmed his heart.

The desire to ask his family if perhaps someday they should return for good became stronger with each passing moment. The boys had their friends back in Canada, their command of the Croatian language was still weak. They would have a hard time adjusting to the school system here. There were just too many things preventing him from making such a drastic move.

"Let's get our luggage on the boat and then we'll head to town." He clapped his hands. "One more night on the town with all of us together and tomorrow the long haul back."

"Boys," Kate called. "Can each of you take one small bag?"

Matthias watched in amazement as they obeyed. The little nanny he'd employed, and fallen madly in love with, had warned him on her first day that the boys needed to learn how to do things for themselves and by themselves. The same girl who had changed their lives would soon be his wife.

"Are you coming?" Kate adjusted the strap of the bag on her shoulder and pointed at the floor. "Everything is loaded except for these two large ones."

"I'll get them." One last scan of the place then he picked up the bags and stepped out.

"The fall will set on early this year. I can tell." Kate said, closing the door with a low thud. She turned the key in the lock. "It's a cool day for late August. I had hoped to grab one last swim, but when I dipped my toes in, the sea was cold." She trailed behind him down the steps.

"The boys didn't seem to mind." He stored the luggage next to the already neatly stacked pile. "You did a great job getting your bags down to the boat," he told the boys.

Their faces lit up at his praise.

Teo pulled a book from his bag, settling himself on Kate's lap. "We're having a big gathering at Fortuno's."

"Yes." She stroked his hair. "Many of your cousins won't be able to come for our wedding so they'll see us tonight."

Luka glanced at her over his handheld Play Station. "Why can't they come?"

"Well, it's a long trip and school won't be out by then," Matthias said. "You guys will still be in school, too."

He threw the lines on the deck. His throat dry, he scanned the top of the islet. Emina's spirit roamed happily here. She'd follow them wherever they went, but her entity would lose some of its essence with each day away from this place.

After retrieving the heavy anchor, he inserted the key into the ignition and turned on the engines. The sea foamed around the boat. At a slow speed, the yacht reversed away from the jetty and turned toward the open sea. Dark clouds loomed in the distance. The islet sank from view until only the peak was visible. A heavy weight sat on his heart and choked off his words as the craft sped away.

Two dolphins raced with the boat. Their carefree play chased away his gloom. Though his little family was whole now, he still wasn't ready to let go of Emina's ghost. He just hoped Kate would understand.

CHAPTER 16

Kate kissed the boys goodbye in the schoolyard as the school bell rang for the second time. The children lined up in front of the doors. Their knapsacks bounced on their backs as they disappeared inside the building. Holding the door open, their young teacher waved to her. When the last of the grade-one students passed through, the teacher followed them inside, closing the wide door behind her.

Kate's cell phone rang for the fifth time in the last hour. She pulled it from her raincoat pocket and glanced at the display. It was the catering company. She pushed the button and pressed the device to her ear. "Hello."

"Miss Rokov, please," the man's flat voice demanded.

She glanced at the sky. Heavy clouds threatened and she scurried to the car. April showers had arrived. "Speaking."

He cleared his throat. "I checked our files again, and I can't find any record or your payment."

Anger spiralled through her. Incompetent people! What had they done with her money? "I paid. And according to the bank, you received it."

"Sorry, but we don't have it." He sighed. "Look, it's the wedding season. We are swamped with business. Send your payment or find another catering company."

"Check your records again. I'm tying the knot in a month." Her voice rose with each word and her feet took longer strides. "Where am I going to find another caterer now?"

"I'm very sorry, but I can't spare another day digging through the paperwork. If you can produce a copy of the receipt, we may honor it."

"I need to speak with your manag—"

The man ended the call. She groaned and flipped the phone closed, shoving the mobile back in the pocket.

The short drive home didn't calm her frayed nerves. Though her tan-lines had faded long ago, the image of the shrinking Earth underneath the plane leaving Croatia still stirred sadness in her. The overcast sky had welcomed them with a downpour as soon as they'd disembarked from the transcontinental flight in Canada.

Winter had settled in early and had kept its grip until last week. With each snowfall she'd warmed her body in Matthias's arms and her soul with the thoughts of the beautiful summer she'd spent on the islet, along with the promise of many more with her husband and children there by the sea.

Matthias had assumed Fortuno would put their wedding together, as always, but she was Matthias's *new* bride. Things should not be the same as when he married Emina. Kate wanted to do all of the preparations herself and had stood her ground. She needed to put her personal touch in every detail. After all, it was said that the variety was the spice of life.

The light on the answering machine flashed as she entered the kitchen. Now what? She pressed the button and groaned as the florist's message added to her already overflowing frustration. They wouldn't be able to do white roses and lilies and would she like to go with yellow, which—since they were brought in from a faraway nursery—would cost more?

She exhaled in exasperation. The cost of the wedding mounted higher and higher with every passing day and while the expense didn't seem to bother Matthias, it gave her headaches.

Lightning flashed and loud thunder rolled, causing her to flinch. She glanced at the window. The sky grew darker as the rain poured down.

Although she was on the brink of caving in and allowing Matthias to let Fortuno take over, she couldn't bring herself to show her weakness. Not even Matthias's demanding stares could get her to change her mind. Although, he might have succeeded the last time if he had only kept his eyes locked on hers another minute. No, she would do this herself. It wasn't as if she'd get to be married to him six times. Besides, if putting the occasion together caused this much trouble, she'd rather marry just once.

The shrill sound of the phone ring made her jump. *The Bridal Shoppe* displayed on the screen. What could they possibly want? Her dress was almost finished.

"Yes," Kate answered with a frustration churning her stomach.

"Miss Rokov." The woman's voice blared in her ear. "Can I get you to come in for another measurement?"

Kate closed her eyes. This couldn't be happening. "Why? The last time I was there you said the dress would be done."

"Well, as it seems we took in too much. But, don't panic. It can be fixed. I just need you to come in again."

"I'll be there in an hour." Kate slammed the phone and cradled her head in the folds of her arms. A hint in the shop owner's voice told her the mistake they made wouldn't be reparable. No, not the dress. Her gown was the only thing coming along smoothly. She wouldn't be able to keep herself together if it was ruined, too.

More rain washed over the pavement. On her way after picking the boys up from school, Kate struggled to keep her eyes on the road through the heavy veil of water as the wipers swished over the windshield at the full speed. Strapped into their booster seats in the back, the boys sang a silly song, ignoring her request to stay quiet.

"Please, guys." She glanced in the rear view mirror. "I asked you to quit singing about gross bodily functions." What was it with the boys of this age and their bathroom humour?

Luka stuck his tongue out and blew air through the gaps in between his missing teeth. Her grip on the steering wheel tightened as her annoyance quickly turned into anger. Twisting from the waist, she spun in his direction and slapped his leg. In an instant, she regretted her action.

Teo's eyes widened. "Mommy, watch out," he shrieked, pointing.

Her foot slammed on the brake. The SUV swerved. As the driver of the car from the oncoming traffic lane laid on the horn, Kate brought the vehicle to a stop on the shoulder, narrowly avoiding a head on collision.

Fingers gripping the steering wheel, she panted as the traffic zoomed by, her heart slamming in wild rhythm. She drew in a long breath and held it as her furiously beating heart slowed down.

She exhaled. "Everyone all right?" Looking in the mirror again, she saw three terrified faces. Their fear intensified her guilt. "Are you all okay?"

They nodded but said nothing.

"I'm so sorry, guys." Her glance went to Luka. Tears sat in the corners of his eyes and melted her anger. "Luka, honey, Mommy didn't mean to hit you. Can you please forgive me?"

"We're sorry, Mommy." Ivan's frown coaxed a smile to her face.

"Sing your song, I'd like to hear the rest, but with your nice voices." The engine revved as she pulled back on the road, but the boys stayed quiet.

Within minutes, she pulled up in the driveway, next to the Audi that was parked in the garage. She dragged herself out of the car and unbuckled the boys. They scurried inside the house and she leaned on the hood. The clicking under it calmed her down.

The side door opened and Matthias stepped out. "There you are. What are you doing here all alone?"

"I'm so stressed I almost caused the accident and killed us all." Her hands shook as she relived a brief moment of facing the car in the lane of oncoming traffic. It had taken her a flash of a second to lose her grip on her cool.

His chest rose and fell with his loud breath. "Shouldn't let things get to you."

"Nothing is going right, Matthias. Now, my dress is ruined. I was so looking forward to wearing the replica of Galadriel's gown, with French lace and Swarovski crystals."

The seamstress had tried to convince her the silk on the waist wouldn't show the stitching done in error, but Kate had spotted the mistake at the door of the shop.

Matthias pulled her into his embrace and his comforting scent was like a balm on her frayed nerves. "I know you had your heart set on that dress. But what can you do now? Buy a finished one."

"I'll have to. They can't sew another one from the scratch now. The only one they have that I kind of like is two thousand dollars more." She inhaled his musky scent once more. All he had to do was to rent a tux while she felt like a circus lion, jumping through the hoops.

"Don't worry about the money." His words only churned her upset stomach worse.

"We're blowing some serious cash. And maybe your budget is unlimited, but it hurts me to see money being mishandled, and no one seems to care. What is this, Matthias?"

"Kate, love." His breath tickled her neck. "You need to take a break from all of this. Where in the world would you like to have me all to yourself for two weeks?"

"Matthias, we can't leave." What was she saying? He wanted to whisk her away. This was her chance to forget about the wedding blues and spend some time alone with him.

He pulled back. "We must. It's for your own good, and I won't take no for an answer."

"What about the boys?" She hadn't been away from them since her vacation in Croatia. How could she leave them now? But the thought of her and Matthias alone, someplace away from the civilization, clouded her mind.

"Fortuno and Adriana will be happy to have them." His lips curled with a smile. "So where are you taking me?"

"Aba Vela, where else?" She heard her voice before she realized it was she who spoke. Once again, she had caved under his tenderness and let him have his way.

He gave her a little pat on the behind. "Go pack. We're leaving tonight."

Her eyes narrowed as she gathered her thoughts. "You'll let Fortuno take over the wedding preparations while we're gone. Won't you?"

Matthias furrowed his brows. "No. I won't, unless you want me to."

"Do you think he could get the money back?" She lowered her gaze to the ground, not willing to show how miserably she failed.

He cradled her chin in his fingers, tilting her head up. "I know he can and lots of freebies, too, but I have to get him on it soon."

A hint of pride surfaced. She should show those caterers who really was the boss here. "Then let him."

The twin engines of *The Pearl* roared as Matthias glided the yacht through the sea.

The light of the full moon washed the waters around him in silver. Thanks to Petar who had prepared the yacht for the navigation, they would dock on Aba Vela soon.

Kate had barely woken since he put her in the airport limo, though the drive to Zadar's marina had taken an hour on the empty roads.

Now that they were in Croatia, his plan was simple. She wanted the full reception. Since her friends and family were all here, why not wed here? Fortuno would fly the boys over on the next flight and open the restaurant in time. The only thing that remained was Kate's dress, but Matthias was sure she'd find one she'd fall in love with.

So far so good. No one knew they'd arrived and he planned to keep their homecoming a secret for as long as he could. After all, he had whisked her away to spend this time with her. She'd be his and no one else's.

The outline of Aba Vela appeared in front of him and he shut the engines, allowing the craft to coast on its wake. After docking the cruiser, he carried the luggage to the house. Kate exhaled loudly as he scooped her up from the bed in the master cabin.

He carried her up the familiar stone steps. Her head rolled on his shoulder with every stair he climbed.

"Are we home?" she whispered.

"Yes, love, we're home." The lights on the patio flickered to life as he unlocked the glass door. *Home*, she'd called this place, rekindling his hope of a permanent return. They'd spent their happy days of summer here and this was where they belonged.

The musty scent of an air-tight house assaulted his nostrils as he stepped inside. After placing her on his big bed, he opened a few windows. The salty air, carried on the gentle breeze would soon replace the smell of disuse.

When he climbed into the large bed, Kate snuggled up to him. He spooned her against him, closed his eyes, and drifted off to sleep.

It was still dark when he opened his eyes. Or had it gotten dark again? How long had he slept? He rolled his head to the side. Kate stared at him. Her chest rose and fell as she breathed. He kissed her lips, but she plunged her tongue deep into his mouth. Her moan turned him hard in an instant. When she straddled him, blood drained from his head and surged into his groin. There was something in the air he couldn't put his finger on. An animal-like urge he couldn't control.

He yanked on the fabric of her shirt. Little buttons clicked as they scattered over the hardwood floor. She cried out with the release of her bra strap her nipples forming firm peaks in his fingers.

The sharp sound of his jeans' zipper opening pierced the air. Scrambling out of his pants with one hand, he pulled the shirt over his head with the other, then pushed her trembling body back onto the mattress.

"Ah, Matthias," she whispered, her sighs growing more urgent with every kiss he pressed on her, from her chin, in between her breasts, down her belly, to her pubic mound.

Settling in between her knees, he cupped her buttocks and she parted her legs wider. Her back arched as his tongue swiped the soft folds of her labia. Bed sheets were clutched in her hands as she squirmed, but he kept on teasing, paying special attention to her tender spot until her fingers dug into his hair.

"Matthias, I won't last long like this."

He ignored her pleas, darting his tongue in and out. Her buttocks squeezed, shoving her hips against his mouth over and over until she screamed, her whole body tightening like a fist and convulsing, before slowly relaxing again.

"Matthias," she heaved as her shudders ceased. "Oh, sweet Jesus, that was good."

"We're not done. Turn over," he demanded. A low hiss escaped him as she obeyed. His hands slid to her supple buttocks. He lifted her hips and his hardness slid inside her with ease, pinning her to the mattress.

"Yes," she moaned. "I want you to love me, Matthias."

"Talk dirty to me." He slipped his hands underneath her and cupped her breasts, thrusting inside her like an animal in rutting season. His orgasm mounted fast with her risqué whispers until he exploded inside her.

His body quivering, he braced his weight on his elbows so he wouldn't crush her. "Kate, my love," he whispered, brushing his lips over her shoulder. "What did you do to me?"

She panted beneath him. "I enjoyed you."

"God, what force came over me?" He rolled onto his back, pulling her against his chest. "I can't remember making love with such vigour before."

With her head on his chest, she wrapped one arm around him. "I hope this force comes over you again."

He raked his fingers through her hair and closed his eyes. "You exhausted me. I'll have to sleep."

"I'm falling asleep too." Her soft kiss on his chest coaxed another moan out of him as two short beeps pierced the silence. Her head rose. "Is that a fax machine I hear?"

"Sounds like it," he slurred, half a sleep. "I'll get it later."

"Who knows we're here? Maybe it's Fortuno. What if something happened and they couldn't reach us over the phone with us pleasing each other like animals?"

"Nothing's happened, love. My phone is right here." Matthias pointed to the night stand then continued combing his fingers through her long hair. "Besides, there are other ways my minion can reach me, if not by the conventional ones. Go to sleep now. It's nothing important, I'm sure."

A long breath escaped her, but she lowered her head to his chest again. The feeling of her smooth skin against his comforted him as sleep claimed him.

When Matthias woke, the room was washed in golden sunlight. Kate slept on her side of the bed, hugging the pillow. The faint scent of their lovemaking still lingered in the air.

The aroma of freshly brewed coffee drifted to him. Good. He had timed the machine right. The brew called to him and he rolled out of the bed.

With a cup in his hand, he strolled to the patio doors then remembered the facsimile. After retrieving the sheet from the tray, he returned to his java. The cushion on the

chair sank under him as he sat on the patio and cast his
glance over the Adriatic washed in sunlight.

As he started to read the fax in his hand, he choked on
the hot liquid. No, it couldn't be! He must have read it
wrong. Kate couldn't even think of such betrayal. What
kind of sick joke was this? He crumpled the paper in his
hand and threw the fax on the floor.

Could she have faked her love? No, she would have to
be one hell of an actress. And last night's loving couldn't be
pretentious. He picked the paper off the floor and uncurled
the sheet then read the fax again, hoping this time the
words would somehow change. Alas, they stayed the same.

His hands balled into fists, losing their grip on his cup.
The heavy mug shattered on the stone patio. Hot coffee
scolded his hand, adding to his anger. He mustn't base his
assumption on one fax, but re-reading the short message
for the seventh time made the seeds of doubt that had
sprout grow into something vicious and hard.

Her laptop, he thought. She'd been spending hours on
the computer. Maybe she had not spent all her time
booking the banquet hall and taking care of wedding details
after all. When he couldn't find her carry-on among their
luggage he had brought from the yacht, he scurried out to
the jetty. The boat stood still in the calm morning.

He found Kate's bag stored under the seat, the laptop
inside. There was enough charge to power the Dell up. His
heart drummed. This was wrong. If Kate had anything to
hide, she'd have her computer protected by a password. He
had to stop his insane quest to prove her infidelity.

But when the screen lit up, he couldn't resist looking.
First, he checked the Email, but found nothing in the
Inbox to confirm his suspicions. The Sent Mail folder
produced the same result. Spam bin contained numerous
messages between Kate and her ex-husband. The oldest
one going back to mid-March. This type of Web mail

automatically deleted messages older than thirty days. For all he knew, they could have been corresponding for months.

Matthias's heart hardened as a wave of anger, jealousy, and rage swept over him. In the three centuries he'd lived on the Earth, he had seen the goriness of wars, the cruelty of disease, drought, and famine, but nothing made him as sick as the sight of this. Then again, he had never been cheated on by a woman before. Damn her!

CHAPTER 17

Kate inhaled a long breath and smiled. The crumpled bedding rustled as she stretched her naked body under the sheets. Her nipples hardened at the thought of Matthias's lovemaking and silent laughter shook her. They'd been like animals. The dirty things she whispered to him drove him wild. She slid her hands down her stomach and pressed them to her tender mound. Never before had he thrust inside her like last night.

Her womb felt heavy with a new surge of desire for him. If they continued on like this, in two weeks she might dispute the brain-cells-rejuvenating theory of Doctor Leone. She turned to the side. Where was Matthias this fine morning?

Should she dress and go look for him or should she wait naked in the bed till he came to her? With a strand of her hair twirled around her finger, she opted to get out of the bed.

An eerie silence settled over the living area. Matthias should have music blaring from his iPhone by now. The shattered mug on the patio drew her attention, and she crouched to pick the sharp pieces. A hint of nervousness settled in her stomach. Something was amiss here.

"Matthias," she called, but there was no reply.

Maybe he was in the rec room pumping his muscles. Her bare feet threaded on the terracotta tiles as she dashed across the floor and down the marble steps. The exercise machines stood still. Where could he have gone? Cold air brushed her exposed skin. Instinct to her to follow the current.

It led her out of the house and up the path to Emina's grave Where Matthias stood, staring at the marker. His back was turned to Kate.

"Here you are," she said. "I was beginning to worry." A lump formed in her throat when he didn't turn around. "Matthias," she managed to whisper. "What's the matter?"

"Emina was wrong." The coldness of his voice shot terror into her heart.

"What was she wrong about?" She took a step closer to him. They'd had occasional fights, but now he appeared as if he hated her.

At the faint sound of engines, he turned his head toward the sea. "Fortuno is here. Pack your things and leave with him."

Kate felt as if a heavy fist had slammed into her stomach. She tried to speak but her breath caught. Swallowing hard, she tried again. "What?" It was all she could force out of her tight throat. Only the thought of her world disintegrating gave her the courage to fight back. "Look at me, Matthias. What have I done?"

Could he be angry because of the dirty talk in bed last night? But he'd provoked her to say those things and he knew she didn't have such foul mouth.

No answer came from him.

"Damn it, Matthias. You owe me some explanation." Tears stung her, but she pushed them away. "Why is Fortuno here? Where are the boys?"

He spun around and faced her, his eyes cold and hard. "I'm looking at you and what do I see? A betrayal. Get your stuff and leave. I need the time alone with Emina."

Kate clapped her hand over her mouth. This was a nightmare and she'd wake any minute now. It couldn't be real. She must have projected her fears that the fairy-tale would end into her dreams.

"Go. Fortuno can't wait for long."

No. She could never have a dream where Matthias's voice sounded so cruel and hateful. This terrible scene was real.

"Matthias." Sobs broke through her defenses. Her confused mind went over every detail of her life since she'd met him. Did she somehow say or do something in the past he suddenly remembered? No, Matthias would clear any misunderstandings right away. He didn't hold grudges.

"I don't owe you anything." He turned back to Emina's grave and stared at the marble headstone. "Leave."

Kate stood frozen to the spot. She'd have pinched herself but the pain in her heart was all too real. He was serious. With her tears running freely down her cheeks, she took first few steps on the path, looking over her shoulder, hoping he'd realize what he had done and stop her.

Emina, help me now. Kate waited for some sign from the ghost but she couldn't detect anything. Why would Emina show her to Matthias if she didn't want to help her?

If he needed time alone to sort out his feelings, he should have asked, explained. She would have understood. Having premarital jitters was normal. She had them, too.

She started to run. When she reached the house, she saw Fortuno on the patio under the pergola. His shoulder lowered as he exhaled and he closed his eyes, shaking his head.

"Do you know what on Earth is going on with him?" she demanded, anger mixing with her disbelief.

"He wouldn't tell me," Fortuno said solemnly.

His presence here so early meant Matthias had called him while she was still asleep. The realization that Matthias wanted her gone struck her hard. Up until now, she tried to believe this was all a simple mistake.

"I don't have much to pack."

She slipped inside and went into the bedroom where just a few hours ago he loved her so hard and deep. What could have happened to turn his heart so cold? Maybe some evil spirit took the possession of him and the real Matthias fought to come out. As she dressed and packed, she kept looking for him to return to the house, to tell her is was a mistake. But he didn't come. She picked up her suitcase and walked out.

From the stern of Fortuno's yacht, she watched Matthias's islet sinking into the distance. A terrible sadness burdened both her spirit and her body as unanswered questions swam in her head. Would she ever understand any of this?

Fortuno's big hand landed on her shoulder. "Don't do anything rash. I promise you, I'll get to the bottom of this, if it's the last thing I do."

Fresh tears poured from her eyes, washing off the dried ones. She couldn't speak. All she could do was to nod.

He took her hand. "Matthias always acts out around the time of Emina's death. It could be a passing phase, and he'll come crawling back on all fours, begging for your forgiveness."

"I hope you are right." Grief tore at her heart and turned her voice into a high pitched squeal. Mingling with immortals was dangerous. She understood that. Nonetheless, she had allowed herself to plunge into their world, knowing she could be hurt. Now she was the one being sent away without an explanation, her will for living crushed.

Left alone with her misery when Fortuno returned to the navigations, she retreated below. Out of the high wind, she sat in the lounge and focused her stare on the replica of Fortuno's unreadable letter, hanging above the bar.

The words emerged before her eyes.

Tonight I die, but this is not the end. For those I've lived with would carry a piece of me in their memories.

Her desperation allowed her to decipher the writing. A smile broke through her tight throat easing some of the pain. Fortuno was right, no matter what was going on with Matthias, she'd stay in his memory and he'd never leave hers.

The dark clouds covered the sky. The storm brewed above Matthias's head as he towered motionless over Emina's grave. If he stared hard enough maybe she'd spring out of the dark soil to be with him and their boys again. The way their life should have been. How could his beloved Emina steer him in to the wrong woman?

It confirmed his fears that neither he nor Emina knew that much about mortals. The money got in between him and Kate. Had the payments for the wedding really gone amiss or had she stashed the cash somewhere? The dollar amount didn't matter to him. It was her betrayal that stung as did the fact that she'd run back to her ex-husband after what he had done to her. Why then had she cried on Matthias's shoulder about it? She had almost made a total fool of him, but he would not make the same mistake again.

His neck was stiff and sore from staring at one spot when he finally glanced over his shoulder. Fortuno stood silently, a few feet away. Matthias swallowed. His friend was the last one to see Kate. "Did she cry?"

"Of course she cried." Fortuno cleared his throat. "Won't you tell me what brought this on?"

Matthias pulled the crumpled fax from his pocket and pressed it to Fortuno's chest. "All she had to do was to ask, and I would have given her the money."

Fortuno shook his head as he scanned the paper. "No, no, no and no. This is not Kate."

"The hell it isn't. That man hurt her in a worst way possible and all she wants to do is to run to him. With my money. I cannot allow this. I have three sons to consider."

"Kate wouldn't do this." Fortuno waved the paper in front of Matthias's face, raising his voice.

"Do not address me in such matter, minion," Matthias growled, glaring at Fortuno. The mortal woman had turned his only friend against him. "You are not to speak of her in my presence anymore. Nor are you permitted to say a word of this to her."

Fortuno stepped back. "Think, Master. Put things together. Why would Kate risk her life to save Teo?"

"Teo might not have been in any real danger. Her bumping her head that hard might have not been planned but that was all for show to get on my good side." The rolling thunder muffled Matthias's last words. Large raindrops splashed over the islet and the sea. Winds crashed the high waves against the sharp rocks.

"Let me be." Matthias dismissed Fortuno and collapsed over Emina's grave, allowing the heavy rain to wash over him. No mortal's love could compare to the one he had had with Emina. Yet, like some fool he had caved in to his craving for Kate and lost his heart. No one to blame but himself. But what had made him fall in love with her this madly?

Kate rested her chin on her knuckles. Dark sunglasses not only shielded her eyes from the late afternoon soon coming in through the glass wall of the building but also hid her red and puffy eyes. Dyane shifted uncomfortably in her seat across from Kate. In the two hours at the airport, she barely exchanged ten words with Dyane. Guilt stung her. Her poor emotional state and her lack of will to carry on a conversation must have made Dyane feel awkward. Though Kate appreciated her friend's attempts to cheer her up, she couldn't bring herself to crack a smile.

Though the pain of the loss was unbearable, she found a tiny bit of comfort that she'd had her one love in life. Their fire had burned too intense. It couldn't have lasted.

Even as she thought it, she knew it wasn't true. He had fallen out of love with her, but *why*? What had she done?

For the past two weeks she had driven herself insane trying to figure out how she had betrayed him. Would she ever get to tremble in his arms again? Tears threatened again over that last thought, and she forced her mind to focus on her future without him.

The first announcement of her flight came through the PI, but she ignored the pleasant voice coming through the speakers. There'd be one more before she had to board.

Dyane stroked her arm. "You didn't touch your espresso."

Kate stared at the small coffee cup on the low table. "The smell of coffee churns my stomach."

Her friend sighed. "I'll come and visit you in June. In the meantime, stay strong."

Kate nodded. "I'll tie up loose ends in Canada then return home. No point me staying there." Anxiety filled her. An impossible hint of hope that perhaps Matthias would come to his senses and would join her on the trip back filled her, but she dismissed it. Maybe in another lifetime. He was immortal. She might be re-born in the next century, but that would be a different Kate, not her. Memories were all she had left to hold on to.

She glanced at the gate's entrance. No sign of him. Stupid. She was stupid for even thinking it. Would Fortuno keep his promise and find out the reason for Matthias's actions?

Her flight was announced a second time. "You have to go. Now." Dyane stood, taking Kate's carry-on luggage in her hand.

With a heavy sigh Kate stood, too. She knew the way she dragged her feet behind Dyane to the boarding gate would make people think she was seeing Dyane off.

"Passengers only from here."

Tears welled in Kate's eyes as she hugged Dyane.

"Have faith, Kate." Dyane gazed toward ceiling, swiping her finger under her eyes. "This will turn out for the best. You must believe me. It's in the cards. Had I known this was coming, I'd have protected you." Kate gasped. Witchery may be just what she needed. "I'm inclined to believe in anything just to get him back. Is the ghost still with me?"

Dyane nodded. "She wouldn't leave you now."

"I don't see how she can help me. If she could, why didn't she help me right away?" Would this confusion ever end? But if anyone knew the "ghostly business" it would be Dyane. Kate struggled to stay calm and find the strength to believe in her friend's words. With a sniff, she took her bag from Dyane. "I must go now or the plane will leave without me."

Dyane nodded through her tears. "Bye," she croaked. "Toni and I will see you as soon as our visas arrive."

Kate followed the crowd down the narrow corridor. She stopped, glanced over her shoulder, and waved to Dyane one last time. Her friend raised her hand, wiggling her fingers.

Passengers snapped their seatbelts while Kate cringed in her seat. Pre-flight preparations always made her nervous. Her stomach flipped as the plane taxied to the runway then the bottom of her chair vibrated with the roar of the engines as the craft gained speed.

As soon as they reached the cruising altitude and the seat belt signs went off, Kate scurried to the lavatory. She barely kept the burning acid down while she locked the door. Take offs and landings were never pleasant for her, but this was the first time the sensations made her vomit.

After cleaning up, she returned to her seat and settled down with an in-flight magazine. Her eyelids drooped. No matter how upset she was, in the past two weeks or so she could fall asleep anytime and anyplace. For such light sleeper, she was pretty zonked out most of the time. This wasn't like her, especially when she was stressed out. She wondered if her poor emotional state could also be causing the never ending nausea. The slightest smell of food churned her stomach and made her dizzy.

Kate peered through the peephole. Dyane's face stared back at her while Toni stood behind her.

Still in her pyjamas, despite the late afternoon, Kate unlocked the bolt and pulled the apartment door open.

"Sorry I couldn't come to the airport, guys." She hugged Dyane and her husband.

"We found you easy enough. The cab driver was very helpful." Dyane stepped aside, shaking her head, while Toni carried in their suitcases. "Sweetie, you don't look so good. Are you still battling the stomach flu?"

"Yeah, I can't seem to get over this very persistent virus. I'm so wiped out all the time. All I have the energy for is sleep and more sleep."

Dyane removed her shoes in the tiny foyer. "Have you seen the doctor?"

Kate snorted. "What for? So I can be told it's a virus and it will run its course." Besides, she had lost all her faith in doctors and didn't have any desire to see one again—ever.

"Indulge me. How long you've been sick?"

"Since I've returned. Maybe I picked something on the plane." Kate gestured with her hand for them to sit on the couch. "How was your flight? Can I get you something?"

"The flight was pretty smooth and we were fed plenty." Dyane sat next to Toni, placing her hand on his knee. "Really, you should see a doctor."

"Fine, Dyane. If it will make you feel better, I'll go to the clinic tomorrow. How's that?" Knowing her friend could be right, Kate caved in. This flu could be a bacterial infection. At the very least, she might be prescribed an antibiotic.

Dyane patted Kate's hand. "Do you want me to come with you?"

Kate shook her head. "You guys sleep in. I'll take the couch and you can have my bed." She pointed to the double mattress in the corner of her flat. Emptiness swept through her at the thought of nestling there in Matthias's arms.

Dyane scanned over the one room apartment. "Kate, have you checked on the sale of your book?"

Kate gasped. "What sale?"

"People back home found the link and are ordering it through Amazon." Toni said as he shifted in his seat.

Really? She pursed her lips as she watched Toni try to find a comfortable spot of her second-hand couch. Those notification emails she deleted, thinking they were spam, now made sense. *And yes, I'm aware the couch has lumps.* But maybe she didn't need to pinch her pennies, after all. "I'll look into it. God, I'm tired already and it's not even seven o'clock in the evening." She stifled another yawn. "Would you mind if I lay down?"

"Of course not, silly." Dyane stood, pulling Toni up by the hand. "I think we'll make it an early night too. Good night, then."

"Night," Kate mumbled. Sleep claimed her and she wasn't sure if Dyane's last words were addressed to her or Toni.

The next morning Kate dragged herself to her feet. The sight of Dyane snuggled against Toni in her bed made Kate's heart ache. Not so long ago, she spooned with Matthias. On her tiptoes, she went to the bathroom and got in the shower. Hopefully there wouldn't be a long line at the clinic. She was not in the mood to wait for hours before her name was called.

Sitting in the exam room, a long while later, she tapped her foot impatiently on the ceramic tile floor. The smell of the clinic worsened her nausea. Where the hell was the doctor? After an hour of standing in line before the clinic opened, she spent another one flipping through the old magazines in the waiting room.

Then a nurse had led her into this tiny room almost twenty minutes ago and told her the doctor would see her right away. With a loud sigh, Kate stood and grabbed her purse. No use wasting another minute here. The doctor would just tell her what she suspected all along.

As she reached for the knob, the door opened and the balding man in white coat entered. "How may I help you?"

Kate returned to her seat. "Well, I flew from Europe almost two months ago and can't get over the stomach flu."

The skinny doctor sat on the round stool. "Any runs or diarrhoea?"

"No, just nausea and tiredness—no matter how much I sleep." The doctor peered at her over his glasses. "I see. The first day of your last menstrual period was?"

"That's another thing. I've been cramping for over a week now and still no period."

The doctor stood and opened the cupboard above his head. "I need a urine sample." He handed her a plastic cup. "The washroom is down the hall. When you are done, leave the specimen on the counter."

Fine, she'd pee in a cup. But how would that help her stomach flu? Seated on the toilet, the realization hit her and she almost dropped the container. The doctor suspected she might be pregnant. She left the bathroom and placed the container on the form with her name. The check mark next to pregnancy box make her hands shake. How could it even be possible?

"You can return to the examination room and wait for the doctor," the nurse said and ushered her away from the counter.

Kate fidgeted with her fingers. Her heart drummed. A pregnancy test shouldn't take this long. She snickered at the absurd thought. Though her first pregnancy had lasted less than fifteen weeks, she knew what being 'a little bit pregnant' felt like. What she had was very different. But it was said no two pregnancies were alike. And, the entire time with Matthias, she had never bothered using any contraception. If she hadn't conceived in all that time, why would she at the end?

The door opened again and the doctor stepped in. "Your test is positive."

Her already racing heart sped up. She licked her dry lips. "W—What did you just say?"

"You're pregnant."

CHAPTER 18

The white walls of the clinic's small examination room closed in on Kate. She tugged on the collar of her shirt. Suddenly, there wasn't enough air in here. *'You're pregnant.'* The doctor's words still rang in her ears.

"Miss." His voice snapped her back. "Do you need some time alone?"

Alone? No. Solitude wouldn't be good for her right now. She shook her head.

"I—" She swallowed another wave of nausea. "I can't be pregnant. I'll get my period any second now. The cramps I've been having feel like menstrual cramping."

"There is a slight chance the test is a false positive. The blood test would tell us for sure. But that cramping you feel is probably the uterus stretching to accommodate the growth of the baby."

"No—I mean." Her eyes search for something to focus on so she could steady her mind and she stared at the poster tacked to the wall. It was a poster showing the anatomy of a human body. "I was left with some scar tissue after a D and C procedure. I was told it would prevent me from conceiving."

He ceased checking the boxes on the form and spun on the stool to face her. "How long ago was that?"

"Over three years ago." She tore her gaze away from the poster over his shoulder and met his eyes. "No, four actually."

"The damage must have healed. This often happens. From your look, I conclude you haven't been told this."

"No, I have not." Fear gripped her with the thought that some clerk would make the same mistake again.

"Since you can't remember the date of your last period, do you know how long since you've been sexually active?"

The thought of Matthias's body covering hers, him thrusting inside her while she clung to his broad shoulders, sprang to her mind and sent heat to her cheeks.

The doctor pushed the desk calendar towards her. She flipped the page back to May. Pain stabbed her heart as her finger traced over the date of their wedding day that never happened. More guilt filled her as she glanced at previous month. The boys' birthday had passed. Their party had been booked at their favorite play place. She wondered if Matthias had gone ahead with it. "It would have to be around this time," she said, her finger circling the second weekend of April.

The doctor stood and stepped to the examining table. The thin paper sheet crinkled as he spread the covering over the top. "Can I have you lie down here?"

Dazed, she obeyed. He raised the t-shirt and opened her jeans to reveal her stomach. Cold jelly spread over her skin.

He placed the earpieces of the stethoscope inside his ears and glided the hollow disk over her abdomen. "Here it is. Loud and clear."

He pressed another disk to her lower belly. Static sound filled the room but was soon replaced by a fast thumping.

"Hear that?" The doctor smiled for the first time. "There's no mistaking it. It's the baby's heartbeat."

A cry escaped her. Matthias's heart beat inside her. She pressed her hand over her mouth.

The doctor squeezed her shoulder. "Miss, are you going to be all right?"

Am I going to be all right? She was having Matthias's baby. She'd be better than all right. Except for the tiny matter of letting him know he was about to become dad again.

Frustrated, Kate stared at the glass of orange juice. She had exhausted all ideas of how to approach Matthias, and she didn't know what to do.

She glanced around the small coffee shop. Staying in public places rather than being confined in her small flat did her good. In the coffee shop, she was not likely to freak out and have an emotional melt down. But, given her delicate condition, she had every right to.

"You have to tell him." The glass scraped along table's top as Dyane pushed the drink toward Kate. "You'd be surprised how men react when they find out."

"When it comes to Matthias, I have my doubts." Kate wrapped her fingers around the glass. "Men are all the same, immortal or not."

Dyane blew on her steaming cup of herbal tea. "Have you had any contact with him?"

"He sent Fortuno over with my stuff and let me keep the Cherokee." Kate forced a sip down her throat. "Fortuno urged me to stay patient till he finds out what is going on, but it will take time. Matthias is stubborn."

"You can still opt to—"

Kate shook her head. "I'm keeping my baby, Dyane. You should have heard its little heart beat inside me." After the loss of her fist baby, Kate had wanted nothing of life but to crawl inside a hole and die. She wouldn't survive the same experience again. "I'm going to have this pea in the pod."

"Then you have to tell him," Dyane hissed. "It's his child, too. You have to tell him regardless of your decision. The boys too need to know they'll have a little brother or sister soon."

Kate crossed her arms. "I don't think he'd care." She decided not to mention that her little angels would go wild if they knew their mom would give them a baby. She shook the thought away. It wouldn't happen, no use to daydream. "Not after the way he treated me."

Dyane patted Kate's stomach. "I wouldn't be surprised if that child inherits stubbornness from both of you."

A slight nausea swiped through Kate. Unsure whether the hormones or the thought of Emina stirred the feeling, she chased the sickness down with a long gulp of juice. "Is the ghost still with me?"

Dyane darted her glance to Kate's left. "And she's happy too. Maybe this was her unfinished earthly business. To give you comfort during this time."

Kate smiled, grateful Emina was still with her. The fact the ghost approved of her choice gave her strength to go through the pregnancy on her own and possibly single motherhood, too. Many women raised their children without the support of men, Kate could too.

"So how far along are you?" Dyane's smile set Kate at ease.

"Since the baby's heartbeat can be detected with the Doppler, the doctor said at least eight weeks, maybe longer. He is sending me for an ultrasound to determine for sure, but according to his calculations, baby is due mid-December." It could be the hormones of pregnancy that caused Kate to feel anxious, but dread filled her mind at the thought of the ultrasound examination.

Dyane leaned over the table and dropped her voice to a whisper as a couple took the seats next to them. "Did he explain how it was possible you conceived?"

Kate nodded, taking another sip. "I don't want to get into the technical details now, but he said scar tissue is for the most part self-healing." Kate's thoughts returned to the ultrasound. Emina was with her, and she'd make sure nothing bad happened to this baby.

The way Dyane was looking at her made Kate nervous. "What's the matter? Is there orange juice on my chin?"

"I envy you, you know. Toni and I've been trying since our wedding and nothing."

"Dyane, these things seem happen when you least expect them. I know it will happen for you, too."

Kate rubbed her belly, smiling at the thought how big she'd get. Matthias would love to see her puffing under the weight of his baby. But fear of how he'd react if she told him replaced her joy. After the way he accused her of betraying him, he'd probably think she cheated on him, too. No, she couldn't tell him. If she did have to be a single mom then she'd manage. The sale of her book had earned her enough to survive for some time. Matthias didn't need to know.

Matthias stared at the page of his book, but in the past hour, he had not read a single word. Without Kate's sweet laughter the whole house seemed empty. Christmas was upon them again, and his thoughts drifted to last year's festive season. The huge tree had decorated the hallway, presents piled up high under the Douglas fir. This year, he just hadn't had the will in him to celebrate. There was nothing, not even a single ribbon.

"The boys are asleep, Mr. Zrin." The maid's voice startled him.

"Yes, thank you," he said without raising his head from the text.

The disappointment on the boys' faces and their silent treatment because Kate was gone stabbed his heart each time he looked at them. They avoided him for the most part and would retreat to their room if he approached them. He had immersed himself in work, but his thoughts constantly drifted to Kate.

How would he find her? After sending her from the islet, he had severed all connection with her. She had moved away and he had lost track of her. In some false hope she'd call him, he had kept his phone number the same. But, why would she want to see him after the way he had treated her?

He had acted on impulse and if his actions had driven her back to her ex-husband then let her be happy.

The heavy picture on the wall behind him came crushing down onto the hardwood floor. Matthias sprang to his feet. "Emina, is that you?"

The cold air spiralled around him. '*Your study.*' Emina's voice came through as if from the deep well.

"What is in my study?" His pulse quickened.

'*Go,*' the voice whispered and he scurried out of the room. The dim light under the door of his office sent shivers through him. *A burglar?* He tapped his jean's pocket and felt the cell through the fabric. If he called the police, they'd arrive with blaring sirens, wake the boys, and scare them.

The muffled voice of the maid came through the study door. She knew she should not be in there. He pushed the door open. On her knees in front of the safe, she held the phone to her ear with one hand and turned the dial with the other. "It's not working. I'm trying but this combination is wrong," she hissed in low whisper. "Listen, Wilkins, I will not put up with your crap."

Matthias struggled to keep calm, but his jaw tightened as he clenched his fists. "Who are you?"

"Shit." The strands of her bleached hair fell from her clip when she whirled around, dropping the phone from her hand.

With two steps, he closed the distance and grabbed the mobile from the floor. A click, followed by dead silence confirmed whoever was on the other end had hung up. "What business do you have with Wilkins?"

She crossed her arms and frowned, her thin lips stained with faded lipstick.

Matthias glared at the large woman. "Are you two working together?"

"I can't tell you."

Her snide smile enraged him. "That missing woman in the news, she was from Nannies' Care. Was she sent here? Did Wilkins do something to her?"

The maid, or Wilkins's accomplice, shrugged. "I can't say."

Matthias dialed. "I'm calling the police."

She pulled a gun from under her apron and inched around him. "They'd have to catch me first. And just for your information, Wilkins is on his way to harm your former nanny."

His stomach dropped. "Kate," he whispered.

The maid's index finger wrapped around the trigger. Both of her shaky hands clutched the pistol's handle, pointing the barrel at him. "Drop the phone, if you want her to live."

"Wilkins has abandoned you. If you know how to stop him, now is the time. Earn some points for the jury." His mind raced. His only chance was to make this woman understand the game was over for her, and Wilkins would try to save only his own hide. "Do you know where has he gone?"

She took a step backwards. "I can't tell you."

He sent out a message on the mental channel. *'Danger in the Master's house!'*

Fortuno replied in his own way.

Matthias stepped closer to the woman. A realization struck him. He was turning human so a bullet could kill him for real this time. Her shivering confirmed she wasn't a cold-blooded murderer. She didn't have it in her to pull the trigger.

"Don't come closer," she ordered "I'll shoot."

He opened his arms wide. "Go ahead."

Hesitation flashed in her eyes. With one quick move, he disarmed her. She fell to her knees, sobbing. "Wilkins made me watch when he killed the other maid. He said the same thing would happen to me."

Police sirens blared in the distance. Fortuno arrived at the house a few minutes before the first officer.

Matthias squeezed Fortuno's bicep. "Kate's in danger. We must find her."

Fortuno gasped. "I don't know where to start looking for her. She moved from her last place."

Matthias paced the hallway. "If Emina is still here, she'll know." He paused, watching the policemen cuff the loud woman. "Emina won't show her presence with them here. Come."

He led Fortuno to the library. "Emina, are you still here?" Matthias strained to hear as the sound of hollow wind filled the room.

'Mount Sinai.' Her voice was no more than an eerie whisper. Emina's ghost seemed to have to use a great deal

of strength to reach the world of living through this gateway.

"She's in the hospital in downtown Toronto." Matthias tapped the computer mouse and the screen lit up. He quickly Googled the hospital's phone number. Why would Kate be in a hospital? He dialed the number but slammed the receiver when he got an automatic greeting. "I don't have time to listen to their new menu carefully. I need to speak with a real person."

He lunged to his feet and ran out to the police officer in the hallway. "Constable, the woman's accomplice is on his way to harm another person. Can I get your escort to Mount Sinai hospital?"

"It is out of our jurisdiction, Mr. Zrin." The young officer took the radio clipped to his shoulder. "I'll alert the dispatch, but I will give you an escort as far as I can then another cruiser will continue on with you."

"Let's go." Matthias shoved Fortuno into the back of the cruiser. He sat next to him and whispered, "We need to get there fast and this will be the fastest way."

Three hi-speed cruisers with blaring sirens later, Matthias ran to the reception desk, his feet slipping on the polished hospital floor. "Kate," he demanded, ignoring the warning to clean his hands with the sanitizing foam provided. "Kate Rokov, which room is she in?"

"How do you spell the last name of the patient?" the nurse asked, turning to her keyboard.

"It's R-O-K-O-V." Matthias tapped his fingers on the desk, while the admin nurse peered at her computer screen through her square glasses.

"Did you say Rokoff?"

"No. Rokov."

"Can you spell that for me again, please? Ah, never mind. Here it is. Yes, Kate Rokov." After adjusting her glasses she turned to him again. "Sir, are you the father?"

He frowned and cut a glance at Fortuno then returned his gaze to the nurse. "I am."

"She's on the seventh floor. The staff in the triage will know exact room." She stood and pointed with her thick arm. "Elevators are over there."

He grabbed Fortuno's arm. "Let's go."

The bell chimed announcing the arrival of the lift. People rushed out as the two of them stepped in. Matthias leaned on the mirrored wall behind him, counting the months backward in his mind. "Dear God," he gasped. "The last time I was with Kate." He swallowed past the lump in his throat. "She could be having my baby. That's what the nurse at the reception meant."

The elevator stopped with a jerk on the seventh floor. The doors slid open. White letters on a black post spelled out *Labor and Delivery.* He scurried out of the elevator, only to be stopped by the security guard at the glass entrance.

A tall guy in a white shirt put his hand up. "We're having a situation here. No one's allowed in."

"Is this about Miss Rokov?" Matthias's pulse quickened.

The man's eyes narrowed. "Yes it is."

"I'm the baby's father." Assuming the fatherhood based on his rough calculation was rash, but deep down he knew he was right. Emina wouldn't have warned him if Kate was having someone else's child.

The static buzz poured from the handheld transmitter when the security guy pressed the button. "We have the baby's father here, over." He spoke into the mesh in front of the device. More static came through. "Copy that. Send him here, slow and steady, over."

"Sir, you can go in. Follow the directions from the other guards."

Matthias nodded, ordering Fortuno to stay on guard.

Another security man motioned for Matthias to come closer and stay quiet. Matthias pressed his back against the wall, but couldn't see inside Kate's room through the drawn curtains.

"The man hasn't hurt her yet, but he is on the edge." The guard kept his voice low. "If she as much as glances at us, he will know we are here and he'll act out."

"Please don't." The fear in Kate's plea broke Matthias's heart. She sounded terrified. "I'm not worth killing, Mr. Wilkins. You'd spent the rest of your life in prison."

The guard leaned sideways. "She is standing on the other side of the bed, trying to pull the IV out."

Matthias closed his eyes and prayed. If the cannula broke off a fragment could enter the venous system and cause an embolism.

"I'm not afraid of prison," Wilkins snarled, his voice dark with rage.

"Why are you doing this?" Kate's words were broken by sobs.

"His wife cost me my first and only good paying job. That's right. Zrin and I go way back. The nurse I sent to tend to the Mrs. thought overdosing her would keep her asleep and she could gain access to his bank account for me."

"You killed Emina?" Kate screamed out.

Wilkins kicked the bed. "Lies! I never touched her."

'*Stay calm, Kate. Don't provoke him.*' Matthias attempted to reconnect with her but their special bond remained useless. The man in Kate's room was responsible for Emina's death. How could someone like Wilkins bring an end to an immortal? Matthias's mind raced. He couldn't recall anyone mentioning Wilkins, let alone seeing his face during Emina's pregnancy.

"How do you think it feels to watch your child die of leukemia?" Agony mixed with the anger in Wilkins's voice. "When I lost my medical coverage the hospital kicked my little girl out. Doctors said they couldn't do anything for her, but I never believed it. They turned their backs and she died in my arms."

"I feel your anger, Mr. Wilkins. I do." The fear in her voice intensified.

"The hell you do." Enraged, Wilkins slammed the hospital bed on its coasters against the wall. The sound of broken glass made everyone flinch.

Kate's horrified scream ripped through Matthias. He would have to act soon if the hospital's security team didn't do something. No way could he live with himself if Wilkins harmed Kate or the baby.

"What do you want me to do, Mr. Wilkins?" Kate sobbed.

Matthias forced air into his tightening chest. With his back pressed to the wall, he glanced at the spotlights on the high ceiling. He should be in there with Kate, helping her through the pain of contractions. '*Stay strong, my love.*' He tried the bond once more without success.

"To suffer, and from the look of it I'll have to do the job myself. The moron got himself arrested in the ally. The other guy I paid to shove you off the solar circle in Croatia failed. The hole I dug couldn't kill you."

Damn Wilkins! Kate had been right when she suspected him, but Matthias had dismissed the notion, asked her not to think about the recruiting agent again. A realization struck Matthias. He had made the same mistake when he had forbidden Emina from trying to conceive. After three centuries, he thought he knew it all, but he knew nothing. Though Wilkins was angered by his tragedies, neither Emina nor Kate had caused them.

Matthias clenched his fists. He'd be damned if he'd let the man succeed.

"The emails I started with your ex worked and the good doctor sent you on your merry way, didn't he?" Wilkins demanded. His voice had calmed down and he seemed to regain his composure. "Later, all it took was but one fax on my part."

"I blocked the sender," Kate shouted.

A tidal wave of guilt washed over Matthias. How could he have believed so blindly that Kate would have plotted to get his money? Wilkins must have gained the access to her computer the day she fell in the hole.

"Stupid girl. I knew you weren't email savvy. Have you checked your Spam folder? Of course not. I blind cc'd myself to coach the maid how to reply to your ex. He latched on, thinking he'd get rich. You never knew of the conversation. A word of advice. If you are going to leave your computer lying around, protect it with a password. But, enough talking. I'm just going to put this in your IV. You won't feel a thing once the industrial strength bleach from this syringe gets into your bloodstream. Man, this stuff dissolves anything. That's his bastard in you, isn't it?"

"No, it's not," Kate shrieked. "It's someone else's."

"Whose?"

Her silence told Matthias the baby was his.

"You lying bitch!"

It sounded like Wilkins put his fist through the wall. Matthias took a step closer, but the guard next to him blocked his way.

"You thought I'd spare you if the gnome inside you is someone else's. But, it's Zrin's. Another foreigner's imp will be born Canadian. Now, look what you've done. You're bleeding all over."

"She pulled the IV out. He's distracted." The security guard motioned with his head. Men poured into the small delivery room and seized Wilkins, pushing him to the floor.

Matthias dashed in and wrapped his arms protectively around Kate. "Did he hurt you?"

Bewilderment quickly replaced the fear on her face. She shook her head. "What are you doing here, Matthias?"

"This is where I belong."

"Damn you all. Damn you!" Wilkins shouted as he fought the burly guys pinning him down. "I'm not going to jail. Not if I can help it." With one swift movement, he jabbed the needle into his neck, emptying the syringe

Matthias pressed Kate's face to his chest as Wilkins's body twitched. The two security guards dragged him out of the room, needle still stuck deep in his skin.

Matthias stroked her hair. "They'll have to move you into different room. There's broken glass everywhere here."

With a crumpled face, she pushed her fists into her back. "Will Mr. Wilkins be alright?"

"Don't worry about him now. He's in good hands. Are you having a contraction?"

She nodded, blowing her breath out in short pants.

"How are we doing here?" An Oriental doctor came in, slipping on the latex gloves. "We need to get you back into bed. Nurse," he called.

A tall nurse with corn-colored braids hurried into the room, pushing wheelchair and stepped toward Kate.

"She's having a contraction." Matthias rubbed his hand on Kate's trembling back as he helped her into the wheelchair.

The short doctor examined the monitor screens. "The baby is happy even after mom went through such an ordeal. Good thing she didn't pull the electrodes off her belly." He turned to Kate sitting in the wheelchair, being tended to by the nurse. "Let's get you in a clean room and so I can see how you are progressing."

After helping her down the hall and onto the fresh bed, the nurse spread the sheet over Kate's belly. "Relax your knees."

Kate bit her lip as doctor examined her.

Matthias caressed her arm. "It'll be over soon."

The doctor straightened. "This baby is coming now. Are you ready?"

"No, I'm not," Kate cried out. Beads of sweat rolled down her forehead. "I'll never be."

"Listen to Doctor Chan's instructions." The nurse said. She spoke with a Caribbean accent. With a press of the button, she lowered the bed.

"At the top of the contraction, you'll grab your knees and push, using the stomach muscles." Doctor Chan stood and positioned Kate's feet wider apart. "Ready?"

A scream replaced Kate's long groan. "I can't do this."

With gauze the nurse handed to him, Matthias wiped her forehead. "Kate, love. No one can do this for you."

"Screaming never helps." The nurse told her. "But cursing the man who did this to you, does."

"Curse me all you want, love." Matthias said with a chuckle. "I deserve it."

Doctor Chan pulled the stool closer to the foot of the bed. "Let's try harder with the next contraction."

"The next one is coming," Kate gasped and grabbed her knees.

"Push now, push." Doctor Chan's voice rose. "You're doing a good job."

"Another one is coming." Kate's face turned red. "I can't handle them."

"It is normal. The contractions are coming on fast because you had to be induced." The nurse squeezed Kate's free hand.

Doctor Chan raised his head and looked away from the monitor. He stood and tapped Matthias's shoulder then motioned to him to come closer. "The baby's heart rate has dropped. It is not dangerous but she has to deliver soon. With her next attempt, can you coax her to try harder?"

Matthias inhaled, glancing at Kate. Exhaustion was etched on her face. "I'll try." He grabbed her shoulders. "Come on, love, you didn't survive Wilkins just to give up now."

Determination flashed in her eyes. "Let's do this."

The nurse smiled. "That's the spirit."

Kate slouched forward. Her body shook, and small groans escaped her. Sweat mixed with her tears. She strained, threw her head back, and squeezed Matthias's hand. "Damn you, Matthias," she gasped when she came up for air.

The nurse grabbed the towel. "She's started to curse you, won't be long now."

"The baby is crowning," Doctor Chan announced. "Don't stop now. Keep it up. Here we go, one more push should do it, and—"

A loud scream ripped out of Kate.

"She's out. Time of birth is nine-fifty p.m." Doctor Chan clamped the umbilical cord.

Matthias gasped at the sight of his daughter. "She is beautiful. Just like her mother."

"Why isn't she crying?" Panic written on her face, Kate stared at Matthias.

"Give her a second." The nurse said.

The baby's soft cry pierced the air.

"There she is." Matthias couldn't contain his grin at the sweet sound of his newborn daughter. The urge to plant a kiss on Kate's lips was unbearable. Though the happiness overwhelmed him, the question of whether or not she would take him back pressed heavily on his mind.

"Would Dad like to cut the cord?" Doctor Chan's voice pulled Matthias's eyes away from Kate.

"I would, thank you." He slipped on the gloves the nurse handed him and took the surgical scissors.

Doctor Chan raised the part of the purple cord. "In between my fingers."

With surgical precision, Matthias cut the life giving thread.

The nurse whisked the baby under the warmer. "You have a beautiful little girl," she announced, wiping off the screaming infant.

Doctor Chan stared at Matthias over the mask. "You must be a surgeon?"

"Yes, Doctor Matthias Zrin." He shook hands with Doctor Chan. "But I'm here as a dad."

"That's why you look familiar." Doctor Chan pointed at him. "You made my wife happy. And when she's happy, I'm happy." He made a half circle motion with his hands on his chest.

Matthias recognized the universal sign for breast enhancement. "I see."

"The birth weight is seven pounds, nine ounces," the nurse called out and took the baby from the scale. "Here's the little one." She passed the baby, wrapped in a green towel, to Kate.

Kate's hands instantly caressed her child's back and kissed her little head.

"Okay, one more kiss then I have to take her," the nurse said. "Once the paediatrician sees her and we take measurements and bathe her, she'd be all yours. Did you bring clothes for her?"

"Yes, I gave them to the other nurse." Kate brushed her lips on the baby's little check. She was already sucking on her tiny fingers.

"The clothes will be in the nursery. Come dear." The Jamaican nurse took the baby in her hands. "You'll eat later."

A lump formed in Matthias's throat as the nurse strode out of the room with his daughter in her arms. Would he get to see the little girl again?

Doctor Chan stood and stepped closer to Kate. "You did great."

Kate smiled tiredly. "Thank you."

"Don't mention it. I love my job." He turned to Matthias. "I'll leave now. There are many babies to deliver, and so little time."

Matthias nodded. "Thank you Doctor Chan. I truly appreciate your help."

With a heavy heart, he took the chair next to Kate's bed. She stared at him in silence for an immeasurable amount of time. He took her hand in his then kissed her fingertips. "I guess I should start."

"I must've dialed your number at least a hundred times each day." Her voice quivered.

"I said I should start."

"And I composed dozens of emails."

A soft smile escaped him. How he had missed her and all her funny little quirks. "All right then, I guess you'll start."

"But I hung up before the phone rang." Tears ran down her cheeks. "I was scared of you, Matthias."

Her words gouged a hole in his heart. He whispered, "Don't ever be afraid of me, Kate. Never." Her tears stabbed at his conscience. "I was a fool, I know, and if you forgive me I'll make it up to you. I swear." What in the world could he give her that would measure up to a daughter?

The sadness in her eyes killed him. "You're not angry with me anymore?"

"No my love, I'm not. I was wrong to be angry with you in the first place. I'm praying you'll forgive me and take me back. I cannot go on without you. The boys miss you. Teo has retreated into his own world again. Oh, they'll be crazy with happiness when they find out they have a little sister." With a soft squeeze on her hand, he waited for her answer.

"You hurt me, Matthias." Her solemn words almost destroyed any hint of hope he had. "But I cannot go on without you either. I missed you and the boys."

"I still need to hear it from your lips. Will you take me back?"

A wide smile replaced her frown. "I will."

Joy surged through him. He stood and cupped her face in his palms. His lips crushed hers. She was back where she belonged, in his arms.

"Here she is." Another nurse entered the room with his newborn child. The baby was crying. "We'll be moving you to a proper room soon. In the meantime there's someone who's ferociously hungry." Kate took the pink bundle in her arms. The nurse helped her latch the baby onto her nipple. "Oh, she is gorgeous, just gorgeous. I know I say this to all new moms, but this time I mean it. And look at all that black hair."

"Thank you." Kate smiled as her baby made sucking noises.

"You're doing fine." The nurse glanced at the clock on the wall. "I'll leave you for now."

Kate shot a glance from the baby to Matthias. "What shall we call her?"

He couldn't take his eyes off Kate, nursing his daughter. Breast-feeding came so naturally to her. "Today is Saint Lucia."

"So, you want to call her Lucia? We already have Luka." The baby's tiny fingers wrapped around Kate's slender one and she kissed the little hand, flashing him a smile.

'We.' The simple little word she spoke warmed his heart. "And now we'll have Lucia. Or Luce for short."

Kate lowered her gaze to the nursing infant. "What do you think, Luce? I like it. So Luce you are."

Luce let go of Kate's nipple. Matthias itched to hold his daughter in his arms.

Kate smiled at the sight of Luce sucking eagerly on her little fingers. "I think daddy wants to hold you."

He extended his hands to the bundled infant, cradled her, and pulled her to his chest.

"First you have to burp her." Kate's soft smile—the one he had missed like crazy—returned to her face, so he planted a kiss on her lips.

"Hello. I'm your Papa," he told Luce. His body swayed, as he held his newborn child for the first time. "I wish I had known you were on your way."

Luce replied by sticking her milk covered tongue out and releasing the gas.

"Can I come in?" A knock on the door and Fortuno's voice made Matthias jerk his eyes away from the cherub with Kate's face.

"Fortuno." Kate reached out to him. "I missed you, big guy."

"Congratulations." Fortuno crossed the room in two long strides and hugged her then peered at Luce in Matthias's arms. "She's a blessed fruit. But I have to head back. The boys are up. Adriana told them and they are jumping on their beds."

Kate chuckled. "Tell them I said you'll bring them here tomorrow but only if they go back to sleep."

Matthias nodded. "I know they'll listen if the order comes from Kate." He leaned toward her. "You'll have to teach me all your secrets."

She cocked her head. "I may yet put you on the straight and narrow."

"Finally. Someone should," Fortuno mumbled. "I'm off then and not in the back of the police cruiser."

Wide-eyed, Kate turned to Matthias. "What is he talking about?"

CHAPTER 19

The stretch limo pulled up in front the Saint James Cathedral. Butterflies assaulted Kate's stomach, partly from the realization that everyone's eyes would be on her as soon as the music started, but mostly because she'd see Matthias waiting by the altar.

Dyane straightened Kate's veil. "You look amazing. Wish I was the one getting married. Don't forget your bouquet."

Kate wrapped the white fur shawl around her bare shoulders, pressed her nose on the soft petals, and drew a long breath. "Aren't these roses beautiful?"

"Everything is." The charms on Dyane's bracelet chimed as she bustled around Kate, getting the ringlets of her hair in the right place. "Matthias has spared no expense on this event. Look at all the limousines he hired to get us here. And you guys are getting married in another Diocese."

She lowered her hands to her lap. "There, now you look like a bride."

Kate smiled and hugged her. "What would I do without you?"

"Don't mention it." Dyane pulled back, swiping her fingers under her eyes. "I'm glad you are all back home for good."

Cold air seeped inside the heated car as the chauffer held the door open. Kate stepped out into the sunny December day. Dyane danced around her, smoothing down the creases of the dress.

Kate pulled her up by her elbow. "Dyane, it's fine. Don't worry."

"You don't want the train to drag on the floor." Dyane bent sideways to grab the hem. Her small pregnant belly stuck out.

"I'll do it." Kate was faster, picking the silk off the floor. "Toni would kill me if something happens to you. So, you just relax and don't strain yourself."

"I wish everyone stops treating me as if I'm sick." Dyane sounded hurt. "I'm pregnant, nothing more."

Kate hugged her. "Take care of yourself and the baby. You know the troubles you've gone through."

Dyane pulled back. "But I'm fine now."

"And I want you to stay that way." Kate squeezed Dyane's hand, giving her a nervous smile. "Let's get married."

The Renaissance cathedral loomed over her as she ascended the wide set of stairs towards the main portal with its two intricate stone rosettes. Since Lucia's baptismal, Kate had dreamed of getting married here. She couldn't get the cathedral out of her mind—marble and limestone worked by skilled local masons, patterned after the early Italian masters. With the extrasensory link between her and Matthias fully restored, he had been aware of her desire and surprised her, arranging their wedding in this UNESCO World Heritage site.

Kate held Dyane's hand and stepped through the wide doors with carved Bible motifs. Toni waved to his wife from the procession line.

"Will you be okay walking down the aisle on your own?" Dyane did a last minute check around Kate, smoothing the dress with her hands.

"I will, Dyane. Now go stand next to Toni."

Kate removed her fur shawl and handed it to an usher. The hum hushed as the thud of the inner double doors announced the beginning of the ceremony. Angelic voices of the children's choir on the upper cloister preformed the Trans-Siberian Orchestra's *The Christmas Canon,* keeping their wedding in the spirit of the season.

"Remember, don't let your eyes wonder away from Matthias and you'll be fine." Dyane pulled the sheer fabric of the veil down over Kate's face and scurried to Toni.

One by one the bride's maids in silver dresses joined their partners and headed down the aisle until Kate stood alone at the doorway. She blew out her breath, staring down at the white roses of her bouquet.

The vast interior with four large columns supporting the archways spread in front of her. The main altar with semi-circular stairs stood at the end of the long aisle, washed in sunlight coming through the glass dome. The exceptional works of goldsmiths and miniaturists set into shell-shaped niches decorated the walls and sides of the pulpit.

Children's voices joined in again with the orchestra and usher nodded to her. Her heart drummed as she took her first step down the marble floor decorated with silver and grey diamond pattern. Putting one foot in front of the other, she headed for Matthias.

As she approached the pews in the middle decorated with white ribbons, she felt everyone's eyes on her while hers stayed on Matthias. He stood transfixed in front of the altar. Fortuno, by his side, tugged on the sleeves of his jacket.

The sight of Matthias steadied her legs, but the altar still appeared miles away. She wished she could close the distance in a few long strides instead of marching slowly to the music. With her gaze locked on her handsome husband-to-be, she continued walking until she stood next to him.

She handed the bouquet to Dyane and placed her hand in Matthias's. Everyone faced Father Shanto who was standing on the stairs with a book in his hand. He waited till the guests in the pews took their seats and the voices calmed down.

When only the occasional clearing of the throat or a cough was heard, he began. "Dearly beloved, we have gathered here today in the sight of God, to join this man and this woman in a holy matrimony..."

Kate struggled to keep her face straight under the veil and to listen to the priest's baritone voice. Matthias squeezed her hand, pressing his lips together. His expression almost made her lose control but she took a deep breath and fixed her stare on the man she was marrying.

Tonight and every night from now on, she'd be his wife in true sense, and he, her husband. She blushed at the many different ways she'd shown him her love and bit her lip. Those crystal blue crescents of his narrowed and a corner of his lips curved. He'd heard her.

The raspy clearing of Father Shanto's throat snapped her back. She glanced over at him. His double chin shook. "I repeat. Do you, Matthias, take this woman to be your lawfully wedded wife?"

Matthias's proud smile melted her insides. He faced the round priest and said, "I do."

Father switched his attention to her. "Do you, Kate, take this man to be your lawfully wedded husband?"

She gazed deep into Matthias's eyes, staring at his smiling face for a couple of seconds before she said firmly, "I do." Warmth filled her chest. Now, if Father would only skip straight to the kissing part.

Teo stepped forward, holding a heart-shaped cushion with two matching rings pinned to the lace.

Matthias slipped the ring on her finger, repeating after Father Shanto. "I, Matthias, give to you, Kate, this ring, as a symbol of my commitment to love, honor, and respect you."

Teo stepped to her and she took Matthias's ring and slid the band on his finger, saying her vow. "With this ring I wed you and bind our lives together for all time."

The book thudded as the Father closed the black leather volume. Arms opened wide, he leaned forward. "And now, I pronounce you husband and wife." He turned to Matthias. "You may kiss your bride."

Matthias slowly raised the veil over her head. He towered over her as they stared at each other for a few seconds. With one arm wrapped around her waist and the other on her hip, he pulled her close and seized her lips with his. Her hands inched along his arms till she wrapped them around his neck. As his tongue plunged into her mouth, she closed her eyes. When her knees buckled, he tightened his hold.

Applause broke out. His lips still lingered on hers when she opened her eyes. With a loud sigh, she pulled back and faced the priest again.

With two fingers in the air, Father Shanto made the Sign of the Cross above their heads. "May peace be with you."

"And also with you." The small congregation replied in unison.

After the formalities and congratulations, Matthias led Kate out of the cathedral and to the long line of limousines parked on the street. The chauffeurs shut the car doors as guests got into their vehicles.

The leather seat caressed her back. She couldn't take her eyes of three emeralds set in gold on her finger.

Her newlywed husband slid in next to her and gave her a peck on the cheek. "They match your eyes."

"Really?" Nestled against him, she laid her head on his shoulder.

"The closest match I could find and those stones are the highest in purity." His fingers brushed her knuckles, causing her to tremble. "But your eyes are the purest of all emeralds."

Her insides melted. Just when she got used to his newest compliment, he surprised her with another. She shifted closer to him. "I know you heard my thoughts during the ceremony."

"Hmmm." A mischievous smile played on his lips as he pressed the button. The dark divider glass slid up. "We have an hour's drive to the reception hall."

His fingers caressed the back of her neck. Their mouths met. With a click of the clasp, the top of her dress loosened. She moaned. The soft material slid down, revealing her heaving chest.

Both his hand cupped her breasts and he sucked on her nipples, until they peaked.

"Careful," she whispered. "Luce is barely weaned off."

"You know how much I love your nectar," he murmured, teasing her nipple with his teeth. Weaning him off may not be as easy.

After finding his pants zipper, she slid the metal down and reached her hand in. Through the fabric of his boxers, her hand pressed on his hardness. He hissed, sliding down the leather seat and undoing his belt in haste.

Hands gripping his trousers, she yanked them down his hips, pulling the underwear along. The size of his erection widened her eyes and surged her with wetness.

She straddled him, pressing her palms to the limo's low ceiling as the vehicle rounded a bend. His hands slid under her dress. His middle fingers tucked inside her thong, he pulled the underwear up. More wetness flooded her with the fabric wedged between her legs.

With a hard pull, he ripped her panties off. She sucked the air as he yanked the ruined lace out and tossed it onto the floor. He slid his finger along her folds, quickly finding her tender spot. Her back arched with his feathery touch.

"Do you like that?" The hoarse whisper he uttered in her ear drove her wild.

"I love it," she whispered back.

The limousine sped along the highway. With raised hips, she positioned herself over his staff. Sensual friction coupled with the motion of the vehicle and its tight interior, intensified her arousal.

His hands held her hips while her muscles closed around him. Her body bobbed in response to his erection thrusting deep inside her. The delicate fabric of her dress, crumpled between their bodies, rustled with each movement.

The windows steamed up as passion overwhelmed her. "Matthias," she cried. An intense orgasm surged through her, bringing blessed relief.

Flooded with ecstasy, she collapsed on top him. As her breathing calmed, she became aware of Christmas music coming in from the speakers. She couldn't ask for anything more this festive season. Santa had been more than gracious to her.

"This is the way to travel." Matthias pressed a kiss to her neck. "But we're exiting the highway." He nudged her, frowning. "Time to get decent."

A moan of satisfaction seeped out of her. The smell of their lovemaking mixed with her flowery perfume. "I want to stay like this for another second."

"And I want to stay like this for an eternity."

She trembled as his hands caressed her bare back. "Unfortunately, we can't."

By the time the chauffer pulled into the parking lot of the hotel and banquet hall, Kate had straightened her dress and reapplied her lipstick.

Matthias pocketed her ripped panties. "The good thing is I came prepared." He pulled a clean pair of silky thongs out of his tux's inner pocket and handed them to her. "Slip them on. I want to watch."

"Black," Kate twirled the underwear around her finger. "I'm wearing white. The panties will show through."

"You can't complain." He shrugged, pinching her cheek. "We can cross one more thing off our bucket list."

"You are right." Under his intense stare, she pulled the black pair on then smoothed her dress. "Happy now?"

His hand clasping hers, he kissed her palm then cupped her face. "The happiest."

"I think all our guests have arrived. Let's go in." Satisfied with her appearance after glancing in the mirror, she stored the makeup in the bridal emergency kit. Bless her maid of honor's heart. Dyane knew just what to put in. Kate would have to thank to Fortuno. The man was right. The stuff he'd put in her hair cemented her do. Not even Matthias's busy fingers could ruin her coiffure.

Matthias knocked on the divider and the driver got out and opened the door. The chauffer held his hand out for her. The last ray of sun spread over the parking lot as she stepped out, Matthias behind her.

"Let the merriment abound," he said as he led her toward the glass entrance.

Kate basked in the afterglow of their lovemaking as the limo rolled down the parking lot.

"Ladies and Gentlemen, put your hands together for Mr. and Mrs. Matthias Zrin." The DJ announced and applause broke throughout the reception hall. Kate's cheeks burned. Aware of the grin on her face, she hoped the train of her dress wouldn't snag on something as Matthias led her to the dance floor.

The piano melody of their song filled the hall. Thank to Dyane's musical training. She performed the sweet song Kate heard so many times while in Matthias's embrace. He wrapped his arm around her waist and seized her hand with his free one. The buttons of his vest drew her attention. She'd be undoing them tonight.

"So, Mrs. Zrin?" He pulled her close to him. "How does your new name sound to you?"

"I keep hearing that name so it must be true." She gazed into Matthias's blue crescents. "But, who is she?"

"A girl I married today." He winked, casting her smile that would have melted the ice caps.

"She's one lucky girl."

"Um-hm." Matthias trailed his thumb along her collarbone, raising goose bumps on her skin. "And she made me one lucky guy."

Other couples slowly joined them on the dance floor. The song changed to an upbeat one, but Kate swayed her hips to the same slow rhythm of their song. Matthias stopped his feet, but his hips continued with hers.

"The professor faxed me the results of your blood test," Matthias paused. "The enzymes passed from me to your blood through Lucia have slowed down your aging. You'll appear thirty years old for quite some time."

Joy filled her. Though he was turning mortal, he still aged at much slower pace compared to an ordinary human. She threw her arms around his neck. "Our little thunder thighs? Thanks to her I get to stay young with you for a long time?"

"Yes, you do." He gave her a gentle squeeze and a kiss on cheek. "We'll age slow and steady together."

"Can the Best Man have this dance?" Fortuno asked, tapping Matthias on his shoulder.

"Not this one. The next one, maybe." Matthias wrapped his arm tighter around Kate's waist and pulled her closer.

"I should dance with him once." Kate winked at Matthias. "To thank him for putting this grand event together, and most importantly, helping me lose all the baby fat so I can get into this dress." She glanced down her halter-top with its long skirt, decorated with pearl beads, cascading over her legs to her toes. Fortuno knew how to dress a girl like a princess.

"And a wonderful gown it is." Matthias placed a soft kiss on her lips. "But, it's who is inside that matters the most. I helped getting you into it, didn't I?"

Kate giggled and nodded, heat searing her cheeks. Matthias spun her around. She exchanged smiles with Dyane, happy in Toni's embrace, her little baby-bump proudly on display.

"It's just the stubborn row of fat on my lower belly that I can't lose." Kate sighed. He had made it clear she was not to ask him to perform any surgeries on her for nonmedical reasons.

"I know what you are hinting at and the answer remains no. The little roll of fat on your lower belly is what makes you a woman and it drives me wild." He slid his hands on her buttocks and pulled her against his pelvis. His breath tickled her neck, sending the tingling to her hips. No matter how recently they made love, she was always ready for more.

She moaned while he trailed his tongue down her neck. "I noticed you like that spot."

"Yes, I do." He grunted. "Besides, now that you are something of an immortal, the liposuction wouldn't work on you."

A different thought crossed her mind and she raised her head from his shoulder. "Matthias?"

"Hm?" The way his eyebrows arched ignited heat below her belly.

"I don't think we made a good impression on Father Shanto."

He blinked, shaking his head. "Why do you say that?"

"Well, first he baptized our daughter in June and today, he married us. We did it backwards."

"But we did it. Let's not even think about what could've been." He gave her another gentle squeeze and pressed his forehead on hers. "Don't worry about the Father. We might've caused him to make a Sign of the Cross more than his usual, but I'm sure he's happy for us."

"If you say so," she said through her laughter then lost herself in the depths of his eyes. His lips pressed to her forehead quickened her pulse. "Did you get to speak with the foreman? I know Petar and Ana are glad we live with them, but I can't wait to move into our house."

"Yes, I spoke with him today. He assured me we'll be in before the summer." Matthias shrugged. "Once the plumbing and electrical is done, the rest will go fast."

"Summer?" A hint of disappointment slithered through her. Though the neglected property they fell in love with while house hunting in Zadar needed lots of work, she hoped to move in sooner.

His feathery hair brushed her neck as he pulled her closer and pressed his cheek to hers. "It takes time to renovate a seventeenth century villa. The building didn't even have a roof when we became the proud owners."

"I know." The expression of the real-estate agent still stirred giggles in her, when he had realized the two of them had been serious about *"sinking money"* into the neighbourhood dumpsite. She trailed her finger down his chest, thinking of the love they gave each other in the limo. "It's just I want to make love to you in our bed, under our own sheets. When I want to."

"You will." He spun her around as the song came to the end. "But until then, we'll have to sneak around like teenagers. I kind of like it, knowing any minute someone could walk in on us. Risqué."

"Just you wait until Lucia turns into a teenager." Kate scowled. "I bet you won't like risqué then."

Color drained from his face. "Yes, one day I'll have to approve of the man she wants to spend the rest of her life with, but she'll be my little cherub for quite some time."

A rock song replaced the upbeat one and guests poured onto the dance floor.

"We should sit this one out," Matthias said. "I can't see myself dancing to this." One arm wrapped around her waist, he led her to the head table.

"I think the boys would like to bid us goodnight." She glanced at the three chocolate covered faces. "Did you have fun today?"

"Yes, this is the best Christmas ever. Can we do this every year?" Luka bounced on his chair, excitement in his eyes.

"Somehow I don't think so." Laughter shook her shoulders as she reached for the napkin and wiped their faces. They squirmed when she kissed their cheeks. Her angels made her whole. Now she understood there was a reason for everything. She had a dream to be someone's wife and to be a mother and in fulfilling her wish, she made their dreams come true as well.

"You look so beautiful, Mama." Teo settled himself on her lap.

"Thank you. You know how to make a girl feel special." Her heart melted at the sight of her boys. "Now it's off to bed for you."

"Aw," they replied in unison. "Can't we stay till you cut your cake? Please?"

Matthias tapped his wristwatch. "Five more minutes won't hurt."

"I guess we should cut the cake." Kate turned to Matthias. "It's a piece of art, shame to eat it."

"I'm supposed to shove a piece in your mouth." Matthias signalled Fortuno.

"You try and you'll be wearing it." She tapped Teo to get off her lap when DJ announced for everyone to gather around the dessert table.

"We'll be civil about it."

Matthias took a knife with ribbons tied to its handle. Kate placed her hands over his and followed his movements, cutting their very first slice. After sharing the almond cream layered piece with him, she served plates to the three boys. They dug in with gusto, smearing the pastry over their freshly cleaned faces.

"Boys, it's way past your bed time." Matthias gathered them for another kiss. "You've had your cake, off to bed, no more dilly-dallying."

"Be quiet when you go into your suite and don't wake your sister." Unable to resist, Kate ruffled their gelled spikes.

"Or your grandma," Matthias added, turning to Kate. "Can't blame them, they love their little sister too much and they are so fond of nana."

"We will." They ran off after Fortuno to the hotel lobby.

Kate smiled, watching them scurry to the hotel elevators, their untied shoelaces dragging on the carpet. White shirts didn't stay tucked in their little tuxedo trousers for long.

"But you." She wagged her finger at Matthias. "Are the worst when it comes to spoiling her. I know she's your little princes, but the indulgence must stop."

His hands wrapped around her waist. "You're right—to teach her how to be independent is the best gift I can give her, but when it comes to my two favorite girls in the world, I lose all my control."

Kate shivered as a cold air brushed over her bare arms and shoulders.

Matthias pulled her closer. "I felt it too."

"It's Emina. I see her." Kate stared at the apparition before her. A beautiful young woman stood, holding a baby. Her mouth moved, she said something but Kate couldn't hear.

Matthias squeezed Kate's hand. "It took her a while to find him in Heaven. She named him Antun. You don't mind?"

"Of course not. My lost baby." Kate swallowed, her tight throat, and fought back the tears. "In my heart I knew it was a little boy, and I'm glad he's not alone. He's got Emina."

Transfixed, Kate stared at Emina. This was the woman who steered her to Matthias and made her love him as she did. She stood by her side when all seemed lost and darkness had closed in on her.

She gave her three boys to raise and cherish, and the least Kate could do was to allow her to do the same. Let her keep the baby Kate had longed for but that was stolen from her.

She gave Emina a nod of approval. Emina's angelic image faded away and the light she stepped through, closed.

"She crossed over. She's gone." Kate stared into the space where just a second ago a most beautiful and inviting white glow had been.

A peaceful feeling settled on her as the realization hit her. Emina's mission was accomplished. She was free to cross over.

"We have Emina's blessing." Matthias pulled Kate into his embrace. She wrapped her arms around his neck and their lips met.

Her knees buckled with his kisses and she tightened her hold as his arms pulled her closer. Bonded by love and crimson to her husband and children, and this land, she'd welcomed each day of their long life together.

THE END

ABOUT THE AUTHOR

Zrinka Jelic lives in Ontario, Canada, with her husband and two children. A member of the Romance Writers of America and its chapter Fantasy Futuristic &Paranormal, as well as Savvy Authors, she writes contemporary fiction—which leans toward the paranormal—and adds a pinch of history. Her characters come from all walks of life, and although she prefers red, romance comes in many colors. Given Jelic's love for her native Croatia and the Adriatic Sea, her characters usually find themselves dealing with a fair amount of sunshine, but that's about the only break they get. "Alas," Jelic says, with a grin. "Some rain must fall in everyone's life."